CLOSER TO THE SUN

ALSO BY PETER GADOL

The Mystery Roast
Coyote

Picador USA
New York

CLOSER
TO THE
SUN

Peter Gadol

Picador ® is a U.S. registered trademark and is used by St. Martin's Press under license from Pan Books Limited.

Design by Ellen R. Sasahara

Library of Congress Cataloging-in-Publication Data

Gadol, Peter.
    Closer to the sun / Peter Gadol.—1st ed.
        p.   cm.
    ISBN 0-312-14084-3
    I. Title.
PS3557.A285C58   1995
813'.54—dc20   95-41422
                                                CIP

First Picador USA Edition: January 1996

10   9   8   7   6   5   4   3   2   1

For Stephen

CLOSER TO THE SUN

ONE

Late in the last year of his life, my grandfather made a pilgrimage to the city of his youth, where he set a house on fire in the middle of the night. It was a house which in the half-century since it had been abandoned had inspired myriad rumors among the children of the neighborhood, who would dare one another to ride their bikes up the driveway and throw stones at an upstairs window, the perch from which a hermit allegedly cast hexes upon anyone who came too close, a never-seen bitter old man, it was said, who could somehow be blamed for every misfortune that befell the quiet street, for the disease that killed off all of the shade trees one year, for the unsolved murder of a young woman a few blocks away, for every flat tire, for every runaway cat, for every carton of milk gone sour. Now and then a volunteer gardener had mowed the lawn or cut back the overgrown hedges, but no one ever repaired the clapboard that fell aslant and no one replaced the shingles that slid off the roof after a storm. Occasionally older kids broke in and threw a party, and in time the house became known by word of mouth as a free hostel where people drifting through town could spend a night or two, especially during the winter, when they burned the staircase balusters and the kitchen cabinets to keep warm.

No one in the neighborhood knew who my grandfather was when his picture ran in the local paper after the police charged him with arson and resisting arrest (several officers reportedly had to restrain him when he tried to prevent the firemen from putting out his fire)—that is, no one in the neighborhood was old enough to remember him. I knew that my grandfather had grown up on the other side of the city, but I had no idea that he had also lived elsewhere in this town as a young man, no idea that while spending the rest of his life a continent away he had continued to pay property taxes on an abandoned house all these years, that he had built that house according to his own design and then left it for dead in the wake of a devastating loss. I did not know that before the war and before he married my grand-mother, he had been married to someone else.

A woman whom my grandfather had known since child-hood; the only girl he had ever dated; his true love with whom he planned to raise a family and grow old in this mod-est house. And then one day a few weeks after they were married, his wife was trying to indicate to the movers in which bedroom they should place a certain heavy bureau or inherited rolltop desk when, to get out of the way, she lost her footing and slipped down the long flight of stairs. She hit her head on the landing, which in a matter of hours would have been protected by a runner that might have soft-ened her fall; she hit her head and never regained con-sciousness. My grandfather, telling me this story when my father and I came to bail him out of jail and take him home with us, did not say how long his first wife had lingered in the hospital, but after she died he decided that he could not live in the house. Nor could he sell it because he could not bear for anyone else to live there either, lest they possibly enjoy the happiness that he had never known in these rooms, which was why when an old acquaintance informed him that strangers were regularly lounging by the hearth on winter nights, my grandfather decided to burn the house down. And I should have done it years ago, he said.

I was fifteen that year and I remember asking my grandfather if he had a picture of his first wife and being disappointed when he claimed that he did not. I wanted to know how he had gotten over her, how anyone ever recovered from losing a childhood sweetheart. How could he continue living? My grandfather's response came easily, astonishingly easily despite the fact that he had about used up the remainder of his living strength to burn the house down. He said, All of a sudden there was a war to fight and I personally could not wait to enlist. And then after the war, he said, people needed houses and I was building houses for them—my grandfather was an architect—and you might say that I just fell into the sweep of time. I said, You did not sell that house and yet you remarried right after the war, and my grandfather replied, That was the way it was, you married, you had a job, you had a family. I fell into the sweep of time, he said.

These words haunted me because I never quite understood what my grandfather meant, not until I was older and in college and I fell in love with a man and believed that I would spend the rest of my life with him. Not until, after seven years, I lost him. Such is the fate of the men in my family (my mother died when I was five and my father remarried): Our first lovers strand us, they slip from our hold. My lover died, and when he died, he took with him my rudder and my sail. And I found that in a perverse way I almost longed for a war to join like the one my grandfather had joined, or even a war to rebel against like the one my father as a young man had rebelled against. I longed for the collective loss that accompanies any war, the cold current of a river that rushes by you and swallows your own inexplicable and private loss into the deeper all-encompassing flow and rapids of history.

Unlike my grandfather, I did not fall into any sweep of time. Time stopped. Unlike him, I could not go on. And I began to wander, I began to drift. I lost track of the days and the weeks, and eventually I headed west. I lost track of the years, two years to be precise.

I wandered and I drifted and then I came to California and to a western canyon. Because I had never lived in a canyon before, I had no way of knowing that within the world of a mountain-fold, your every whisper, your most silent thought, your most secret longing can slip away from you and plunge into the gorge, where it will be magnified into an echo and illuminated by a white sun and float down into the brush, where it will eventually become as integral to the terrain as the wildflowers and the chaparral.

I came to a half-burned-out canyon, where it appeared that a man and a woman were building a house atop a slope of ash, sculpting it and shaping it from the ash itself, or so it seemed during the last light of the day, and I knew, I somehow knew early on that this was a house toward which I would be drawn in the middle of the night years later to set on fire.

That was the season of record rain when flash floods washed out canyon after canyon along the Pacific coast. Mountain roads collapsed in sudden sighs of mud, houses slid down the hills one after another like children on sleds, and drivers who were foolish enough to brave these daily tempests often found themselves wading away from stranded cars as the ocean reclaimed the shoreline that it had gradually ceded for a millennium, as the ocean spilled back into the basin of the city. The rain had its moods—it gusted, it spat, it gusted again—and soon after I arrived that winter during a fleeting reprieve of drizzle and mist, soon after I drove up to a large house at the summit of Encantado Canyon, the downpour began again, the hard rain, the determined rain. I fast discovered that I was going nowhere. Mud clogged the road at the mouth of the canyon so there was no heading south, and the ENTER AT YOUR OWN RISK signs posted along the highway down into the deluged valley discouraged travel north. I did not know what the canyon truly looked like because all I could see through the rain was a vast chasm of drenched flora, nothing but green slopes beneath green skies.

I remember that I did not do much of anything during those first long days in California. I slept in the afternoons and then got up and swam in the pool even when it was pouring. I swam my laps and added a few each day as if I were in training for a distance swim, and I suppose that I was in training, having wandered all that I could wander, having come to the edge of the continent and the edge of reason. I needed to be strong enough to swim out into the ocean and swim far enough so that I would not be able to turn back toward the shore. If that was what I wanted. These were dark days for me, empty and uncertain days, and the rain did not help, the cold rain pounding the long pool. I sank to the floor of the deep end and hugged my knees and held myself there in the enticing sleep of the deep water. Inevitably I surfaced, but I dreamed of drowning.

And then the rains abated unexpectedly one night and ceased completely before morning. I remember being awakened by murmurs in the fog, voices diluted by the canyon echo, the voices of breakfast conversations, the recounted reveries of troubled sleep. Then I heard a dog barking and another dog answering it and the crescendoing hum of a truck on the coast road. I heard gulls returning to the shore, the squawking birds all blown about in the giddy breeze. I heard laughter tripping back and forth. I heard someone practicing piano scales. And I heard the buzz of a saw, then hammering.

By the time I got out of bed that first arid morning, the fog was lifting, and I could begin to survey the dimensions of the canyon, its generous width, its histrionic depth. I pulled on a pair of shorts and made a pot of strong coffee and stood out on the deck off the kitchen. A wind weedy with sage and rosemary washed over me. I smelled lemons. One by one, the houses dotting the hills were revealed to me, square white houses riding flat terraces and houses set into the steep mountainside like shells embedded in the sand after an ebb tide. Suddenly there was color: mustard bluffs and falls of magenta bougainvillea and bloodred poppies everywhere, golden poppies bowing in the breeze, and the green brush that I had been observing all along, the dense brush expanding imperially after the rains. Then at long last I could take in the entire landscape in one breath and look down on the slopes wooded with oak, down past flaking coral trees to the lower barren cliffs, down all the way to the slithering highway squeezed into a two-lane bend, down to a stand of inebriate palms and the narrow perimeter of white sand and the swollen tide rushing beneath houses on stilts, down to the cold surf, the limitless reach of water and a remote gray horizon that barely delineated the blue of the sky from the blue of the Pacific.

Now I understood the topography of Encantado Canyon, a hidden gulch forty miles west of Los Angeles and just beyond the Ventura County line. In order to really see the gorge, you had to follow Encantado Canyon Road up its first formidable hill and then, just as you caught a first glimpse of the entire glacial bowl, take a sharp right turn to continue the climb—as opposed to driving along the willow-lined westward tine which was Las Patas Glen—and only then, with each higher plateau and panorama, could you measure the scope of the divide between the two passages, the two roads each winding away from each other, restlessly curving and rising toward two matching, opposed promontories of equal altitude—the house that I was sitting straddled the eastern peak—before wending downhill and toward each other until they closed a circle of sorts and merged into the scenic drive that ran along the spine of the Santa Monica range, the road that connected this canyon with all of the other canyons along the latitude. The city to the east was only vaguely in view where the coast yawned south.

Now I understood that there were actually two landscapes contained within the single canyon—one lush and one charred—because the western half of the divide had been destroyed by a wildfire, and while all of the homes along Las Patas Glen had burned to the ground, the firefighters had evidently made their stand right down the middle of the vale and protected the Encantado Canyon Road side from the blaze. The mudslide at the mouth of the canyon, at the fork in the road, was partly the result of a lack of roots, the roots of scrub and trees that might have held the soil in place against the flow of the winter runoff. A crew of tractors was now clearing the road and men in hard hats were constructing a great wall of sandbags. The other side of the canyon was a different world entirely, a gray and lonesome scape of ash that had seen little regrowth since the fire, maybe a patch of green here or there, spotty regermination at best along a lunar frontier. Even a mountain clear-cut for lumber holds on to some of its green, its reds, its browns, some measure of life, but here was a wasteland that had been scorched to its nude geology, its rocks and inclines punctured with daggers of tree trunks and gnarled fragments of unspent brush. Instead of square white houses angled toward the ocean, I could see only the outlines of houses, the lots of rubble and queer freestanding chimneys and twisted metal where houses once stood. Some of these

lots had been bulldozed flat, prepared for resale or rebuilding, although no one had returned to that side of Encantado
Canyon and it looked as though no one ever would live
there again.

And yet these ruins in the distance, however gray, however somber, appealed to me in the way that I was attracted
to ruins of any sort, the lone columns and half-pediment
atop an ancient cliff, the abandoned house with a caved-in
roof in the middle of an empty prairie, and now the ashen
shadows of hillside homes, the crumbling foundation walls,
the stray hearths. Call me morose, call me gloomy—losing
the love of my life had made me morose and gloomy—but
I found myself in a place that matched, that appeared to be
a stage set for my sobered worldview, and I think that whenever we find ourselves in such a landscape, we feel, I felt,
strangely and gratifyingly at home.

That first morning after the rain, the air was preternat-
urally clear, and because I could see so far in all directions—I could see the entire archipelago of the Channel
Islands floating off the coast to the north—I believed that I
would be able to track the voices and the dog barks and the
pianos that I heard. While I could, for instance, stare down
onto the pool and patio of a neighbor down the canyon
road and watch a woman in a bikini smear her arms and
legs with a white lotion, I could not determine where these
sounds were coming from at all. I could not connect what
I could hear with what I could see except for the sawing and
hammering, which had become louder as the morning pro-
gressed and which, just as I was about to give up, I traced
due west across the canyon to the facing paw of rock. I
picked out a few faint vertical brown lines spiked against
the sky.

Wood, I thought. The first studs of a new house, someone finally rebuilding after all. Someone was building a
house across the canyon, that was what I guessed and

guessed correctly, although I would have to drag the living room telescope into the kitchen before I knew that I was right, and I did not do that until the end of the day.

I dressed and climbed into my car and headed down the canyon road. I spilled out onto the coast road and did not need to step on the gas for what seemed like miles. I spent the day exploring.

It was quite breezy in the city that morning. I drove through Malibu and past the Moderne buildings of Santa Monica, the hotels that looked like ocean liners, in and out the Oz of Century City, east along the boulevards striping the La Brea basin, east and west again and east, tacking according to the whim of the wind. Eventually I stopped using a map and relied on a natural compass instead: the mountains to the north, the water to the west. I covered so much ground that I felt quite small and insignificant in the big city, and I was glad to drive west beyond the sprawl and honk of Los Angeles proper, west to a remote canyon that most people who traveled up and down the coast did not know existed.

On the way home, I stopped off at a diner on the coast road just east of Encantado Canyon, the only place to eat for miles, a classic old truck stop and semi-chic surfer's den that faced a strip of beach houses, the garages of which were all you saw from the highway. The Paradise Diner was a convenient walk from the nearby state beach, but there was no one there toward the end of the day and I had the place to myself. You know this diner even if you have never eaten there, a diner with its wall of red booths and its long counter, where I sat on a chrome stool and played with the straw dispenser until I could nod hello to a waitress and order a club sandwich and soup and coffee and yawn contentedly at the prospect of dining on basic food in a well-lit dive opposite the ocean at dusk.

The day was easy, I could improvise a day, but the night

was a different game, its rules eluded me. The night was as long as the Pacific coast. At night I drank too much and took myself even more seriously than I did during the day, were that possible, and it was always at night that my mourning became unbearable and I decided once and for all to drown myself. But as I made my way back up Encantado Canyon Road—it was a minor miracle that my wreck of a car, almost as old as I was, survived that last long ascent up the private drive off the main road—the night ahead, the night alone did not fill me with dread. Maybe that was because I got to watch my first sunset in a canyon after a season of rain.

First the brighter colors of the ravine dissolved until there was the blue sky and bluer sea and patchy green hillside, that dimming palette then stippled with pearls of white light from the homes lining the canyon and from the headlights of cars driving down the coast. The sun eased itself into the Pacific like an old man lowering himself into a bath, although once the sun did begin to disappear, it was gone quickly, casting an auric wash when it went, gilding all of the trees and the bluffs and the shoreline and even the burned-out slopes with a fragile splendor. For a moment the world seemed cast in a thin precious metal that could be misshapen by the heat of my breath, for a moment the world gloamed gold. And I remember that this was when I knew that I was not alone after all.

I was alone in the sense that after two years of wandering in a nomad trance, I believed that I would always be alone, and I was literally alone when I stood out on the deck of a borrowed house and bounced on my toes to keep warm. But I was not alone or as alone as I had been because when I returned to the house, I glanced west across the canyon toward the opposite cliff and thought that I saw a figure, two figures standing on the edge of that bald rock.

I carried the telescope into the kitchen. It was a brass refracting telescope which at its best focus was still fairly weak and only slightly enhanced my vision, but I could confirm that someone was constructing a house across the canyon— a corner had been framed from what I could tell—and that a man and a woman sat on the edge of the cliff and watched the sunset with me. The man was wearing light-colored clothing, which made it easier for me to follow him in the fading day, to watch him rest his elbows on his knees and drag on a cigarette while the woman knelt behind him and massaged his shoulders. When it was dark, they both stood and circled the framed corner and tapped the studs of wood with their hands before they climbed into a pickup truck and disappeared down Las Patas Glen Road.

We would watch a dozen sunsets like this, together and yet apart, before we finally met.

After Dean died, I had not wanted to stay in the New York apartment where we had lived for the latter three of our seven years together. I kept bumping into him at every turn. I would notice the jar of Mediterranean sand that he used as a paperweight on his desk. I found a bananawood votive figure on a shelf behind some books, an evidently impotent goddess of good health from who remembered where, from a certain jungle nation, from a certain trip. His shirts were hanging in the closet, his linens and his paisleys. His watches were lined up on top of his dresser, each with the same roman-numeraled face, in silver, in gold, with a brown leather band, with a black one. Not to mention his cameras everywhere. His cumbersome camera on its tripod, a camera that was all hood and billows. The countless cameras that he had picked up at flea markets and never gotten around to repairing. A dozen cameras and, on every wall and in stacks leaning against the walls, his photographs, his livelihood and his passion.

He specialized in landscapes. At the time of his death, he had begun to achieve a degree of fame with a series of big sepia prints of ancient ruins. Photographs of tombs and temples and stone walls. They were artful snapshots from our travels—that was one way of looking at them, that was how I looked at them, our life of constant movement. I could not take them down, although there came a month when I had to; the gallery wanted them, the executor who was Dean's gallery director wanted them. And then I was left with the ghost rectangles on the walls where the sun had not faded the paint. I could have repainted the walls, of course, the deep forest green in the living room, the deep brown of the study, colors that Dean had chosen because—and he was the first to admit it—they complemented his own dark coloring, his autumnal good looks. I could have hired a crew of painters with the money suddenly at my disposal, but I knew that no matter how many coats of white and off-white they applied, Dean's dark colors would eventually seep through and that it would be impossible for me to live amid my own pale betrayal.

So I made it known among my friends that I did not want to stay in the apartment, and that was how I ended up house-sitting in a roomy converted barn up the Hudson. That was a two-week stay. And then I house-sat for another friend, a beach house this time, for another two weeks. Then there was another beach house and another, and one gig led to the next and I house-sat for friends of friends. I let the lease run out on my apartment, so I had to either move into a new place or make plans to house-sit for someone else and put my few belongings in storage. To my surprise, there was not much to store once the photographs were gone and once I had, in one ruthless and later-regretted sweep, disposed of mementos like the jar of sand and the votive figure. Before long I was taking care of the houses that belonged to friends twice and thrice removed, for people whom I may have met at a party but did not necessarily remember meeting, for people whom I had never met, and I was living for a week here, for three weeks there. I began to work my way cross-country, and at some point, it became impossible for me to trace my current hosts back to the original generosity of the friends who I did know, the friends with whom I had chosen to lose touch after Dean died. It is alarmingly easy to become a fugitive from the people who know you.

A month was the longest that I remained in any one place. I became the man you would see sorting through lettuces in your grocery store, the man who sat alone in the back of your local cinema, who browsed novels in your favorite bookstore, who lazed shirtless on the lawn of your park, the man who seemed friendly enough to say hello to and to strike up a conversation with but who, just as you were about to introduce yourself, vanished from the scene, the man who disappeared and was never seen again.

And that was how I came to Encantado Canyon, to the second home of a man and a woman who had two teenage boys and were in the middle of a protracted divorce. As part of a complicated settlement, they had agreed to sell off their weekend house, but they were trying to unload it during a rather poor time to sell real estate in California, and because both the man and the woman had known Dean and liked him and missed him—I honestly did not remember ever meeting this man before he offered me his home—I was told that I could stay in their house as long as I wanted, until the place was sold. My only favor in return was to keep the place looking stunning—the owner's word—for prospective buyers whom a real-estate agent might bring by with little or no notice.

It was a cavernous house, a house of obscene scale, a house with white stucco walls inside and out. It had a red-tiled roof for the hacienda effect. Hardwood floors, Mexican rugs. A few nonflowering plants that I had not been asked to but would water. Each room had cathedral-high ceilings with exposed beams, each room was painted bone-white. The furniture was overstuffed and white, and the tables and bureaus were all a light pine. The walls were decorated with a decent collection of photographs but not one with any unifying sense of ardor or curiosity. And was that the connection to Dean, were they collectors?

I found two large prints on a wall in the master bedroom. One was from Dean's wave series—he had photographed seas and oceans and bays in black and white, and the stark and frozen patterns of the tides created a minimal, almost abstract picture—and the second was a wide view of the ruins of an Egyptian temple, of flower-fluted columns rendered in daguerre-browns. I knew that I was being childish when I removed the photographs from the walls and stored them in a closet. I felt as though Dean had tracked me down, as if he had found me. Not that I had ever really escaped his shade, not that I wanted to. I despised this house, this septic cold house, and finding the photographs did not help. I decided that I would leave after no more than a day or two.

But I stayed, and I think that I stayed because of the view. Wide decks wrapped around both floors of the white house; most of the windows were sliding doors. And there was the pool off the living room, facing the ocean. Dean and I were going to build a house in the country, that had been the dream that had sustained us before he got sick, and our house was going to have a pool, a simple and serene pool like this one.

Often when I house-sat, I took care of cats or fed the children's goldfish or watered plants, and sometimes I drove the old family car around town to keep the motor running well.

Sometimes I was asked to paint a room, and I frankly was happy to do the work, but I had no such responsibilities or chores at the canyon house. So I made the garden around the house my purview despite the fact that the rosemary and lavender and agave did not need my checking up on them after a season of rain. I remember that during that first dry weekend in the canyon, I created tasks for myself, shoring up the berm of a date sapling, pruning a laurel bush that did not need pruning, so that the gardener who came once a week had little to do when he showed up a few days later. He removed some of the dead petals of the bright-blooming birds-of-paradise by the pool and called it a day.

And throughout that weekend, as long as there was daylight, an incessant bang of carpentry drifted across the canyon. From the echo of it, I expected to find a team of workers pounding away to get the house framed in record time for an impatient family, but when I looked through the telescope, I only saw the same two workers whom I had noticed before, the same man and woman responsible for all of that clamor. They had no helpers, and when I checked on them in the week ahead, I made the same observation. One man and one woman—a couple, I decided—building a house alone. The man continued to dress in light-colored clothing, white like the pickup truck that they drove, and he was generally a blondish figure when I had him in my cross hairs. The woman was a darker presence on the cliff and harder for me to follow with the telescope, although I did watch her become angry at something that the man had done—witness the way she clutched what looked like blueprints and pointed, You see, you see, at a certain corner of the unfurled page with a hammer. And although the man tried to stop her, the woman proceeded to rip out some of the framing that they had just installed. They had erected more of the frame and braced the studs with angled planks of wood, they had made measurable progress, but I began to suspect that they were not your everyday carpenters and that this house that they were constructing had to be their own house because no one would ever hire them. The more I watched them, the more I wondered who they were, what sort of people would undertake a project they were so clearly unqualified for.

It rained again for two days, but not so hard, not so angrily, and the clear air that followed was worth the wait. This climate spawned hope. You woke up and you believed that you would be remembering that day for some time to come. You knew that you would sleep well that night. This was memorable weather, although I do not exactly remember what I did in the days that followed.

I decided that if I was not going to drown myself just yet, then I should look for work. Dean had left me some money and I had lived on it, but I wanted to save the remainder for what Dean and I had been saving for together, the house that we were going to buy and renovate or build from scratch. So in each new place that I came to, I promised myself that I would get a bookstore job or a position at an art gallery, but I never did. Dean and I had talked about the many things that I could do with my life other than being his assistant, like becoming a travel writer, since we spent so much time far from home. My chronic ambitionlessness made him crazy. When he died, I had not become the travel writer that he wanted me to be nor had I become anything else nor did I want to.

Once again, I did not look for a job, and instead I took day trips along country roads to the north and to the east of the canyon, far north into the valleys where the hills were extravagantly painted with blooming wildflowers, entire slopes dressed in thick velvets of poppies and heather and golden-rod, far east into the desert, also in bloom, the pale plains there adorned with bright cactus blooms and flames of petals on the spindly ocotillo. I drove nowhere in particular but kept changing the direction in which I was traveling—long roads that led nowhere troubled me now when they never used to trouble me—and turned back toward the city and made it back to my canyon in time to check out what progress the couple building the house had made that day.

They continued to work painfully slowly. They framed one wall, they began another. I found myself talking to them. Very good, another corner framed, I would say. Now how about going for an entire wall in a single day? But my cheerleading seemed to have an adverse effect because they tended to build a section one day only to rip it down and redo it the next. One day when I was late getting back to the canyon from a long drive and it was too dark to determine what the couple had accomplished, I was frustrated to have missed a day in the life of the house-in-progress, bothered enough so that I slept worse than usual. I woke up early to look through the telescope and see what they had done.

The reason that I was late returning to the canyon was because I had almost purchased a tract of land, a sliver of an acre with a trailer home on it about fifty miles north of Joshua Tree. As I had moved around the country, I had collected odd bits of land, if these minor investments taken together could be called a collection, which was one way of fulfilling Dean's desire that his money be used to acquire a piece of earth of somewhere remote. I never paid more than a thousand dollars, and usually the property came with a dilapidated fixer-upper or sometimes a cottage that had been condemned. My first purchase was a slender lot of utter flatness in the dead-middle of the country and a good hundred miles away from the farmhouse that I was sitting at the time, a lot that I happened to pass on one of my aimless day trips. The land had a one-bedroom house with no roof to speak of and some sheds. I thought I could live there. I thought that when I became tired of moving around, I could settle down and make a life on the outskirts of the middle-of-nowhere. But as soon as I had moved on to my next house-sitting assignment, I lost interest in the prairie real estate and impulsively purchased some other undesirable property in a swamp or at the base of a mesa or wherever. I knew that it was a frivolous habit, a squandering of finite resources, but I had my stack of deeds and titles, my land. I had somewhere to go.

The piece of the desert that I wanted to add to this collection was actually larger than most of the properties that I had purchased, and I imagined that I would not be able to afford it. The sardine can of a trailer would have to go, but I appreciated the land itself because life survived on it—a few yuccas, a plump cactus, and at least one lizard, which darted from the shade of a yucca to the cactus via the shadow of my leg. The FOR SALE sign listed a phone number and I had to drive some twenty miles before I found a convenience store with a phone booth. No one answered when I made my call, and because I kept trying the number whenever I saw a phone booth on the way back to Los Angeles, I was late returning to the canyon. If I gave too much thought to these land purchases, I came to my senses and did not spend the money, and so I never bought the property in the desert.

Another day I went to the County Museum. I was sitting on a bench trying to make sense of a recent untitled abstract mural when I realized that a man with blond hair pulled into a ponytail was not sketching the painting as I had thought he was, but sketching me staring at the painting. I was attracted to his hands and the way his fingers manipulated a charcoal pencil across the broad page of his sketch pad. I acknowledged him with a smile, but I did not turn my head toward him so as not to ruin the pose. I was flattered when he told me that I had wonderful shadows. I said that this was because I was an insomniac. He rubbed the pad with the side of his pinky, working my shadows I guessed. He never showed me the drawing.

We lunched in the cafeteria. He laughed easily. He told me about his art classes and his job in the museum store, which, since I had once worked in a museum store myself, allowed us to swap dull anecdotes and express mutual despair about the decline of museums in the age of blockbuster exhibitions. I was bullshitting, but it did not seem to matter because so was he. He was the bold one who suggested that I probably had wonderful shadows all over my body and asked if he could draw me. Can I draw you?

How long had it been, how long. Can I draw you? We would go to his apartment. I would take off my clothes and try to be cool and coquettish, but I would be hard, and after he had been sketching me for a while, I would tell him that I wanted to draw him, too, and he would ask me if I had ever taken any life-drawing classes, and I would have to say that, no, I had not, and as he slipped out of his black shirt and black jeans, as he tossed me a pad and a pencil, he would say, You know, you really should, everyone should, in order to appreciate the human form.

And I appreciated his form, I did, I did. But I lied and said that I had to be somewhere. A tired line: I have to meet some friends. And our conversation, which had been so fluent and refreshing, became awkward. The man left me in the cafeteria.

I followed him out and then followed his car. I drove as far as his house and watched him talk to a friend on the street before he went inside. And I came close to knocking on his door, to apologizing for my sudden change in weather. There are dark clouds over my head, I would say, but they're clearing up. I had the door of my car open, one foot on the street. I would like you to draw me. Please. Yes, and I know of some land that we can go to in the desert; we could build a small house there. You can paint all day and I will mix us margaritas at dusk. We will go into the city once a year to sell your paintings but otherwise never leave the desert. I had my foot on the street. I drove away.

When Dean died, I thought that I would get over him in time, but that was not the case; the more time passed, the more I missed him. I missed the meals that we cooked for ourselves, the instant wok dinners, the marathon lasagnas. I missed our talk, our sex. I missed the way that he would teach me whatever radio song of the moment he had taught himself; I had no voice and a bad memory for lyrics, but he was a patient teacher. I missed these songs and the way that they ran through my head and made me think of him. Now when I thought of Dean, there was no music, only a stone of sorrow lodged in my chest.

When I got back to the canyon, I swam until I did not have the strength in my shoulders to continue, and then I dragged the telescope out to the deck and watched the builders in turn watch the sunset. I think that we create puzzles for ourselves to keep us going from day to day, and a house under construction is an epic riddle solved slowly but never completely solved, of course, until someone moves in. The parallel studs and crossbeams perpendicular to the studs began to form a skeleton, the fish bones of a house, but enough of a skeleton now to define a rectangular structure.

Would it lie low against the landscape and follow the contour of the canyon peak? Would it have wide and open windows and broad terraces and blend into the natural terrain? Or would it emerge as an abstract structure with a neat, self-assured geometry in contrast to the non-euclidean mountain? Would it be a white box which during the day looked heavy and solid but pure and pristine and which in the evening seemed just the opposite, light and electrified, a beacon of a house that appeared to defy gravity and hover and float toward the stars? Or maybe what was going up across the canyon was just another easy-eaved bungalow, shingle-sided and shingle-roofed. Maybe it would be a tall and gabled gothic mansion with emaciated windows and witch-hat turrets. Or maybe it would be a cold metal cube with shiny railings and mesh follies. Or one of those beach houses that were becoming common again, lime-bleached houses meant to look wind-swept and sand-swept. Maybe it would be a tile-roofed stucco palace like the house that I was sitting, with all of its colonialist pretensions. Maybe it would be an adobe, a throwback cliff dwelling. Maybe it would be painted pink, a palazzo in the rough. What kind of a house would it be?

A confession: There was a time when I wanted to be an architect. Architecture, after all, was a part of my heritage. My father spent his working life as an urban planner, redesigning downtowns to include parks with zoos. However, he never achieved the kind of prominence that my grandfather did, my grandfather whose legacy was widespread and whose influence could be best measured in the suburbs of America. Blame him in part for the proliferation of the split-level and blame him in part for the kind of neighborhoods where there are one or two model homes and dozens and dozens of clones.

I did not spend much time visiting my father at his projects, but when I was young I did go and see my grandfather on the job. He would wad a scarf into a hard hat and place it firmly on my head. He let me carry a long tube of blueprints. I stuffed pens into my shirt pocket the way he did, and everything seemed so large—his life was played out on a movie lot—the bulldozers clearing vast hills for development, the trucks rolling in with stacks of lumber, the scores of bustling workers slapping together whole houses in a day, or so it seemed. I was too young to understand what was sacrificed in the name of my grandfather's grand projects, the forests, the rivers. He was who I wanted to be.

In junior high school, I took a semester elective of drafting, and when I told my grandfather that I enjoyed drafting, he made a face. It gets much more interesting than drafting, he said. Why don't you try drawing a house? I used his T square and right triangles and drew the floor plans for a house in one-to-one-quarter-inch scale. My grandfather encouraged me to do more, and I began to apply my allowance toward mechanical pencils and templates and compasses and proportional dividers. I set up a modest atelier in my bedroom and, when I was done with my homework on weeknights and all night on Friday and Saturday, I stayed up late doodling houses and then transforming these doodles into rough blueprints, first on graph paper and then on velum.

I drew houses for families to live in, although I never imagined the family itself, big, big houses with big, big rooms. I wonder what ever happened to all of those drawings, hours and hours of precocious drawings. I subscribed to architecture digests and read up on all of the working deans of American design. All alone in my room, but imagining myself at the helm of an important firm, I drew house after house for fictional sites, but one day I abruptly stopped drawing and never took it up again.

My grandfather, who loudly lauded each and every plan that I ever showed him, died during that time; I lost his encouragement, but that was not why I stopped. I think that my father, who had never had the warmest of rapports with his father, was rather critical of my efforts, but that was not it, either. Probably I became more of a social creature and started hanging out with my peers and going to the shore once one of us could drive, and that was why my life as an amateur architect came to an end. I suppose the real question is why I did not pursue architecture again in college or after college.

I made the mistake of telling Dean all about my adolescent drawing, and then he encouraged me to go to graduate school; he nagged me about it until we had a rather unseemly row one afternoon on a beach somewhere. I was nasty and childish, kicking sand if I remember correctly, and after that he left me alone.

But when we talked about the house that we were going to build in the country, our mythic retreat, he let me take the lead, he let me construct a model of it at the foot of our bed. The magazine that he was reading stood for the living room, which would be designed around a great stone hearth, the alarm clock, and also aligned with the pool, the book that I was reading, and one steep wall of the main room would be lined with floor-to-ceiling bookshelves—pass me that highlighter pen, please—and then instead of a formal dining room, we would think of the eating area, a tissue box, as an extension of the kitchen. . . . And so on. Dean watched me assemble a sprawling heap of objects on the quilt, and he never told me to pare down my construction or that the house that I was imagining was too large for us and beyond our means; he would try not to smile too obviously, but his delight was more than obvious, it warmed the bedroom, and that was why I kept piling on the television remote and the telephone and the address book, rooms on top of rooms on top of rooms. At Dean's memorial service, an architect friend of his pulled me aside and confessed that it was Dean's expressed wish that I somehow be sucked into my alleged calling by becoming deeply involved in the design process of our dream house; as if this man needed to tell me what Dean wanted, as if I did not know.

Some of the people for whom I would house-sit subscribed to interior design magazines and I would plunk down in an armchair at night with nothing but a reading lamp turned on and read these magazines from cover to cover; design magazines were my pulp fiction. When I went to bookstores, I always flipped through the expensive architecture books that I could never afford. And I will admit that now and then I still thought about becoming an architect—I mean going to school, taking the boards, apprenticing with some reputable maverick—but these were thoughts that expired when my shower ended or I was done swimming laps. Now a couple was building a house across a canyon, and when I watched them work—eventually they finished framing the walls and began framing a low-pitched roof—a vague and ancient longing ached deep in my gut as if I had run into an old flame on a crowded city street and, during a brief and awkward exchange, instantly recalled the very beginning of that distant affair, not the denouement and disappointment but the first uncomplicated encounter and the desire that carried me toward it, the careless rush, the drive, the naked risk. The risk.

Days went by, it was April, warmer days of avid bloom when the canyon wind was fragrant to the point of mawkish with wild roses. One night, I waited until the man had smoked his cigarette and the woman had massaged his shoulders—the man massaged her shoulders affectionately, too—until after they had driven their truck out of the canyon, and then I got in my car and tore down Encantado Canyon Road (realizing too late that it probably would have been faster to travel in the other direction, along the mountain road that I never took), and when I hit Las Patas Glen Road, I headed up and into the unexplored other half of the canyon.

Las Patas Glen proved to be a narrower rise than I had expected, and the tributary private drives that speared off toward the burned-out lots fell away from the road so sharply that, even without any trees or foliage, it was difficult for me to see where they went and if I had driven past the turn-off that I wanted. Also there were no streetlights, only the occasional stump of a streetlight, but my ears were popping and so I knew that I was still rising toward higher ground. Now and then I could see the cascade of lit homes across the divide. Driving up a canyon is like swimming underwater, you push and push and finally emerge with a gasp and see how far you've gone. I spotted a road veering off to the right and a gate—I had not counted on a gate, although I should have since the private drive up to my house had one—but fortunately the gate had been left wide open.

I steered up an even darker road, an unpaved and bumpy road, and already I was making excuses for when the man and the woman showed up the next day and I had to explain my presence and ask for a lift to a telephone to call for a tow truck. At one point, I made a severe left turn, and had I been traveling ten miles an hour faster, I might have plunged into the canyon. It was a treacherous turn along the edge of the cliff, a cliff turn without a guard railing at that. I followed a final straightaway and reached a plateau and the house under construction.

I had left my house in haste and forgotten a flashlight, so I aimed the headlights of my car at the house, illuminating the frame with twin sulfuric beams. I had to watch my step because there were tools strewn everywhere, a hammer here, a box of nails there, a power tool of some kind, not to mention a veritable obstacle course of woodpiles covered in plastic alongside piles of other materials which were unidentifiable beneath tarps. There was some kind of heavy machinery draped in canvas. Finally I reached the house itself.

A revelation: The house had two floors. From my vantage looking west all this time, I had been unable to see that there were two levels which, from what I could tell now in the dark, formed an L. The upper level, where I was standing, ran east and west and stood on the highest ground of the property; this was the floor that I had wrongly assumed to be the entire house. What I had not noticed before was the lower perpendicular level built into the slope of the hill, a floor that faced south and that was backed by a cement wall that I had not noticed either, presumably a retaining wall engineered to hold the rock and soil in place. The flooring and framing of the upper steppe overlapped the framing of the lower level, but I could not figure how to get down there since stairs had not yet been constructed.

The floor felt solid underfoot, solid like the frame which I banged with my fist, and the walls had openings where the windows and doors probably would go, but there were no interior walls, not that I could tell, and I could not arrive at a basic understanding of how someone would occupy this space. The site smelled like a forest after a storm. Sweet like a cedar chest. I wanted to get down to that lower level, but the only apparent way was to climb down the frame as if it were a ladder, which was what I did, trusting that the beams would hold me.

I nearly lost my footing and ended up jumping halfway down. I was dizzy for a moment after I removed a large splinter from under my right thumbnail. I did not know enough about house construction to extrapolate what movement or trend I should assign the ultimate architecture, and it was difficult for me to estimate the size of the house in the dark, although I was certain that it would be a considerably more humble dwelling than my current lodgings. I looked back at my house in all its glory—I had left all of the lights on and the place was aglow—and it did not look nearly as ghastly at night, just large, like an old hotel. Most houses at night, if illuminated from within, possess an inviting warmth; they are reduced to their essence, they are shelters. The rest of the canyon appeared as it did from the vista that I already knew, the spread of lights falling away from me, the blue-black blanket studded with opaline gems of varying luster, a blanket that covered something alive, something that breathed, a beast that slept.

I stepped toward the center of the—the what?—the living room, a bedroom, a studio, where I lay down on my back and looked up through the roofless roof at a low moon and the evening's constellations, the stars arranged into connect-the-dot figures with attendant myths which I struggled to remember from that time in mid-childhood when I knew them all and could recite them with ease.

There was a certain breeze of loss in the night air on this side of the canyon, a treeless rustle that was absent on the side where I lived. I must have suspected that this was a house that was being put up by people who had lost a great deal and who had more to lose if they failed to build it. I know this now, but I knew it then, too.

A few days later, I went to the state beach down the coast road. I spent a morning naked under a parching sun watching the surfers in their rubber suits teeter to shore and wade back into the waves. I fell asleep and burned my back and headed up to the Paradise Diner for lunch. There was a line out the door of hungry people all waiting for booths to open up, but there were several available stools in the center of the counter.

I left a seat between me and a dark-haired woman who seemed to be engaged in a going-nowhere argument with a blondish man next to her. The man was in the process of smearing a dollop of jam over a triangle of toast with confident and grand swipes of his knife, as if to emphasize the certainty with which he could defend a point that he had made. The woman was wearing a white sleeveless turtleneck, which accentuated her mocha complexion. She had a tape measure clipped to a belt loop of her blue jeans. She withdrew a piece of toast from their mutual pile and dunked it into her plate of eggs.

When the waitress approached me from the other side of the counter and pulled out a pad from her apron, I pointed to what the arguing man and woman were eating to indicate that I wanted the same.

The man and I, I noticed, were almost identically dressed. Both us wore white T-shirts under our untucked white shirts, both of us had slung tennis sweaters over our shoulders like shawls. He wore chinos and I wore khaki shorts, he wore dark brown shoes while I was in sneakers, but if I had not gone to the beach, I would have had on long pants like his and maybe bucks like his, too. The woman tucked her chestnut bob behind her ears and concentrated on the rest of her breakfast-for-lunch, chasing home fries around an oval plate. She had downed a cup of coffee in the minutes since I arrived and politely raised her cup to signal the waitress she was ready for a refill.

She swiveled her stool toward the man and said, in a softer and less argumentative voice, "We have to read more carefully, that's all."

"I hate arguing about it," the man said to her.

"Me, too," she said.

"I just want to do it, and I don't want to keep retracing our steps," he added.

"I know," she said, agreeing, "me neither."

He said, "I just don't know if I can do this anymore."

She said, "You shouldn't talk that way."

"I don't want to give up," the man said, "but I don't know if I can do this anymore."

"Look," the woman said, "we have made progress. You have to give me that."

I was attracted to her voice. Low and weary as if she had been talking for hours, low and knowing. My platter of eggs and toast and potatoes came, my deep mug of coffee, and I was suddenly very happy.

"Do you want that?" the man asked the woman about a last scrap of toast.

"It wasn't very good," the woman said, pushing the plate his way.

"You would think that they would know how to make better toast," he said, eating it anyway, sans jam this time.

"How hard is it to make decent toast?" the woman asked.

"It was soggy," he said.

"Too much butter," she said.

I sampled the toast myself and indeed it was rather limp, but I had eaten fine and crisp and certainly adequate toast in the Paradise Diner on many previous outings.

"Too much butter isn't very good for us," the man pointed out.

"Please," the woman said, "neither are the eggs or the potatoes with all that grease."

"I can make better toast than this," the man said. "And I don't have to read a book about how to do it," he added.

"And then read the book wrong and have to retoast the bread," she said.

"Usually they make better toast here," I said.

At first I thought that the couple would ignore me, uncertain whether I had spoken to them, and in the seconds before they acknowledged me, I felt my face flood with blush. In all of the diners and cafés that I had frequented in all of the cities that I had called home for any length of time, I had listened in on the mindless chatter of an untold number of strangers and never let on that I was eavesdropping. Why I spoke then, I will never know. But I had made it clear that I was listening in on their conversation and that I had an opinion about the day's toast and there was no going back.

The woman cocked her head and looked at me with

chocolate eyes, and she said, "You are absolutely right. They're just having an off day."

The man leaned forward on his elbow and looked my way, too.

"I think it's the bread," I said. "You know, the kind of bread you start with."

"The man knows his toast," the woman said to the man.

"It sounds that way," the man said.

He needed a shave, his hair was all windblown. There was something approachable about him, an easygoing bearishness to him; not that he was large, he was my size, lankier. And he dressed the way I dressed, but the woman and I could have been brother and sister. Our hair and our skin and our dark eyes were alike. More than that, the hollowness of her glance, her high cheekbones; my admired shadows. I was overwhelmed with the desire to rest my head on her bare shoulder. Both of them looked to be about my age, maybe two or three years older, thirty, thirty-one at most

The man looked like the kind of person to whom you handed over your car keys hoping that he might figure out what was wrong with your transmission merely by driving the car a few miles. He was the man who taught other people how to drive a stick shift. The one whom you wanted to teach you something, like the rules to a team sport, even if you already understood the game. He played the guitar with great passion but was not very good at it, yet he had a sweet voice when he sang. And she was a fellow insomniac, I knew it right away. Her mind was cluttered with trivia, the years of the reigns of enlightened kings, the moons of the planets. She picked up languages from bookstore primers. She could identify trees by their leaves, and she always won at cards. You wanted to make bread with her. That was what I was thinking: that we could make bread, she and I, the kind of bread that would make good toast, to be sure.

"And let's be fair," the woman said, "the eggs were superb."

"The fries were tasty, too," the man chimed.

"Okay, we can come back," the woman said.

"We have to come back," the man said, tapping the counter as if he were playing the bongos, "because it's the only place for miles."

"We should get back to work," the woman said. "It was nice meeting you," she added, although we had not really met.

It was at that point, shaking her hand and smiling stupidly, that I looked out a diner window at the parking lot and saw a familiar white pickup parked among the four-wheel-drives and small trucks and sedans. Not just any white pickup. My heart raced.

"You haven't heard a word I said," the man said. "I can't just go back and—"

"Let's go for a walk on the beach and talk about it," the woman said.

"I don't want to talk about it," he said. "All we do is talk about it."

"We never take walks on the beach anymore," the woman said.

The man pulled coins from his pocket and added them to the crumpled bills the woman had already placed on the counter.

"We used to take long walks. We used to collect shells," she said.

"That's not true and you know it," the man said.

"I know. We never collected anything," the woman said. "Do you think we should have collected something? Would that have helped? Do you think we should collect anything now? Pottery or folk art or old toys or . . . or what?"

"I don't know," the man said. "I don't really want to collect anything."

I could not convince myself that they were the blurry figures in the distance at whom I had trained my telescope all these weeks. I could not connect their subtle gestures now at close range—the way he combed his hair back with his fingers, the way she ironed the cash with the side of her hand—with the more athletic movement which I associated with them, the sawing of wood, the hammering of wood.

"We're going for a walk on the beach," the woman said to me.

"But you won't collect shells," I said.

"Definitely not," the woman said.

"I'll join you," I said.

"Great," the man said. "We can discuss the coffee."

"I think the coffee is pretty good for a diner," I said, paying my check.

"The coffee is excellent," the woman concurred.

We waited for the traffic to subside and then we bolted across the two lanes of the highway. The man lit a cigarette.

"Don't smoke," the woman said to him. "It's bad for you."

"Yeah, and so were the eggs, I hear," the man replied.

"Let's take a shortcut," the woman said.

"I don't think so," the man said.

"Oh, come on," the woman said.

The walk to the beach was a good quarter-mile, and you had to climb down a rocky slope to get to the sand; to avoid the rocks, you needed to use the official entrance to the state beach, yet that was a half-mile away at least. The alternative was to walk up the shoulder of the highway to the north a ways, but there again, you had to climb down an uninviting tumble of boulders to reach the shore. The beach was public but access to it was private along the strip opposite the Paradise Diner, and the fastest route would have been to leap over one of the walls of the houses that were lined up next to each other without a break between them.

The woman walked past the garage of one house and approached the gate to the left of it.

"Do you live here?" I asked her.

Sitting in the Paradise Diner a few days back, I had noticed that when people pulled into the truncated driveways off the highway and did not park in the garages, they tended to open the gates to the beach houses without using keys. They were lazy about locking up, it seemed, or the residents of the beachfront properties left the doors unlocked so that they could receive guests without having to get up out of their chaises on their decks. The woman tried the gate door, but it was locked, and so the man and I followed her over to the next house and the next garage and gate beyond it, which was also locked.

"You don't live here?" I asked, although I knew what she was doing.

"This is insane," the man said. "Come on," he said and pulled my arm away from the woman. "We'll climb down the rocks."

The woman had walked four houses down in the opposite direction from us.

"Has she done this before?" I asked.

"She's only threatened to," the man said.

At last the woman found a door that would open. She pulled it back a crack and peeked in and waited for the man and me to join her. Which we did and, behind her, I saw only a series of bridged walkways reaching across an atrium to the house itself. The woman waited until a car whizzed by and then she said, "If we run into someone, we'll apologize and say that the door was open and that we must have the wrong address."

"I don't believe this," the man said and dragged on his cigarette one last time before stamping it out.

That day I behaved in a way I never had before, interrupting the conversation of total strangers in a diner and then willfully breaking into a beach house with them. And I realize in retrospect that what was weird was that I never for a moment worried that we would be discovered trespassing. When I followed them down a set of stairs from the street level to a patio of potted plants which were all dying in the salt air, when I stopped long enough to peer through the sliding doors of a two-story beach home and look across a sparsely furnished room to the sliding doors leading out to a deck on the other side of the house, a deck where an unsuspecting man was lying in the sun and talking on a cordless phone, I did not believe that we would get caught.

"Fuck," the man said when he saw the man on the deck. "Let's get out of—"

The woman shushed him. "Which way to the beach?" she whispered to me.

And I knew how to answer her. I had never entered a beach house compound like this before, but after two years of house-sitting, I had developed an intuitive understanding of houses and their layouts, and so I led the way down a narrow passage off the atrium, where there were many doors to choose from. The first door I tried opened onto a closet containing a washing machine and dryer. The second door was another closet, this one packed with rafts and folding chairs and beach umbrellas. A pair of bright blue flippers fell out onto the boarded walkway and I picked them up and shut the door. Finally, at the end of a long corridor off the atrium, I found the door we wanted, and we trotted down the warped wooden stairs that dipped under the stilts holding the house up over the shore. We stayed close to the stilts of the abutting house just to be sure that the man on the deck of the house did not see us and get suspicious.

When we had walked a safe distance, the man said, "Man, oh, man, oh, man."

The afternoon winds had kicked in and the woman

grabbed the man's sweater and pulled it over her head. I realized that I was still holding on to the pair of blue flippers.

The woman said, "He may know his toast, but he's a common thief."

I winged each flipper back toward the beach house. "Hey," I said, "it was your idea to break in."

"Man, oh, man," the man said, kicking off his shoes, tugging at his socks.

"You should have taken one of those rafts, if you had to steal something," the woman said to me.

The wind was behind us and pushed us along. In a few weeks, with warmer weather, the shore would shrink and there would be less of a beach to walk on even at low tide, but that afternoon, the shoreline was still at its winter width. Rock formations divided stretches of the beach and these rocks were covered with all matter of marine life, with black mussels, with spongy urchins that spurted water and shriveled when you nudged them with your toe, with burgundy starfish and brown starfish sucking the boulders and waiting for the next tide to carry them back to sea.

"Did I hear you say you had to get back to work?" I asked.

The woman nodded.

"Do you work around here?"

"Sort of," she said. "But it's not work like you mean work."

"I'm house-sitting at the top of Encantado Canyon in that big white house with the red roof," I said.

"We know that house," the man said.

I could not be coy with them; I knew who they were. That afternoon I was prone to easy confessions, me who never confided in anyone. I said, "I sort of have an unrequited love of architecture."

The man stopped walking and looked at me. The woman took his arm and stood close to him.

"My grandfather was an architect," I went on. "You would

know his houses if you've spent any time in the suburbs. I thought about becoming an architect myself, and when I was fourteen I stayed up late all alone in my room drawing houses, which probably sounds pretentious, but that was what I liked to do. But I never did become an architect, and I've been . . . See, there's this telescope in the house that I'm sitting, and I couldn't help but notice that you're building a house on the Las Patas Glen peak. . . . I mean, it's the only house going up after the fire, it seems. And I—"

"You've been watching us," the man said, squinting.

I thought he would tell me off. I thought that he was going to tell me I was creepy, and suddenly I felt a little creepy.

The woman covered her eyes with her hand. "I'm so embarrassed, I'm mortified. We must look like total idiots," she said.

"We don't know what we're doing," the man said.

"You're building a house," I said, heading down the beach again, "and I've been sort of fascinated because I never really understood how a house was put together before."

"Join the club," the woman said.

"Well, you look like you know what you're doing to me," I lied.

The woman laughed. "That's very flattering," she said.

"We lost our house in the Ventura fire last year," the man explained.

"We lost everything," the woman said. "Everything," stretching the word.

"I'm very sorry," I said.

"Don't be sorry for too long," the woman said. "We loved our view and we still have our view."

"And so you're rebuilding your house yourselves," I said.

"It's a lot cheaper than hiring a contractor," the woman said.

"It's one way to save a marriage," the man said, staring off into the ocean.

"We wanted to be together all day, every day," the woman said. "So we decided to build our dream house. We had the land—"

"We just need the dream," the man inserted.

I thought about their argument in the diner. Now the woman looked as though she had taken about as much as she could from the man. She rubbed the back of her neck.

The man stopped walking again. "It's not that I want to give up," he said to her. "It's just that—"

"No," I said, "you can't give up."

The man swallowed hard. The woman took his hand.

"The amount that you've accomplished already . . . She's right, the progress that you've made . . . You can't give up, you have to keep going because, well, if you can see it, I mean that if you can picture it, then you can make it: the big living room with the stone hearth and the floor-to-ceiling wall of books and the wall of windows looking out at the long pool. The bedroom that is like an altar with skylights and the enormous kitchen that opens onto a terrace . . ." I felt my face turn red. "I was going to build a house myself once, or have it built. . . . Anyway, you know what I mean," I said. "We all dream about building our own house, but you're actually doing it. You can't give up, you've come too far."

The man was silent. Finally he said, "We'll see," and we walked again.

The woman said, "Honestly, I'm flattered if it looks like we know what we're doing." She pushed up the sleeves of her (his) sweater.

"You must think I'm a horrible voyeur," I said.

The woman caught me off guard. She touched my cheek ever so briefly. "We should get back to work," she said, and this time the man did not respond.

"I'm parked at the beach lot," I said. My face burned where she had touched me.

"We're parked back at the diner," the man said. "But I don't think we should cut through that man's house again," he said.

"Lately I've been wondering how exactly you put a house together," I said. "That's all."

Her name was Helen Zayne and he was Ethan Zayne.

She said, "Stop by sometime." He shook my hand. Then they drifted back the way we had come. I walked in the opposite direction, and when I turned around, they were gone.

When we were living in the West Village, Dean and I used to watch a couple just out of college in an apartment in the building directly across from our brownstone. They tacked up sheets for curtains, and the sheets tended to come down with the merest breeze at night. They burned a lot of candles and their lamps were bright, which made it easy for us to follow them around their apartment as they each adjusted to living with a lover for the first time, as they figured out how to create necessary distance within the close quarters of a Manhattan walk-up, how to occupy different rooms within the same room, how to come together, when to fall out of view onto the mattress on the floor. We made up stories about them for ourselves, it was hard not to; we gave them names, we imagined their conversation when they painted their apartment or had friends over for beer and chili. We did not necessarily find them terribly intriguing, but in our own way, we became attached to them and rooted for them to hang on to each other when they argued. We watched them sit out on their fire escape arm in arm and we may have been jealous. We wanted to return to that first summer after college, that sacred season. But then one night we recognized them in the corner deli and we heard their voices, which were so different from the voices that we had assigned them in our minds. The woman called out the man's name and it was a different name from the one that we had chosen, and our fiction crashed in the time that it took to purchase a pint of ice cream. We stopped watching them after that encounter.

And maybe that was why I did not venture across the canyon the day after I met the Zaynes in the diner nor the day after that, because walking on the beach with them ruined my speculating. I decided that I had spied on them long enough and returned the telescope to the living room, but even then I could hear them—they did keep building after all. I could hear their cutting and banging and I wondered what piece of the puzzle they had fit into place that day. I carried the telescope back into the kitchen and almost expected them to wave hello, but they did not acknowledge me at all. They were too busy ripping out the bit of roofing that they had assembled the previous week.

The real-estate agent charged with selling the house that I was sitting showed up with some prospective buyers, a man and a woman who wore their sunglasses like tiaras, who wore his and hers matching gold watches. It appeared as though they were turned off by the view of the burned-out side of the canyon and only made a superficial tour of the premises, but they looked like they could afford the house and, more significantly, the land that the house stood on. I did not think that about Helen and Ethan Zayne. If someone could afford to live on such expensive property, green or burned, would they really build their dream house themselves? It was more likely that they would hire a team of established architects who would recommend veteran contractors to cater to their every whim. And then maybe, if they were so inclined, they might take the time out from their hectic moneyed lives to help their carpenters build a walk-in closet or a medicine cabinet. The couple shopping for a house only made me wonder even more about the Zaynes and their project across the canyon.

I wanted to visit them, I thought that we had gotten along fairly well, but I was embarrassed by my babble on the beach. Hello, nice to meet you, I have been watching you with a telescope. What kind of stalker did they take me for, what kind of maniac? I had been so alone since Dean died and alone, too, during my life with him, because even in the best marriages there is a certain amount of solitude, an isolation at times. I had never really had the kind of friends I could just loll around with. I was not sure that I knew how to make friends anymore.

The Zaynes were climbing ladders and beginning the roof framing again, and I checked in on them every few hours. And then it rained again one more time, the last rain that April, and they could not build while it stormed, so I did not see them for several days. When it rained, I slipped back into my old routine. Sleeping in the afternoons. Swimming laps in the downpour, swimming as if I were in training, and I was in training again. The rain would not stop.

Finally one night during the storm, I realized that the second anniversary of Dean's death—always in my sights yet somehow forgotten—was the next day, and all I could think about when I swam laps was how Dean at thirty years of age, Dean who had so many more pictures in him, Dean with all of his talent and his charm—Dean who what? Who could have hung on until some new drug was invented to sustain him? Who could have wasted away but lasted until there was a cure to revive him? All I could think about was how Dean had given up so unconditionally and so fast.

Most people when they get sick go in and out of the hospital several times and try a panoply of treatments. They struggle awhile, they put up a fight which Dean did not even pretend to wage. He had gone into the hospital just once; he came back to our apartment at half his weight having decided, having arranged to die. He ordered a hospital bed for the living room; he added codicils to his will. He was weak, yet he had time to write down what music he wanted a lone cellist to play at his memorial service, so why did he surrender so quickly? Was I so easy to leave behind, was I so easy to strand?

These were not new thoughts, and when I had allowed myself to think them before, I had hated myself for being so selfish. I was supposed to say, At least he did not suffer long. I was supposed to say, He would not have wanted to live a life in which his travel would be limited, in which he might go blind and not be able to work his cameras. But the truth of the matter was that I could not forgive him for abandoning me so easily. I watched him gray and thin and grow old without me. He was drugged into oblivion for the last month of his life, and I held his hand every day that month. I kissed his fingers. I would cool my hand in front of a fan and then place it flat against his brow. Did he know that I was there? I could not forgive him.

It was raining hard when I got in my car that night and drove down the canyon road to the coast highway. Raining and thundering when I drove to the rocks beyond the stretch of houses and left my car on the shoulder of the road and, with the rain banging at my back, climbed down that tumble of rocks to the shore. It was a miracle that I did not slip on those rocks. I staggered across the shore and dove into the ocean.

But the line between the shore and the tide can blur during a torrential rain, and so while I thought that I had bounded far enough into the waves to dive, I had in fact only gone partway across the shore. I landed on my stomach, smack on the wet sand, my face in the foam, and the water and the sand were numbingly, paralyzingly cold, and a big wave crashed on the shore and pushed me back, back as I stood up and tried to balance myself, back and stumbling away from the tide, back, back. . . .

I screamed, I was pathetic. I screamed until I was hoarse. Pathetic. And I do not remember how I was able to climb back up the rocks to the shore, but that was what I did, in search of the beach blanket that I had stashed in my backseat; I would warm myself up before trying to drown myself again. I was shivering, my teeth chattering. Dean, Dean, Dean, I shouted. Dean, Dean. As if shouting his name loud enough would either bring him back or banish him from my waking dreams. I leaned on the horn. Dean . . . I had the beach blanket draped over my shoulder and I just wanted to go to bed and sleep for a long time. Pathetic. I drove home.

Once again the rain stopped before dawn and the air was clear the next morning; everything in the canyon had a sharper edge, the oleander with its clusters of white and pink flowers, its shimmering leaves, the gleaming fins of convertibles swimming up the canyon road. When I breathed, I drew in too much oxygen and became faint as if I had traveled to a higher altitude and not yet acclimated to the thinner air, and the usual morning echoes blended together into a pleasing symphony. There would be nothing dissonant about such a day, the kind of day when monuments were dedicated and armistices signed. The kind of day when afternoon lovers lunched alfresco for all the world to witness their passion. This was a climate that made us believe that we were invulnerable, a climate that empowered us with unexpected wherewithal.

When I pulled up the final stretch of the dirt driveway on the other side of the canyon that morning, I saw Helen

Zayne emerge from the house and wave an enthusiastic hello and direct me to park next to the white pickup. She shouted behind her, "Look, our friend the thief came to see us after all." Then Ethan Zayne emerged through the frame of the house as well, both of them looking the same and dressed almost the same as they had been in the Paradise Diner.

"We'll give you a tour," Helen said, closing my car door after me.

"It looks like you've pretty much got the place framed," I said.

"We're raising the roof," Ethan said. He offered me a cigarette which I declined.

They led me toward the house, both of them grabbing my elbow when it looked like I might step on a large splinter of wood or open toolbox. And as I had noticed during my initial reconnaissance, their tools were strewn everywhere like children's toys all across a lawn. Hammers and screwdrivers and block planes. They guided me around the piles of lumber with their plastic wraps peeled back now, around a makeshift table—a board across sawhorses—on which blueprints were spread out and held down with large stones so that they would not blow away.

It was not difficult for me to pretend that this was my first visit because the framing and the property itself proved to be entirely new to me by daylight, the narrow slats of studs against the sky taking on a logic now, the syntax of walls. This side of the canyon was a different wilderness than the one that I had come to know, rockier because of the fire, more arid without trees and shade, but I also saw that more life had taken root or regerminated than I had realized, that the lower cliffs were dusted with an ochre scrub, a redder brush that crept up to the newly poured foundation of the construction, a foundation which included sets of low steps, steps that I had not seen at night, a house situated and designed, I now understood, to take advantage of the maximum reach of a jagged peak, to hover above the divide. The sheer height of the house and the way the world fell away from it took my breath away. This property was all on an incline, and the only level place to stand was in the house itself.

"You just walked in the front door," Ethan said when I stepped up through the frame of the upper floor. "Welcome."

"You realize that you're our first guest," Helen said. She wiped a smudge of sawdust from her cheek.

What had been a lulling breeze elsewhere in the canyon became a fierce wind up here, and I had to keep combing my hair out of my face. A whipping wind which made it difficult for me to speak and to hear Ethan, but I thought he said, "Picture one big room. The kitchen will be run along that wall there, and we will probably want our dining table over there. We'll build a terrace on the lower roof, you see, and so we'll be able to have our dinner out there, if we like." He pointed toward the western end of the house. "The fireplace," he said. "Plenty of room to sit around the fireplace," he added.

I saw that there was already some sort of preparatory masonry in place along the foundation.

"If we replace the piano that we lost," he said, "I would put it where you're standing now and maybe some bookshelves and a good reading chair. Maybe a desk. You get the idea. The stairs will go where the ladder is, and then downstairs—" After you, he motioned.

No, after you, I motioned back and followed him and Helen down the ladder which would have been handy the other night when I had climbed down the frame itself at some risk; I saw how far I would have fallen had I misstepped.

From the lower floor, I discovered the canyon anew. The

falls of lemonade berry, the falls of feathery fuchsia. The Zaynes had sited this part of the house so that entire floor appeared to reach into and float over the glen like a long dock on the edge of a deep lake. The elevation turned out to be noticeably steeper than on my side by a good fifty feet—when I glanced back at my house, I was looking down—and while the perspective that I was accustomed to was certainly spectacular, this vista was entirely proprietary, an arrogant stance from which to survey the ocean. I became convinced that I could see it all from there, the entire Pacific across the curve of the planet.

"The bedroom," Helen said. "Actually, we haven't figured out if we want to cut up the floor into two or three rooms or leave it like this, just one big loft."

"Oh, just one big loft," I blurted, trying to imagine what it would be like to wake up in a room this large, with this view. I stepped around a long pile of lumber.

Helen showed me where she wanted to angle the bed and where she thought they could build a window seat, but she made the point of saying that no matter how they arranged the furniture, they would try to keep the house open and spare. "We hate clutter," she said, and that statement seemed to me less like a strategy of interior design than a revealing declaration of the Zaynes' worldview.

I followed Ethan and Helen up the ladder. They went back to work. I did not want to get in their way, so I stayed on the opposite side of the floor from where they had positioned a second ladder which they took turns climbing up to hammer nails into the occasional joist that spanned the width of the room. I checked out the valleys to the north, where a small white plane flew low over the distant quilt-work of ranches. The band of blue on the northern horizon was another mountain range.

Ethan had belted his sweater around his waist and he wiped his forehead with the shoulder of his sleeve—it was

windy but getting warm—and Helen repositioned the ladder and the two of them proceeded to reinforce all of the ceiling joists before they began the next step, before they lifted
up a long and substantial beam of wood—two beams actually, which they had joined together with metal brackets—
and rested it on the joists. This was the spine of the roof, the
ridge that would run its length. They measured the ridge
with a tape measure and measured it again and drew marks
on the beam with a pencil. Then they each set up a metal
scaffold on either side of the room, pipes of steel or some
sturdy alloy that rose a foot above the joists—it took them
a while to assemble the scaffolding—and then eventually
they lifted the heavy ridge up once again and set it down on
the scaffolding.

Ethan's hair had darkened with sweat, he was down to
his T-shirt, and Helen tied her hair back with a white ker-
chief. She shouted something to me but again I could not
hear what she said. Soon both of them were descending the
ladder to the lower floor, and I was unsure whether I should
follow them down. They took a long time returning, and I
was about to climb down the ladder, too, when Ethan came
back and was about to shove a beam of wood up the ladder
and slide it onto the upper floor where I was standing, and
so I took this beam from him instead. Helen, I noticed, was
right behind him but busy reading a large and thick book.
Ethan lifted five pieces of wood up to me, one after another,
thinner slats than the joists, and I stacked them, and then
he hopped up the ladder and nodded thank you. Helen followed; she put her book down.

"What are they for?" I asked about the beams that I had
handled.

"The rafters," he said.

Helen had carried a portable power saw up the ladder with
her, and after she measured one of the rafters with a metal
L of a ruler, a framing square, she then trimmed the beams,

all five of them at once, with angled cuts while Ethan held them together.

The rafters would run from the beam that connected the studs up to the ridge—that became clear to me when Ethan scrambled up the wobbly rungs of a scaffold with one of the cut beams in hand. From the top of the scaffold, he angled the rafter down to the stud-wall to check the measurements, but when he did this, he had trouble. He needed another set of hands to hold the as yet untethered ridge in place. Helen climbed up the other side of the scaffold—they did not appear to be afraid of heights—and she was able to use her weight to keep the ridge from sliding. But Ethan still had problems, because even with the ridge secure, he could not hold the rafter in place and at the same time manage a hammer.

You need three people to raise a roof. They needed me.

I steadied the ladder against a crossbeam and hesitated before climbing up—I never felt surefooted on a ladder—and I did climb up it and turned my torso ever so slightly so that I could hold on to a stud with one hand and grab hold of the rafter with the other. That accomplished, I cautiously climbed to a higher rung of the ladder and held the rafter snugly in place until Ethan had hammered in his nails. The piece of wood vibrated in my hands when he pounded at it. At the same time that he hammered, the wind died down somewhat, and I could hear him when he asked, "How does it fit?"

"Flush," I said. "Perfectly within your markings."

"Miracles do happen," Helen said.

"Do you think you could tap in a few temporary nails?" Ethan asked.

That these nails were allegedly temporary meant that I could mess up entirely and know that my amateur imprint would be erased, the structural integrity of the house not jeopardized. Would they have let me help them if they knew that before that day, my experience with a hammer was limited to two bookcases that I had slapped together during college, shelves which forever teetered even when laden with books and which had collapsed the first time I tried to move them? The sum total of my carpentry to date had made a splendid fire one winter night.

I climbed down the ladder and found a hammer on the floor and slipped some nails in my pocket and climbed up and drove the nails into the rafter along the angle of the beam, copying the way Ethan had nailed the rafter to the ridge. I was surprised when I took my hand away and the rafter stayed put.

"Nice work," Ethan said. "Let's do the next one."

I rolled up my sleeves and handed him another rafter—he stayed put on the scaffolding while, as instructed, I moved my ladder to the opposite side of the room—and I helped him secure the other leg of the gable in place while Helen continued to hold down the ridge. This time I hammered my thumb; it had to happen, it was my baptism. We assumed the same roles at the other end of the house and positioned four rafters in all, forming two squat scalene triangles which were connected by the ridge and which in turn supported it. This was going to be a roof with a low grade, a gently sloped and unassuming lid to the house.

"Where does the fifth rafter go?" I asked.

"We'll use that one to cut the other rafters," Helen explained, "since we know that it's a perfect fit. That's what our book says to do."

"We're raising the roof," I said. To say it gave me a chill. A roof over one's head was the most fundamental component of any shelter, was it not? I was participating in an ancient rite. Men had gathered to raise the roofs of neighbors everywhere for centuries. It was a ritual of commune and kinship. "We're raising the roof," I said again, giddy.

"Slowly but surely," Helen said, heading down the ladder.

"We got it all wrong before," Ethan said, "but this time I think we'll get it right."

While Ethan and Helen went about the business of removing the rafter stock from a pile of wood and measuring it against the fifth rafter and cutting it all with a large table saw, the machinery previously covered in canvas, I examined the blueprints spread out on the board-and-sawhorse table. Now I could see where the windows went, the doors. It all made sense to me now, the flow from the upper to the lower floor, the way the rooms addressed the landscape, the view. I flipped through additional drawings, roughly scaled sketches of the framing on dozens of other pages of a graph-paper pad, pages and pages of encyclopedic notations, the type of wood to use, where the nails should go, the kind of nails to use—how the frame had to fit together all down to an eighth of an inch and even more exact than that, the math of it all scribbled in the margins. What I could not find among the blueprints, however, were any projections that would have given me some idea of what the exterior of the house was going to look like. The floor plans had to suffice. And then I found the large book that Helen had been reading before.

I do not remember the exact title. It was something clear and to the point, like *How to Build an American House,* a recent copyright, a text which when I flipped through it proved to be exactly what it was billed as, a manual for the common man, the lay carpenter, the amateur with ambition. A bookmark had been inserted into Chapter 5, "The Roof."

"A nice man in the bookstore recommended that one," Helen said, startling me since I had not seen her coming over to me. She said, "Where there's a how, there's a how-to book. Of course, reading the instructions and then reading our plans correctly is another story. There really should be a how-to book on how to read how-to books."

I looked back at the framing and the flooring and the foundation, and I wanted to express my sincere awe for what she and Ethan had built thus far by reading a book, my gratitude although I was not sure what I wanted to thank them for, but Ethan came along carrying some of the freshly cut rafters and saw that I was holding their book.

"Hey, hey, hey," he said, "no looking ahead to see how it ends."

I closed the book and helped him carry the rafters, and then the three of us began to position them against the ridge and against the stud-wall, hammering them permanently into place, stepping over the joists, working our way from the ends of the house in toward the center. Ethan moved his scaffolding, I moved my ladder, Helen shifted the second ladder on the other side of the room from me, and we inched along, the three of us, each bracing the wood and securing the beams in turn. My upper arms began to ache from the hammering, and my forearms were giving out—I doubted that I would have enough strength to keep going—and yet I persevered, we persevered, and we raised the roof, we raised it rafter by rafter.

Gradually I began to understand the design in physical terms; I mean that I did not simply observe how the pieces of a roof came together, that I felt for myself the way the ridge became increasingly sturdier and the way the rafters carried the weight of the frame down to the studs, the studs to the foundation; I mean that when I held on to and pounded the wood, I tapped into the flow of basic physics, the transfer of forces from my biceps to my hammer to the rafter; I mean that something of myself went into that roof that we raised against the blue heft of the sky. One by one, we hammered the rafters to the ridge, and without speech, without stopping to catch our breath, we fell into a rhythm of lifting beams of wood up high and pressing the angle of the cut against the penciled markings and acknowledging

the perfect fit with a nod and taking turns holding the rafter
in place and nailing it down firmly and giving it a good slap
before moving on, a tempo of positioning and hammering
wood that quickened as we worked, a rhythm that included
our every breath and thought, a mechanical rhythm that
was difficult to break when we were done and the rafters
were all in place and the roof was framed, the roof raised.
As fatigued as I was, drained to the point of speechlessness,
I wanted to keep going.

The sun began to set, first across the stripes of rafters and
then down the canyon and out to sea. Ethan pulled himself
up to the ridge and stood up while Helen and I followed him
beneath the rafters, spotting him as he paced back and forth
along the length of the roof and, from each end and at various points in the middle, dropped a plumb line. The red
needle-nosed bob swayed in the breeze and twirled before
it pointed straight down. I was not quite sure how the plumb
line was supposed to work, how you read its dangle, but
Ethan and Helen apparently were able to assess the per-
pendicularity of our efforts, and judging from their smiles,
we had done exactly what we were supposed to do. We had
raised the roof and the house was now a true house.

We sat side by side on the step that projected out from the
eastern side of the upper floor—these steps were a strange
element of the design because they did not lead anywhere,
only down the bluff—and we stared across the canyon.
Ethan smoked a cigarette, Helen reached around him and
massaged his shoulders, then he massaged hers. They both
spoke of the work they still had to do on the roof—it needed
to be sheathed and shingled—and then there was the downstairs roof for another day.

Helen turned to me and said, "But I think we can say we
raised the roof, and so thank you." She began to work her
fingers along my shoulders and neck. The massage was
soothing.

Ethan smiled an easy-breaking grin. He said, "That was a great day."

I asked them if they had designed the house themselves.

"We did," Helen said.

"She did it all," Ethan said.

"We had talked and talked about it," Helen said. "We always used to talk about our old house and what was wrong with it."

"She did it all," Ethan said again. "I just complained. And thanks to you," he said, "I'm still here. We're still here."

I did not know what he meant.

"Because of what you said on the beach," he said. "Or not so much what you said as how you said it. So I told Helen that I would give it one last shot and that if our work went smoothly, I—we would keep going."

"If we fuck up this time," Helen said, "we'll . . . We will sell the land."

"If every day is like today," Ethan said, "we won't have a problem."

"But we can have a bad day now and then," Helen said, "can't we?"

Ethan did not answer her.

She looked at me. "What happened to your house?" she asked. "The one that you said you were building."

"My house," I said. "Well, we never actually got around to designing it, let alone building it, and we wouldn't have built it ourselves anyway. I mean Dean with a hammer"—I laughed—"would be more absurd than me with a hammer, which as you saw . . . Dean died," I said.

Helen touched my arm. "When?"

"Two years ago," I said. "Two years and about ten hours," I said. Dean, Dean, Dean.

Helen held my hand. Ethan took a deep breath, and I expected one of them to say something standard and consoling.

But what Helen said was, "We lost our son."

"Oh, no," I said, "in the fire?"

"No, no, before the fire," she said. "The fire was at the end of last summer and he died the winter before that. He was three."

Later I saw a photograph. The child's name was Wes and he was blond and looked so much like Ethan that I thought at first that Ethan was showing me a snapshot of himself as a boy.

"First you lost your son," I said, "and then you had to go through a fire on top of that." I realized that I was gripping Helen's hand too tightly.

"I was in a car accident," she said. "I was . . ."

I did not want her to have to tell me what had happened if it was painful to relive, and so I said, "I am so sorry," so that she would not have to continue.

And at this point I would have expected Ethan to reach his arm around Helen's shoulder and hold her—or vice versa—but Ethan was silent and seemed very far away from us as he stared out into the canyon.

I had told Helen about Dean but not told her much; she had given me a few unsettling facts about her own life, and that was all I knew. But there is a dialect of loss that only those of us who have dwelled for a time in a province of grief can recognize. She and I were speaking a similar slang. I began to understand much more based on what had not been said—and what I intuited would prove to be correct for the most part—about Ethan's initial reluctance to rebuild, about Helen's convincing him that it was the only way for them to get their life back, to reconstruct it themselves, with their own hands.

I began to feel rather clumsy. I was an intruder. I had arrived without warning and pitched in without asking if I could help; I had insinuated myself and now I was the guest who did not know when to leave the party. I stood and began to phrase an apology.

But Helen said to me, "We really needed you today."

"I should have asked if—"

"We need all the help we can get," she said. "Hey. Are you working right now?"

I suspect that she presumed that if I had time to watch them with a telescope, then I might be unemployed. I shook my head no.

Helen looked at Ethan and Ethan nodded back at her. She asked, "So how are you spending your days?"

"Doing absolutely nothing," I said, "why?"

Helen smiled. "Give us a minute," she said.

I wandered back into the house not really sure what she had in mind. She huddled with Ethan and I could not hear what they said to each other.

Helen called me back. "Brad," she said, "come here. We can't afford to pay you much, just a minimum wage, but we need help, your help, and so if you're interested . . ."

My immediate response was to shout yes. Yes, yes, yes. But instead I said, "Shouldn't you get someone who knows what he's doing, someone with experience?"

Ethan laughed. "Yes," he said. "But we can't afford that person, and so you'll just have to do."

"I'm the one who should pay you," I said. "But I don't know. See, I wasn't planning on staying in Encantado Canyon too much longer—"

"What do you say?" Helen Zayne asked.

Ethan Zayne dragged on his cigarette. He began to nod slowly and approvingly as if I had already made up my mind to join them.

And I started to nod, too, even as I said, "I don't know," even as I said, "I should move on."

TWO

We finished the framing of the lower roof in a sprint. That roof was an easily managed set of rafters that sloped down from the juncture with the upper floor to create a kind of lean-to nestled beneath the main hull of the house. The lower roof covered most but not all of the terrace, and the terrace itself did not extend across the full length of the lower floor. Helen explained that she wanted to leave room for some planters, which she would fill with rosemary and sage and which she hoped would make the bottom tier of the house blend with, indeed disappear into the slope of the canyon. We built out the gables of the upper roof to create overhangs, and we propped up temporary posts between these gables and the extended foundation, which I now understood would provide two shallow porches with four columns each on the east and west sides of the house.

Then we turned to the roof sheathing and hauled measured and cut boards of plywood up the ladder. Ethan pulled himself up to the rafters while Helen and I stood on ladders and held the sheathing so that he could deliver swift smacks of his hammer to nail the boards in place. He kept dropping his nails; dozens of nails rolled off the eave and plummeted into the slope of desiccated brush below us. And even though the roof was pitched at a fairly low slant, we found ourselves slipping when we sheathed the rafters, staggering the sheathing like bricks as we worked from the eave up toward the ridge. I should say Ethan was slipping because he had trouble getting a good hold with his worn-in, worn-soled bucks, not the best choice in footwear for house-building. At one point I was holding on to a rafter with one hand and his ankle with my other hand, and I surprised myself when I volunteered to switch places with him, when I performed a neat gymnastic move which I did not know I was capable of pulling off and lifted myself through the rafters, onto them, and took his hammer as if it were a relay baton and began pounding nails into the sheathing. If I did not look down, I was fine. And I liked the way Helen or Ethan occasionally grasped my calf or heel to make sure that I did not slide into the canyon; I liked knowing that they would catch me if I fell.

My technique was raw. I wasted countless nails merely trying to drive them in straight. I ruined so many nails prying them free from the wood and bending them with the claw of my hammer. I had a lot of catching up to do in terms of my basic hammering method, but Helen graciously demonstrated that if I slid my hand down the handle of the tool, I could get more leverage and force beyond the peen, and that obvious adjustment made a great deal of difference. I would need to learn how to get the best angle on a saw, how to drive a plane smoothly across a board, how to do so much, but even as we sheathed the roof and slowly altered the shadows on the floor beneath us from the stripes of the rafter beams to solid shade, my hammer became less of an alien accessory in my hand and more of an innately evolved limb.

When the sun reached its peak height, we piled into the pickup, Ethan driving and Helen between him and me. It was an old truck with a high rounded hood and manic bugeyes for headlights. The three of us fit quite comfortably on the vinyl seat of the cab, and we drove down to the Paradise Diner, where we ate at the counter.

"Where have you been living?" I asked them.

Ethan named a hotel in Santa Monica.

"That must be expensive," I said.

"Tell me about it," Helen said. She explained that after the fire and after they had returned to the ruins of their house and picked through the rubble with kerchiefs over their mouths, they had decided to treat themselves to a swank hotel and spoil themselves for a while; they had lost everything and felt that they deserved it. The only problem was that they never left.

"That would have made too much sense," Ethan said.

"That would have meant that we would have had to spend our insurance money wisely," Helen said. "Like on wood for the new house."

"It's a very pleasant hotel on the beach," Ethan said. "And someone makes the bed each morning."

"Wait," I said. "You've been staying in a hotel all this time?"

Helen took a bite of her sandwich. Ethan sipped his coffee.

"I love hotels," Helen said. "Or I should say I love hotel lobbies."

"You live for hotel lobbies," Ethan said. "All of the people coming and going."

"All of the people meeting each other," Helen said. "I love hotel bars."

"There has to be a piano," he said.

"And a man playing something cool and moody and mindless," she said.

"You should have found a house-sitting gig," I said. "That's the way to go."

"We should have moved to another state," Ethan said.

Helen: "Let's not start in on that."

Ethan flashed an apologetic grin.

We took the long way to get to the beach for our after-lunch walk because Ethan was unwilling to trespass again even if Helen and I were willing to take the risk. On the beach, Helen hooked Ethan's arm and told me that she had met Ethan in a hotel bar in a city on the East Coast.

"He was waiting for someone else when I sat down in the club chair next to him," she said, "and I bought him a drink, and then he bought me a drink—what were we drinking, darling, do you remember?"

Ethan looked at me and said, "You realize that she's making all of this up."

"And I remember that I had the piano man play a certain song, and even though no one was dancing, Ethan asked me to dance."

"We dated in high school," Ethan told me. "In New Jersey," he said.

"Everyone was watching, and we were dancing this drunken tango, and I think that was when your date showed up, Ethan, and saw us having such a fun time together that she left without even saying hello or good-bye."

"We would take the train into the city together on Friday nights," Ethan said, "and one time, the night of our senior prom, we went into the city and eloped."

"Now he's the one who's lying," Helen said. "You can't just elope without a blood test or license or—"

"And then we stole a car," Ethan said, "her in her gown and me in my rental tux, and we started driving across the country. We drove for days and days, knocking off convenience stores as we went, until we couldn't go any farther, and that was how we ended up here in California."

I knew better than to believe either of them and pretended to sight a whale off the coast in order to change the subject not because I found the breeze with which they willfully deceived me or denied me the truth to be upsetting but, to the contrary, because I was envious of their union, however it may have begun.

Back in the canyon, we finished the sheathing and unfurled sheets of an asphalt paper and used a heavy-duty stapler to affix it to the plywood. And then we began to nail down the shingles, two nails to a shingle. Ethan told me that the house would ultimately be painted white, which meant that the gray shingled roof would almost disappear when you looked at the house from a distance. This would not be a roof that would weigh down too heavily on the house and prevent it from floating above the canyon.

All three of us shingled from various points along the eaves and gradually worked our way up to the ridge, a tedious task, the overlapping of the shingles and the constant checking over what we had done to make sure we were installing them along straight and more or less parallel lines. We shingled and we shingled, and I was amazed when we were bumping elbows in the late afternoon. We worked well together, efficiently, with confidence.

At one point before the sun set, Helen consulted the blueprints to see how and where exactly we were going to attach gutters and downspouts. She shrieked and her scream reverberated throughout the canyon and bounced back at us and enveloped us with her dismay. We had apparently forgotten to carve out the necessary roof openings for the various air and plumbing vents, not to mention a notch for the chimney and, more significantly, the squares for an array of skylights on the upper roof.

I should have seen this coming. I knew how the Zaynes worked. As soon as we would make some headway, we would have to backtrack and rip out all that we had nailed down and start over. Helen became very quiet, and so I was quiet, too. Ethan paced beneath the rafters and stared at the faulty roofing. He walked over to where Helen and I were standing, and I half-expected him to say, Well, that's that. We had our one shot to do it right, and we blew it. We would not only rip out the roofing but also the stud-wall, and then Ethan and Helen would put their land up for sale.

Ethan lit a cigarette. He said, "Tomorrow morning we'll have to go back and cut through the shingles and the paper and the rafters. It's not the end of the world," he said.

Helen could not check a wide smile of relief.

"What?" Ethan asked, exhaling smoke.

"You don't want to, like, divorce me and pretend you never met me?" Helen asked.

Ethan said, "Not at all. Isn't that strange?"

They both stared at me as if I were responsible for their entente. I shrugged.

We lost our light; we had to call it a day. We sat on the cliff and watched the cartoonish puffs of clouds absorb the orange of the sunset, the clouds themselves seemingly descending, and when it was dark and Ethan was done with his cigarette and Helen done massaging his shoulders and neck and I hers—she taught me how to work my fingers as she had taught herself by reading a book—she took out a wad of crisp cash and paid me for my day's work. Not much, but I did not mind. The idea of earning some money was satisfying, the idea of saving money again.

Ethan and Helen got into their pickup and I started my car and we caravaned down Las Patas Glen until we hit the fork with Encantado Canyon Road, where we went our separate ways. At night I went for a swim and tried to read a book but was so exhausted that I fell asleep before nine. That was a typical day. I would meet up with the Zaynes early the next morning.

But before I made it to the top of Las Patas Glen, I veered off the main road and drove down one of the private roads of destroyed homes. Often that was how I began my day that spring, scavenging the rubble still redolent of noxious smoke, picking through the blackened bricks and objects made of metal, andirons and skillets and bike fenders.

What did I find so compelling about these ruins? Why is anyone ever interested in raising a wrecked ship or unearthing the cultish catacombs of lesser antiquity? In the name of history, we say, to complete an ongoing chronicle of time lost. To solve a puzzle, to fit in the missing tiles of a mosaic, because everyone likes a good mystery. We love to ponder the exotic and curious customs of ancient peoples; we want to try on their argot at the same time that we reproach them for their lack of refinement. How quickly we forget that where a city rose, a city also fell. When we sift through the slow avalanche of soil that has buried a city-state whole, we want to get as close as possible to the fate of a civilization without really knowing that fate firsthand.

I can say that my own attraction to ruins was a direct result of Dean's professional preoccupation. He would travel deep into a remote savannah to find the one remaining wall of a temple to a minor deity of the harvest and then circle that wall for hours until he figured out how he wanted to shoot it, what time of day would give him the best shadows, the best flood of light. He could spend a week camped out by that wall. He wanted to photograph every ancient ruin in the world, that was his mission. He would hang out at archaeological digs in order to snap the first glimpses of a freshly unearthed palace. He would follow a stone wall through miles of meadow until he was satisfied that he had seen its entire length and wend.

Once we traveled to a lesser-known Greek island—this was on our first trip together when I was still in school—an island with a mountain and a temple nestled into one flank of that mountain. We had already visited a dozen other islands on that trip, each with its own temple, and I remember asking Dean why we needed to charter yet another boat for more of the same. I suspect that he considered dumping me then and there. I said to him, Tell me, please. It's not that I don't appreciate these temples, too, I do. But why are you so . . . ? Obsessed? he asked back.

Dean never came up with an adequate response, and I put the question to him many times. Sometimes he would tell me that he was drawn to the entire composition of the landscape of which the ruins were only a part. Sometimes he would lecture me and tell me that the Greeks knew what they were doing, setting their temples amid the ideal continuum of the ocean and the mountains. He said that his fascination was rooted partly in the history of what had been lost, but if the truth be told, I think his obsession was primarily an aesthetic one. He was drawn to decline, to collapse, to loss. He liked the hollowness of ruins, the broken lines. If I wanted to annoy him, I would say that there really was not much difference between the ancient ruins we visited and the much newer ruins that you could find closer to home. That made Dean nuts. It's not the same, he would say. Not the same at all.

But they are everywhere you turn in America, although we do not always label them as such. Every small town has at least one abandoned house like my grandfather's house; neighbor kids throw rocks in the windows and build up a local mythology around it. Look at the naked tenements that you will pass along the neglected corridors of any city. We tend not to call these places ruins when we understand how they became ruins; we tend not to be so intrigued by the ashes the more we know about the fire that made them. When I came to Encantado Canyon and finally saw how a wildfire could storm a canyon, all ruins began to lose their allure for me. But that was in the autumn, and back in the spring, I was still intrigued by the torched glen.

I always intended to get to work before Ethan and Helen arrived, but inevitably I stopped off on the way to marvel at the single corner of a house that had survived the fire and not fallen down so many months later, or the chimneys, soot-drenched but still standing, still drawing air up through their shafts and occasionally whistling with wind. I would try to identify the gnarled objects in the debris, and I remember staring at a triangle of metal attached to a handful of pegs for the longest while until I figured out that it was what was left of a piano. And when I found a rim, say eight inches in diameter, for instance, I could never really know whether it belonged to the burner of a stove or the casing of a wall clock. Where did the various pipes that I picked up belong, what had they connected to what? I found a metal rake, the spray nozzle of a garden hose, the spoked wheel of an Exercycle spinning in the breeze, the frame of a lawn chair.

I thought about all of the people returning to the canyon the day after the fire, their mouths masked with bandannas. You did not want religion at a time like that; the rumor of the last millennium was that you might find comfort in the embrace of a church, but religion only meant that there was more to explain, more to justify in a larger cosmic context. The fire had to have happened for a reason, and so you asked yourself why, why me? Even if you could attribute the fire to arson, to some cruel inhuman moment, the striking of a match against the sole of a shoe, you had to ask why a messenger had been sent to test your faith in man. Without religion, you were required to explain nothing; what happened simply happened.

And I could picture Ethan wearing a baseball cap and Helen in dark glasses, and certainly they were devastated by the grim scene and saddened, stepping over the smoldering walls, the ground still hot, through the walls that they could still envision and feel and believe that they were touching. But I could also understand how once the shock subsided, they may have been excited, freed in a sense. They had led charmed lives but that charm had run out and they had known great tragedy. Yet the fire was not their tragedy, and if the truth be told, the fire offered them a way out, a way to start over. Here was their opening to leave the canyon. That was Ethan's take. Or they could start over right where they were standing. That was Helen's spin. This was their dilemma, their peculiar fortune.

Although neither one of them really could admit that losing their home was emancipating, it was too brutal a confession, what with the relief workers wrapping blankets around the hysterical newly homeless people of the canyon, all of the nurses on hand to administer mild sedatives, the news crews poking around, the helicopters swooping in for the close-up. Helen could not say what she was thinking, no one would have believed her, that she was more attracted to the canyon now than before, the canyon rendered even more serene by the fire and more desolate and more remote. I would have believed her if had I been there with her picking through the rubble. When I toured the ruins in the morning, I was certain that I would have come to the same conclusion that she had reached, the same resolve to rebuild.

One property that I visited had been bulldozed flat, all traces of the house rolled smooth, yet there was a car parked in the driveway, a gutted chassis riding phantom wheels. The plastic molding of its signal and parking lights had melted and frozen into red and orange icicles. I walked around the car several times before I got back in my own car and drove off, fast toward the summit of the canyon, at once spooked and exhilarated.

We had to brace the rafters from the underside of the roof and then drill holes through the shingles so that we would know which ones to pull up, where to peel back the asphalt paper and where to carve a square in the sheathing. Then we cut the braced rafters with no room for error, not a fraction of an inch, and we inserted short horizontal pieces of wood to frame the skylights. As we opened the squares of the roof, I thought that the house sighed, that it breathed easier whenever we went back and repaired our mistakes.

Another day, we assembled and installed the troughs of gutters running beneath the eaves and the downspouts that would spill rainwater when there was rain again down the slope of the property. The house started to look strange to me, the roofing in place but the walls only framed and not yet sheathed, see-through walls that were open to the salty sea breeze that rushed through the house starting at about one-thirty each afternoon. The house looked naked to me, naked but wearing a big hat.

"A sombrero," Ethan agreed.

"No, more of a fedora," Helen said.

I expected that we would dress these naked walls next, but I was wrong, we were nowhere near ready to close in the house. Next came the stairs. I had heard it said that the true test of a gourmet was how he or she roasted a duck, that the crispness and the glaze and the moistness of the poultry and the way the sauce brought out the essence of the bird were the best measures of culinary talent. The same could be said about stairs and carpentry. Staircases might look straightforward and basic to anyone who marched up or down them, but they were deceptively complicated, a challenge of math and woodworking.

The longer days were hotter days when April spilled into May, and I did not mind getting out of the sun to work indoors for a while. The sun whitened over the course of a day and from one day to the next, bleaching the beach but at the same time bringing out the more extravagant flowers of the season, the almost neon bottlebrush, the jacaranda trees with their feathery green leaves giving way overnight to lacy and lavender trumpet-shaped blossoms. The jacarandas empurpling the lower rise of the vale.

Helen skimmed the chapter on stairs while I brought the appropriate wood inside and laid it out on the lower floor, while Ethan collected the tools that we needed from around the yard. He and I waited for her to tell us what to do, but Helen appeared to have trouble understanding the recipe. The ingredients were simple enough, but the way they were to be combined was impossible to follow.

"Where are your drawings?" I asked. Helen had drafted meticulous plans for the framing and roofing, specific and thorough treatments that rarely required us to make adjustments when we got down to the actual construction.

"There are no drawings of the stairs," she said. "I never got around to mapping out the interior. We were anxious to get started. We'll make it up as we go along."

She stepped away from where the stairs would rise and squinted. She lifted her legs as if she were actually going to climb the steps that she envisioned. And then she told us to find a piece of one-inch-by-four-inch lumber, which we did, and then position it vertically against the upper floor, which we did; this was our story pole, that was what she called it, and we would mark off the height of each riser on it. Ethan and I both had our pencils at the ready, but Helen rubbed her brow. She chewed on her thumb. She cradled the book in one arm and pointed with her other hand and read aloud, or I should say mumbled aloud, while Ethan and I tried to make sense of her instructions.

She said, "The exact stair height should be . . . But if the second floor is . . . Okay. Right. The height of the risers must be equal. And safe. And if the measured riser does not . . . Well, the stringer will be . . . And the length of the stringer equals . . . Oh, fuck it," she said.

"I overheard a guy in the lumberyard ordering a prefab staircase," Ethan said.

"For how much?" Helen quipped. "We cannot afford some catalog staircase, Ethan, and besides—"

"We want to make it ourselves," I backed her up.

"Listen to our friend the thief," Helen said. She read the book again and her eyes widened. "Oh, I see," she said. "I see, I see."

"What?" Ethan and I both asked.

"Well, it's pretty basic trig," she said. "The square of the rise plus the square of the run equals the square of the stringer. Can you believe it's that simple?"

I understood that the stringer was the main stair support and that we were talking right triangles here, but that was the extent of what I understood. "I get it," I said.

"No, you don't," Ethan said.

Helen began to flutter around the room excitedly, grabbing tools but setting them down, ultimately settling for the framing square, the legs of which she hastily banded with masking tape. She was talking to herself now, oblivious to us, and Ethan and I stepped back to give her room.

"But that doesn't allow for the nosing of the tread," she said, "damn, damn," and pulled off the masking tape and reapplied it elsewhere on the metal rule. She dragged the long piece of lumber out to the center of the floor, the hypotenuse of the staircase, and she crawled alongside the wood while she flipped her framing square leg over leg along the length of the beam. She penciled in some diagonal lines on the wood; she scribbled algebra on the pine. When she glanced up at us, she was all glassy-eyed. She said, "This may take me a few minutes."

"Cool," Ethan said. "Take your time."

"Just a few minutes," she said.

We waited for her, but she was lost in her calculations. Ethan decided to start sheathing the walls with plywood and told me to help Helen. But she did not want me to stand there and watch her think, so she in turn assigned me my first solo task, which was to work on the framing of an interior half-wall and closets on the lower floor.

Until that point, I had done very little measuring of the wood and no sawing, restricting myself to less cerebral tasks like hammering. I read the blueprints and scribbled down a list of exact lengths and I unhinged the yellow folding rule and transferred these measurements to a virgin board and eventually, with Ethan's help, drew the slab of wood across the table saw. Sawdust sprayed back at my goggles and I could not see what I was doing, but I somehow managed to cut straight and evenly against the grain and somehow the plank fit exactly the way it needed to fit, flush between a joist and the floor. I was not always so accurate, sometimes I cut short and sometimes I cut long—at least in the latter case I could correct my mistake with a hand saw—but I had entered a new realm of working with wood.

And it was when I began to shape the lumber that I began to appreciate the qualities of wood. I found myself staring at the grain. We were using two kinds of pine, each with its own landscape. The white pine was striped with wide dark-edged bands, the rivers, and numerous narrow parallel bands around it, the banks running down to the rivers. But the patterns in the ponderosa pine looked more like valleys as seen from a spy plane, like our canyon with its deep trench and the countless steppes descending toward its core, its dry arroyo. Or take the poplar—most of the plywood was made with poplar—and its faint streaks, its smooth blond pattern; the poplar grain reminded me of a beach and the occasional stream trickling down the shore. We had some cherrywood that we were saving for the interior finish work, and the cherrywood made me think of the shifting swells of a desert. When I began to saw the wood, I began to admire its virtues, its sturdiness, its weight. It did not give up easily to my toothed blade, especially when I was not using one of our battery-powered cutters but relying on my own muscle to push and pull a crosscut saw. I sawed and sawed until my shoulders swelled and nearly burst with pain. And the knots, the dark nodes of the bole: Ethan and Helen complained about these imperfections in the lumber, but I must admit that I liked finding them because they reminded me of our arboreal source. A knot signified a branch, after all, the living reach of a tree, a tree sacrificed for a house.

I began to take an interest in the tools we used, too, which were not just any old tools. Ethan and Helen had stumbled across a listing in the classifieds. A Glendale man was retiring from a long career as a handyman and occasional contractor and wanted to sell his tools, all of them at once, to someone who would take care of them and apply them toward good work and generally cherish these instruments that had served him well. He did not like the look of Ethan and Helen when they showed up, he said so, because they hardly appeared to be the artisans to whom he wanted to hand down his tools. But then Helen admired a certain awl or hammer and the way the broken-in grip felt secure in her hand, treating the tool like the artifact that it was, a tool with a blue-painted wood handle, blue with one red stripe mostly chipped away. And Ethan started talking to the man, respectfully inquiring about his life as a craftsman, laughing at a story about a client who wanted a coffin to sleep in because he believed that he was a vampire, sighing at the story about what happened to the old man's son. The son was going to apprentice with his father and go into the trade of fixing cabinets and building bookshelves, but then there was a war and he was called to it and he died far from home.

We will take good care of your tools, Ethan and Helen promised the man, and how he would have cried had he seen the way we scattered the tools as we used them. But then again we were using them, we were using his Paleolithic hatchet and his I beam of a level with its embalmed bubbles; his tools served us well, too. His clunking wrenches and delicate nail sets. All of his worn-threaded clamps and his easily loosened pliers. His files, his chisels, his prized fine-toothed saws for detail work. The old man had shown Ethan how to disassemble his block plane and sharpen its blade on a whetstone and put it back together so that it would shave wood with exceptional smoothness, and Ethan in turn showed me the way to clean the plane. I had expected to use an array of gadgets, all manner of implements designed for one and only one function—in a kitchen, we have so many utensils designated for specific tasks, a melonballer, a grapefruit knife, a garlic press—but beyond the power saws and power drills, there were no fancy gadgets in the toolboxes. All of our labor came down to measuring and sawing and hammering, and these rudimentary tools, these inherited tools more than sufficed.

So I measured and I sawed and I hammered all day long, and I began to notice something narcotic about the work. I woke up needing a fix, my fingers flexing with the desire to fit my hand around a hammer grip and start pounding. I worked all day and yet I found that I had more energy than ever before. Enough extra strength to prune the hedges back at my house and weed the beds of herbs that I bought at a stand on the coast road and found the time to plant. Enough breath for my postprandial swim. And I could hammer and hoe and swim, and still I was not sated; I was not tired enough to sleep. When I looked in a full-length mirror after showering one night, I was amazed to see that my body had begun to take on a new shape, that I had a physique to speak of for the first time in so many years, since those teenage summers when I played tennis nonstop. I had forgotten that I was once strong.

It took me several days, but I made a closet, a closet without a door as of yet. I knew that it was not much, but I was idiotically proud, grinning when Ethan inspected my work and grinning when he gave me more to do, a wall to sheathe, another closet to frame. Meanwhile, Helen was still engaged in the much more complex undertaking of the stairs, and one afternoon when Ethan had gone off to the Ventura lumberyard for some wood that he had ordered or maybe for the cement mix for the chimney, Helen pulled me aside and said, whispering as if Ethan would hear, "I fucked up big-time."

Her stairs did not fit snugly against the wall nor did they rise in even increments; the risers were too steep and the treads too long. She had ended up inserting shims of wood scraps here and there to make up for gaps in her measuring. The stairs were not a complete disaster, they would have sufficed, but she wanted to start over.

"Don't tell Ethan," she said.

"He was cool about the skylights," I reminded her.

"I know," she said. Helen looked at her stairs and bit her lower lip. "Come on," she said. "Let's redo it all before he gets back."

We were still ripping out the first-draft staircase when Ethan returned. Of course he noticed what we were doing, but he did not say anything. He leaned against a corner of the framing and puffed on a cigarette and watched us for a while before wandering off to attend to some other chore.

"Sometimes he surprises me," Helen said. "We might just build a house after all."

This time I worked with her on the stairs. Once again we set up a story pole and marked off where the stairs should fall. This time we took into account the thickness of the floorboards that would eventually be laid over the under-floor. Then we set that pole down on the floor and laid out a fresh beam of wood for a stringer next to it. Helen scribbled her equations on the wood and then used the taped-off framing square to plot out where the triangular notches should be cut for the risers and the treads, checking and rechecking her math. When it came to cutting the wood, we did it all with fine-toothed saws for the greatest precision; we used our well-measured, well-cut stringer as a pattern to measure and cut the remaining stringers; and we actually set up our stairs with only a few temporary nails first to make sure all of the boards fit together; and they did.

This took the better part of a week, but finally we lined up the balusters and railings and the stairs were done. The true test of well-made stairs is whether you take them for granted. If you trip on a step with a fractionally steeper or shorter riser, if you stumble at all going up or down, then you notice the hand of the carpenter and the carpenter has failed. We took several turns trying out the stairs and we did not stumble once. The railing and newel were plain and simple and the balusters neatly parallel. Helen had aimed for and achieved a clean geometry. I hoped that we would not have to finish the staircase off with stain or paint any time soon or ever if we could help it. If no one was going to no-tice our watchwork calibration, then at least Helen's calcu-lations would be preserved in the wild equations that she had scrawled all over the pine. These were stairs adorned with math.

She and I sat on the same step late in the day while Ethan finished sheathing a wall upstairs—we could really speak now of an upstairs and a downstairs—and I asked her what the old house, the one that burned, had looked like.

"It was a cottage," she said. "Quite small, painted green. There were only four rooms, and that's including the kitchen, but it had a big deck that reached out toward the ocean." She extended her arms toward the lower tier of the house that we were building, and I could picture the deck, a deck supported by tall stilts. "The house had a lot of windows but it was not very well ventilated, and so we spent our lives out on the deck."

Her eyes misted and I regretted asking my question. "This house will be much grander," I said.

"Yes," Helen said, "grander."

"You need a larger house now," I said.

"After the fire," she said, "we came back and picked through the rubble of our house, and there was absolutely nothing left, nothing we could identify except for our old iron bed, which was all mangled. And all the keys."

"The keys?" I asked.

"Ethan was always losing his keys," Helen said. "Which was quite a feat, given how small the house was. His house keys and car keys, any key he ever put in his pocket, the key to his bike lock. And then after the fire, we found keys everywhere we looked. Where there had been a desk, under the twisted bed, where there had been bookshelves, everywhere we turned, Ethan's misplaced keys. In the bedroom closet, behind the kitchen stove, keys everywhere, keys to things that no longer existed."

"Now you'll have so much space," I said, "you won't know what to do with it all."

"I did try to save that house, you know," she said. "I mean when the fire came."

I nodded. I stopped trying to coax her out of the past.

"I had the television on and I knew that the fire was coming our way and coming fast. . . . I kept wetting down the roof with a garden hose. Watering all of the shrubs around the house," Helen said. "I drenched the roof and the fire was coming fast—"

"Where was Ethan?" I asked.

"Not there," Helen said.

Where, then? I wondered.

"And I would have stayed right through the fire and kept watering the roof until it passed around me, I would have," she said, "I would have," as if she needed to convince me that her story was true, as if I doubted her bravery. "I would have. But . . ."

"But what?"

"The police came," she said quickly, "and evacuated the canyon and I had to wait on the beach. I could hear the fire, and I could hear all of the houses imploding. I thought that I heard our house go."

"You tried to save it," I said. "And now you're building your dream house."

Helen smiled, she took my hand. We found Ethan upstairs and then the three of us went out to the cliff to watch the sun go down.

Ethan reached into his pocket to pull out his pack of cigarettes, I thought, but withdrew a ring of keys instead. He jangled them for Helen to see, and I wondered how much of our conversation he had heard. One of the keys, I could tell, was a hotel key.

Helen smirked. "Oh, please. Don't pretend," she said to him. "I know that you had to ask the concierge for another key to the suite because we were charged for it. It was on the bill."

Ethan shrugged, So what?

"Don't pretend," she said.

I could feel a spat coming on. I intervened. I said, "Hey, why don't you guys come over for a swim?"

"Now?" Helen asked.

"Come over to my house for a swim, and then I'll make you dinner," I said.

Ethan was game, but for some reason Helen was reluctant.

"It's not your house," Helen said.

"You know what I mean," I said.

"I'm kind of beat," she said.

"It was a great day," I said.

"It was a great day," Ethan concurred with a yawn.

"Let me make you dinner," I said to Helen. "We could make it a great night, too."

As soon as they crossed the threshold, they were off and exploring, Ethan gravitating toward the kitchen and Helen drawn upstairs to the bedrooms. I plopped down into an armchair and watched them drift from room to room with their mouths agape. Helen came downstairs and crossed Ethan's path without comment; Ethan went upstairs. I saw Helen jump up in the dining room; she was unable to touch the wrought iron chandelier. As Ethan checked out each bedroom, he switched on overhead lights and lamps, spilling incandescent puddles into the upstairs hallway.

Helen was the first to return to the living room, where she disappeared into the deeper reaches of a couch. I could only see her sandals when she delivered her verdict. "No one should live in a house this big," she said. "I got lonesome just looking around."

I asked her if she or Ethan had known the couple who was selling the house.

"About two or three times a year," Helen said, "the place was lit up for a party, you know, with paper lanterns everywhere. You could hear the string quartet throughout the canyon. And then the parties stopped, and so we knew that something had happened, but these weren't parties that we were ever invited to, and no, we didn't know the people who lived there. Here, I mean."

We waited for Ethan to join us but he did not surface, and I was ready to send out a search party when he finally came down the stairs. Instead of joining us, he loitered over in the corner of the living room where there was a grand piano. He sat on the bench.

"Do you play?" I asked him.

He pressed a few random keys.

"Does he play?" I asked Helen.

A few more notes, and then Ethan bolted up from the piano and practically charged across the room toward the terrace and the pool.

"Don't bring it up," Helen whispered.

"Why don't you guys take a swim while I make dinner?" I suggested.

"We didn't exactly bring our bathing suits," she pointed out.

"Right," I said. "I'll hurry with dinner."

I slipped into the kitchen and opened my refrigerator on the off-chance that I would find the ingredients for a feast, but one frozen single-serving chicken pot pie would not be enough. Ethan appeared to be content to lounge around the house while Helen and I went to the market in Trancas.

I had no idea what I wanted to cook that night as I headed into the produce section of the grocery and picked through the various alps of greens and tubers but put nothing in my basket. Helen got bored and wandered off to find us some wine. What to cook. Something impressive, something dazzling. I had experimented with various cuisines in recent years—I always tested cookbook recipes that I found in the various kitchens that I had at my disposal—and I was not a bad chef when I had someone to cook for. I panicked. I groped at sun-dried tomatoes and mushrooms thinking I could pull off a wonderful springy sauce to pour over angel's-hair; I would add toasted almond slivers, I would mix in breadcrumbs. No, I was not in the mood for pasta. How about fish. I could poach some salmon in a light lemon-dill-and-caper sauce, or maybe I could grill the fillets and then smear on some pesto and top off the dish with marinated tomatoes. I had made that once and it had turned out well, but it was too complicated. Too many steps. What to cook, what to cook.

Helen returned with a cart full of wine and mineral water—who was supposed to drink all that wine?—and all I had done was throw a bag of onions into my basket, a bulb of garlic. I was a great deliberator about everything except land purchases, but Helen was an impulse shopper.

I managed to put together the makings for a simpler dinner than I had originally intended, and we headed for the checkout line, where Helen offered to pay for the food. I said no, that it was my treat, but she insisted and had given the man at the register a credit card before I could produce the necessary cash. I was a little annoyed by her gesture and did not want her to pay, and when the credit card was deemed unusable because she had exceeded her credit limit, I handed over what I had in my pocket. Which turned out not to be enough money, what with all that wine. Helen gave the man another credit card while I fumbled for my own plastic, discovering that I had left my wallet in my car—we had driven the pickup to the market—and Helen's second credit card was also tapped to its maximum, as was the third and fourth and fifth one she handed over.

The man at the register was getting impatient, a line had formed behind us. Helen made the man try nine credit cards in all, and it was the ninth card that accepted our purchase.

On the way back to the canyon, she said, "I forgot that I ordered the windows and doors. I think that's why I have no credit."

"You paid for the windows and doors with all of your credit cards?" I said.

"No, I put the wood on four of them. The wood so far has cost us the most, and we haven't finished buying it, there's still more to get. Let's see, I put the roofing on another, there was the foundation, some extra tools. . . ."

The Zaynes had financed their construction on credit, and that was my first real inkling that they were broke. "Couldn't you have gotten a bank loan?" I asked.

Helen laughed. "A bank loan," she said. "You're funny."

I had never known anyone who carried as many cards as she did—she also carried charge plates for numerous department stores and countless gas cards—and when I told her this, she said, "I used to be respectable," and changed the subject.

Ethan and Helen sat on opposite counters of the kitchen while I prepared a chicken. It would take a while to roast, but I had been inspired to snip some of the herbs I had recently planted and improvise with the spices. I cleaned the bird and cut up the vegetables, and meanwhile we drank a bottle of dry bordeaux. We were talking about whatever, the progress of our house-building, the changing weather, Southern California versus Northern California, nothing in particular, when we moved on to the second bottle and I got the chicken in the oven. Helen kept refilling my goblet, and I was getting buzzed.

She asked me to give her a tour of the grounds while the chicken cooked, and so we stepped out onto the terraced lawn while Ethan returned to the piano; I heard him tap out a few more notes, holding them longer, and I heard him produce a chord. I switched on all of the outside floodlights, the pool lights, too.

"Tell me about Dean," Helen said.

She had caught me off guard. "He was . . ." I did not know what to say, what adjectives to deploy. "Well . . ." I thought that if I stuttered long enough, she would let me off the hook.

"What did he look like?"

"He was . . ." What was my problem? "He was hand-some," I said. "Quite handsome. He looked good in the rooms of our apartment. He looked good in greens and browns, which was why he painted the walls those colors."

"Heavens," she said.

I did not know why I had told her that; it was the wine. "He was very visual," I said. "He was a photographer, and a good one," I added.

"Interesting," Helen said.

"Why is that interesting?" I asked her.

"It just is," she said. "Never mind."

"He was a brilliant photographer," I said.

"Do you have any of his pictures?"

"I don't, no, but . . ." I hooked her arm and led her back inside. I did not hear Ethan at the piano but did not know where he was. I took Helen upstairs and to the master bed-room wardrobe closet, where I had stashed the two Dean photographs that I had removed from the wall. I laid them out flat on the bed for her to inspect them.

I could not tell whether she admired the wave print and the ruins print—she never really commented on them be-yond issuing a polite ooh and ah—but she noticed the spots on the walls where the frames belonged. I had left the hooks in place.

"Brad," she said softly. "Brad, Brad, Brad."

"What?" I asked.

"Poor Brad," she said and lifted one of the frames off the bed. "Come on," she said. We rehung both photographs.

"I won't be able to sleep with those there," I complained.

"Yes, you will," Helen said.

We returned to the kitchen and found Ethan. He was going through the mail.

"Hey," I said and grabbed the knife that he was using as a letter opener, "stop it. I could get in a lot of trouble." One of my chief responsibilities as a house-sitter naturally was to forward letters and save magazines and sometimes to pay utility bills. Even though the couple selling the house had informed the post office of their departure from the canyon, occasional letters still trickled in along with various sale mailings from local boutiques and invitations to charity benefits. "I have to put that stuff back in the mail," I said, shoving the opened envelopes back into the cardboard box that I left by the front door.

"I read one letter to the woman who lived here," Ethan said without a trace of guilt. "It was from an old boyfriend who said that she should really try to work things out with her husband because he was so rich and because it was a bad time to be alone in America."

"The old boyfriend is right," Helen said. "I mean about being alone in America."

"I can't believe you opened their mail," I said.

"And then I read another postcard from the same old boyfriend," Ethan went on, "telling the woman that he was in a big hotel room all by himself in Honolulu, and that the woman should join him because . . . It was lurid."

"We can handle it," Helen said.

"I can't repeat it," Ethan said. He blushed.

"The old boyfriend wants her back," she said. "He still loves her," she said.

"He was just horny," I said.

"And then I read another letter," Ethan said.

"I can't forward opened mail," I said. "I'll have to throw it out."

"I think that's illegal," Helen said. "What did the other letter say? Was it from the old boyfriend again?"

"Yes," Ethan said, "and this time he basically asked her to disregard his previous correspondence."

"The damned toad met someone else," Helen said.

Ethan nodded.

"It is not a good time to be alone in America," I said.

We drank more wine, we sat down to dinner. Rosemary-and-thyme-and-sage-roasted chicken—what I did was roast the bird the way you would roast any bird, but I rubbed in a lot of garlic and drizzled olive oil over it and squeezed a lemon, too, and then dredged the chicken in the spices—and new potatoes, which I had placed around and beneath the rack in the roasting pan, and a confit of zucchini and caramelized onions and peppers that I had sautéed a tad too long. Plus bread, and that was supper. Maybe it was too simple and too sincere a cuisine without enough flourish or dazzle because neither Ethan nor Helen said a word, they just ate and ate quietly. But when I heard Ethan hum and when Helen winked at me as she added some more dark meat to her plate, I relaxed. Seconds, thirds, more wine. I made coffee. I put out a plate of brownies and a bowl of red-flame grapes.

"The chicken was a religious experience," Ethan said.

"Like the potatoes," Helen said. "And let's not forget about the other vegetables."

"The vegetables were divinely inspired," Ethan said.

"Our friend the thief can really cook," Helen said.

"I'll say," he replied. "And now I'll play the piano."

We retired to the living room. I brought in the candles from the table and set them on the piano. Ethan sat down on the bench and cracked his knuckles and leaned forward and spread his hands over the keys but then did not play. He heaved a dramatic sigh.

"Oh, come on," Helen said, a bit annoyed. "It hasn't been that long."

"We had an upright," Ethan said to me. "It burned."

"It's not like you were playing it much before the fire," Helen said.

"I played," Ethan said defensively, "I played."

"Well, play now," I said.

Ethan closed his eyes and then when he did finally make music, it seemed as if it came from some place other than the piano, as if the music drifted in from the ocean and up the rise of the canyon. Ethan's music was pure breeze. Jazz, blues, a dreamy minor dirge that floated above a rumble of sad chords, floated up to the high ceilings and then settled slowly. He did play the piano, and he played sweetly and confidently as if he were singing.

Helen had not been watching him, she had shut her eyes when he shut his. And when he let the last chord finally fade, she looked at him and he looked at her. She could really smile when she wanted to smile, a radiant and warming grin, a contagious smile. Ethan beamed.

He bounced a bit and then swung into an upbeat medley of old songs, the songs of our grandparents' day, the seamless standards of the middle-century. He was good, very good, and some of the tunes I recognized, most I did not. He played well, enviably well, and when he was done with the second part of his recital, he launched into a showy hand-bouncing rendition of a familiar romantic virtuoso piece. This was Ethan in more moods than I had ever seen him, lamenting and playful and chatty. He was a natural.

Helen and I gave him a standing ovation, which pleased him, I thought.

"It has been a long time," Helen said, and I thought she might leap across the room and hug him—and hold him—but she stayed put.

"Have you ever played professionally?" I asked. "You could," I said.

"That's always been his pipe dream," Helen said.

"You could play in a hotel bar," I said, and I meant that as a compliment although it did not sound so complimentary to me once I had said it; a hotel bar was hardly a concert hall. But these were people who loved hotel bars, after all, and they knew what I meant.

"His pipe dream," Helen said again.

Ethan was playing something again, another song. "I'm not good enough," he said.

"A long time ago," Helen said, "he was going to answer an ad in the paper to play in a lounge, but he chickened out."

"That's not true," Ethan said, "I had to get a real job."

"That was when we had plenty of money," she said. "You chickened out." She sank back in the couch and groaned and said, "I feel completely untalented."

I was quick to point out that she had designed the house we were building.

"No, I mean talented like playing the piano like Ethan," she said.

"Well, I can't play anything either," I said. "I'm completely unmusical."

"But you're a fantastic cook," Helen said.

It had never really occurred to me that my cooking was a talent like piano playing.

"You have talents," Ethan said to her. "You can take apart any computer and make it work like new."

"You can?" I asked.

Helen did not answer me.

"She hasn't told you about her computer company?" Ethan asked.

"No, and we're not going to talk about it," she said.

I was lost and not about to be clued in.

"You dive," Ethan said.

"You had a computer company?" I asked Helen.

"I forgot all about the diving," she said, giggling.

She kicked off her sandals and led us out the living room through the sliding doors, out to the pool, where she shed her sweater, Ethan's sweater, and, still wearing her shorts and her shirt, hopped up to the diving board, stepped to its edge, pivoted so that her back was to the water, raised her arms so that her body formed a Y, bounced once, bounced twice, and jumped up high and leaned back into a graceful arc, hardly making a splash when she pierced the surface of the pool.

Ethan and I applauded loudly. She climbed out of the water and proceeded to trot out to the edge of the diving board again, this time taking off with a single hop and bounce and high launch. She tucked her knees into her gut and somersaulted before plunging into the crisscrossing beams of the pool lights. Her wet clothes clung to her body when she pulled herself out of the water again. Her wet clothes clung to the round shape of her chest, which she usually disguised with a loose shirt.

"She was a champion diver in high school," Ethan told me.

"He was a swimmer," Helen said.

"I was not a champion swimmer," Ethan said.

"He moved to town and joined the swim team," Helen said. "That was when I met him."

So they did know each other in school.

"I can't believe I remember all of these dives," she said.

I was standing next to her, and I admit that I was curious, overtly curious, that I was staring at the taper of waist, the curve of her hips. She turned back toward the deep end but gave me a single strong push first, and before I had a chance to prepare myself for the fall, I was sinking to the bottom of the pool. Ethan thought it was funny, so I splashed him and splashed him, and when he saw Helen charging him, he jumped in.

We swam in the warm pool in our clothes. The air was cool and so Ethan swam laps underwater. Helen dove off the board, got out, and dove again. I treaded water and watched and clapped, and got out of Ethan's way when he frog-kicked by. We swam and dove and splashed around like children in the ocean until we were spent, and then we collapsed on the chaises lined up by the edge of the pool.

Our clothes were plastered against our skin. We started to shiver. I brought them towels and they each went off to a bathroom to slip out of their wet clothes. We reconvened in the laundry room, all of us saronged in the towels, and I put all of our shirts and shorts and underwear in the washer to spin out, then into the dryer. I did not know how late it was, but it had to be very late.

"You guys should stay over," I said.

Helen was staring at the dryer while it tumbled. "I know what you're thinking," she said to Ethan.

"I know that you know what I'm thinking," he said.

"When we were in high school," she said to me, "Ethan would show up at my house in the morning and do his laundry."

"Your family didn't have a washer and dryer?" I asked him.

"No," Helen answered for him, "they did. He never explained it, he just liked to show up and do his laundry at my house before we left for school."

"I don't think I did that more than two or three times," Ethan said.

"He never explained why," Helen said, "but in a weird way, it was flattering. My mother thought he was crazy, but I was flattered. He only did it a few times, but it seemed like he was always doing laundry at my house."

We watched the dryer spin, hypnotized, high on fatigue. I sorted our clothes and Ethan and Helen disappeared into the dark house together, upstairs to one of the many bed-rooms. I went to my bed and, even with Dean's photographs on the wall, slept well.

I woke to the clanging of someone cleaning up the previous evening's dishes in the kitchen, but when I went downstairs, found that Ethan had done little more than stack the pots and pans in the sink. The noise I had heard was him brewing coffee and scrambling eggs and buttering the toast that he was famous among us for making well. Helen was out on the deck off the kitchen.

I had woken up with a bright idea, which, even though it violated the most basic rule of house-sitting, no guests, I pitched to Ethan. "Why don't you guys stay here?" I said. "You'd save money and wouldn't have to drive so far in the morning and at night. You should stay here."

Ethan liked the idea. "Cool," he said. "And you wouldn't mind?"

"I want you to stay here," I said.

"Cool," he said.

I joined Helen on the deck. She was leaning on the railing, leaning on her elbows and looking west across the canyon at the facing cliff of Las Patas Glen and the house that we were building there, admiring our work, I thought, but no doubt ruminating about how far we had to go. In the morning light, the wood house glowed; it looked like it was made of honey.

We constructed the hearth, and just when I thought that I was becoming a decent carpenter, I had to learn how to work with an entirely new genus of tools, a new phylum of materials, concrete and mortar and bricks. Ethan and Helen had poured the foundation for the fireplace at the western end of the upper floor when they had constructed the rest of the house foundation. Now we needed to create a floor for the hearth above this foundation, and so Ethan built a plywood form atop it into which we could pour freshly mixed concrete. Meanwhile I spilled a bag of dusty cement into a wagon and then added ocean water—we had not yet located and reopened the water line at the top of the canyon, so we had to drive down to the shore and fill our buckets with the Pacific blue—and sand—we got sand all over the bay of the truck carrying a trash can of it back from the beach—and lastly a package of stone aggregate. Helen read the recipe aloud and then mixed the goop with a shovel, stirring the thickening mix with both hands as if she were cooking up a vat of stew, enough mess for a regiment.

Summer bloomed early. That was the season of record heat. We wore shorts and Ethan and I tended to take off our shirts during the day. As soon as the sun went down, we still needed sweaters, but during the day, we baked. Helen's skin turned very dark.

Slowly I was gathering facts about my new friends, yet I believed that I knew them well long before I had sorted out their joint and separate chronologies. I got to know them by working alongside them. Helen calculating the amount of space we needed to leave to allow the shell of the fireplace to expand when it was hot; she was a puzzle-solver; she was a fast-thinker who became restless easily and always wanted to dart off to the next problem before the one at hand was necessarily solved. Ethan pouring the concrete and watching it set and dry, smoothing it out again and again with a hand float, checking to make sure that the box that he had inserted to create an ash-pit dump did not slip; Ethan arguing to wait a few extra hours before removing the plywood forms just to be on the safe side; he was cautious, he was deliberate. You would not think that they would get along, let alone be able to work together, and yet Helen determined how the rear wall of the fireplace should be angled, at what degree to achieve the best updraft, and then Ethan chalk-marked that wall on the floor of the hearth and measured and remeasured his lines before we positioned the first brick. Somehow I fit into this balance; I was not sure why; I did not really try to figure out why we collaborated so easily that first month, that second month.

We laid out the bricks on the sides of the fireplace first and then arranged the tapered and forward-sloping back of the hearth, which we had to cement from the rear to keep from falling over. This was delicate work, careful work as we passed the mortar board off to one another, as we slapped on a thin layering of the gray glop before setting the bricks in place, taking turns as we shaped the fireplace, laying a zig-gurat of bricks atop the hearth—the hearth looked to me to be a house unto itself with its own foundation and walls and roof—gradually reaching the flue and the chimney. We passed off bricks to one another, and eventually our chim-ney peeked above the tent of the roof.

Helen always paid me at sunset. It became increasingly awkward for me to take the Zaynes' money after they moved into the house that I was sitting, after I knew for a fact that they had nothing in the bank and had accumulated a huge debt; but Helen insisted, and so technically, I was their em-ployee. I suppose that this was offset by the fact that they were my guests. We piled in the pickup at dusk and drove across the canyon to the gibraltar of a white house. They had moved in the day after I made my offer, but it was hard to tell that they were living with me—I suspect that the real-estate agent who stopped by twice to show the house dur-ing this period did not have a clue—because they owned so few things, just some clothes purchased after the fire, clothes and Helen's books on house design and her drafting board and T square; everything else they had owned had burned.

We worked all day and came back to my house when it

was dark and swam and ate a good dinner which I prepared; that was a typical day. After so much time alone, I relished their company in the evenings. I worried that I did not know when to leave them alone together, and there may have been occasions when I should have slipped off to bed to read a book. I discovered that the Zaynes owned the lot directly below the one they were building on, and that was when I began to fantasize about buying this parcel of land from them. I would build my own house on it in time; we would be neighbors.

Once they moved in with me, their marriage became transparent. They were never very physical—No, that is not accurate, they were intimate, but only after a period of negotiation first. We would be lounging around the living room, for example, talking or flipping through magazines, each of us occupying a separate chair, Ethan stretched out on a couch. Helen would excuse herself to take a dip in the pool, and after swimming and drying off and throwing on a robe, she would rejoin us, this time sitting on the same couch as Ethan, but at the opposite end. A half-hour would pass. Ethan would extend a leg, and Helen would massage his bare foot. She would stop massaging his foot and just hold it in her hand. He inched closer to her; he kept reading his magazine. She had worked her hand up his calf. Another half-hour. He moved closer still. Her hand was up his thigh, exploring his shorts. By that point, he would be sitting up and only pretending to read and he would ease his hand to an equal spot on her leg beneath her robe. And then, but not before then, they would say good night and go upstairs.

One morning I walked past the corner bedroom that they had taken as theirs, the door was ajar, and I saw them sleeping, half-entwined. Another morning when I passed their room, I saw Ethan sleeping alone, his back rising and falling, his head buried beneath a pillow; I found Helen sleeping downstairs on a couch. I tiptoed but woke her anyway, and she explained that she had been tossing and turning and did not want to disturb Ethan. It happened often, my finding Helen on the couch in the morning. Being the light sleeper that I was—when I did sleep—I began to hear Helen when she made her way downstairs; I suppose that I was listening for her. And some nights I followed her down. We went out to the pool and talked there. That was when we had some of our great conversations, on those early summer nights, mornings really. Insomniac mornings by the pool.

She told me that she was seventeen when Ethan's family moved to her town. He was the new kid, and she wanted to know everything about him. He was unlike any other boy that she had ever met.

"He had that killer smile," Helen said. She was lying on a towel by the edge of the pool and running her fingertips along the surface of the water. "You know that smile," she said.

Often she would see him wandering through town with a gas can because he owned a hand-me-down convertible, and he never remembered to put gas in it. He was forever getting stranded and wandering off on foot to a gas station. Helen's friends made fun of him. She made fun of him.

"Sports were required in my high school," she said. "You had to go out for one team or another. Ethan ended up on the swim team. I dove. I was the champion. I was attracted to him, I admit it, attracted purely physically speaking. Ethan in a swimsuit. Lanky. Okay, hung. I started talking to him one day, and he was much more friendly than I would have expected, this boy wandering around town with a gas can.

I got to know him slowly, and I knew that there was something that he was holding back when we talked about his family. It took me a while, but I finally got it out of him. His parents had been separated. Now they were together again, and his father had gotten a new job in a new part of the country and he was making a fresh start with Ethan's mother in this new town."

Ethan had four slightly younger brothers, Helen said, and the Zayne family seemed like a happy family. They had a big Christmas tree with a heap of wrapped presents all around it. They threw a party for the neighborhood, a holiday party with Mr. Zayne's special homemade eggnog. The older kids were allowed to partake in the spiked batch. But toward the end of that party, after everyone had drunk a little too much of the eggnog, the scene became a little weird.

"Mrs. Zayne passed out by the fireplace," Helen said, "and Mr. Zayne kept walking past her and sort of nudging her with his foot. Gently at first, then not so gently, pushing her toward the fireplace . . . It looked like he wanted to roll her right into the fire, it was so weird. Nothing bad happened, but I remember thinking that Mr. Zayne was kind of a creep and that he would have pushed his wife into the fireplace if no one was looking."

"Did they stay together?" I asked.

"They did," Helen said. "But Ethan told me—I finally got this out of him after swim practice, after swim meets—he admitted that he preferred it when his parents were separated and not living together. He preferred his family after it had fallen apart than when it was all reassembled and fixed."

Another early morning by the pool, Helen said, "I was the local chess champion, the state diving champion. I had colleges calling me up, begging me to apply. Pick a college, any college, it was silly. I was going to be this woman of science. I had it all mapped out, the discoveries, the prizes. Ethan had no plans. He was a photonegative of me. He did not know whether he wanted to go to college. He smoked a lot of pot. He would get high and play this electric keyboard he had in his room. I stopped hanging out with my other friends. My mother and father were completely freaked out that I was seeing this boy with hair in his eyes. They had never lectured me about sex before, and now they lectured me whenever they could."

Helen said that instead of going to their prom, she and Ethan took a train into New York and went to a café in the Village and smoked a lot of hand-rolled cigarettes and listened to a woman pay acoustic guitar and sing bad love songs.

"He was a romantic," Helen said, "the real thing. Like with the poetry he would send me when I was in college. We are talking really, really bad poetry. The songs he wrote. Really, really bad songs. He was amazingly loyal during those years, faithful, which is more than I can say for myself. He lived at home and went to a local college off and on until I was done with school and then we eloped the weekend of my graduation. We found an apartment in Boston. And then I made all that money."

I do not remember when exactly I got the full account of Helen's breakneck slalom through corporate America, whether I learned about it all at once during one of our poolside conversations or later in bits and pieces, but it explained how Helen had become the kind of person to whom credit card companies once upon a time gladly extended their welcome.

She had been a science nerd in college—that much I had already gathered—and had taken all kinds of courses in physics and math and computer theory. Her teaching fellow for one computer course was a doctoral candidate who had a few ideas about how computers might be made usable for the common man—this was at the dawn of the revolution in personal computers—and he even had a few thoughts that he believed might be worth patenting, even though he had yet to make these ideas work in practice. Ideas about how to organize the essential operating software of these new machines, how to make them accessible and user-friendly, a new term in the lexicon back then. Helen agreed to work part-time as the man's assistant and help him prepare these ideas and file for patents, and then when the man became interested in forming a company around his patents, he could not afford to pay Helen but wanted her to work for him and gave her a sliver of equity in the new and as yet worthless concern in lieu of a salary.

Then, lo and behold, the man made his ideas work. And every larger computer corporation became very interested in his research, his software breakthrough, his patented breakthrough. So Helen, who had taught herself everything she needed to know about the byzantine world of intellectual property, taught herself about how to license these registered ideas, ideas which were, as she freely admitted, mostly over her head. But one thing was quite clear to her: Their little product had come into being at the right time. The money started to come in, and after a while, the man decided to sell the company, a bigger fish swallowed a smaller fish whole, and when he made his fortune through this sale, Helen's sliver of equity from her days of working for nothing came to something.

Add that sum to the money that Helen had inherited from a well-to-do and childless aunt on her mother's side around that time, and she and Ethan had enough money so that neither of them had to work for a while. They would be able to buy a house somewhere, but first they wanted to wander, which was what they did, to Europe and back, to North Africa and back, to California.

"On the one hand, we were kind of aimless," she said. "But it was a splendid aimlessness."

They lived on this money for a long time, and Helen did some computer consulting now and then, and Ethan taught second grade, and they always had a reserve of cash to fall back on. They had a valuable piece of land in a western canyon. And then Helen had Wes.

"Short for Wesley?" I asked.

"Short for Westlawn," she said. "Westlawn Zayne."

"A family name," I said.

"West. Lawn. The town where Ethan and I met and fell in love," she said.

Now they had a house with a spectacular view and an easy life and a son who was about as miraculous as they come.

"He had so much of his father in him," Helen said. "He was—or would have been—his father's son."

He was a little man more than a boy, she said. He would worry, he would fret about all manner of things. Ethan had planted some saplings on the lower lot, and Wes worried that these trees would not grow in the summer sun.

"I know," Helen said. "I know. He was three and he knew about these things."

So they were happy, the Zaynes of Las Patas Glen, extraordinarily happy for a time.

"Why did our luck run out?" Helen asked me.

I did not know how to answer her.

"Maybe we were never all that lucky. We had just tricked ourselves into believing that we were lucky."

Their bank account, once ample, dwindled fast. Ethan lost his job when the state cut its education budget; he lost it right when they needed the money. In the sagging economy, Helen could not find work in the computer industry. Their money was gone; they were land-poor. And then there was the car accident.

It was a hot morning when Helen began to talk about it

by the pool; the sun was coming up fast. "It was a cloudy day that day," she told me. "Ethan was working on the garden down in the lower lot. . . ." She did not go on.

"You want to tell me about it," I said.

Helen frowned. "No, not really."

She would have to tell me one of these days. I knew that she needed to tell me. Instead of pressing her on it, however, I asked her instead where Ethan was during the fire, if he was not at home helping her hose down their roof.

"He had left me about a month before," Helen said. "We were breaking up. And then when the fire did come, and he heard about it on the news wherever he was . . . Well, I know where he was. He was living out in the desert. He heard about the fire and rushed back to Los Angeles to find me, and he could not get down the Coast Highway because it was blocked off. And he went nuts, he nearly slugged a cop. He had to get to me," Helen said, "and he went absolutely crazy worrying whether I was okay. He knew that he loved me and after all that we had been through . . . He had to find me."

"He found you eventually," I said.

"After the fire, in a shelter set up in a school gym," she said. "That was when we went to the hotel in Santa Monica. That was when we decided to start over."

"That was when you decided to build your house yourselves," I said.

"I think he was starting to stop blaming me for the accident," she said.

"Blaming you? Because you were driving," I said.

"There's more to it than that," Helen said.

"Tell me," I said.

Helen heaved a sigh. She said, "Tit for tat."

This was the way these conversations worked.

"Quid pro quo?" I asked.

"An eye for an eye," she said.

But what was there to say? That I met Dean in college. He was a graduate student, three years older than me. That we met in the usual way. There was a party, I was horny, he was handsome. Dark, sophisticated. We went to his apartment. I was young and he was already out in the world, or so it seemed from my perspective, on his own. I had known plenty of other men and women, too. But I had never spent the night. He was the first person in whose bed I spent the night. And woke up next to. The big cliché. What was there to say? I was young, and yet I knew that I wanted to spend the rest of my life with him; I was young enough to believe that I would.

Helen wanted more. So I told her that he was a city boy and that I came from the hinterland. He had been sexually active since he was fifteen, and he had known older men and had relationships with them that went on for months, for years. I was a change for him, a breath of newness, of refreshing naïveté.

"Part of it was that he liked me because I was impressed with him," I said.

"He liked you for other reasons, I'm sure," Helen said.

"I suppose," I said. "Yes."

Dean was going to be a graphic designer and open up his own firm; photography was a diversion that took over the rest of his life. I was a sophomore majoring in art history. I wanted to be a museum curator back then, if I wanted to be anything. He had some money. He dropped out of graduate school and started traveling here and there to take pictures of ruins. I waited for him to come home. I lived in his apartment. I wore his shirts and drank coffee out of his favorite mug. I hated it when he was away. I lost my mind wondering whether he was being faithful.

"Was he?" Helen asked.

"He's dead," I said. Meaning, how dare she ask such a question now, what did it matter.

"You brought it up," she said.

"I don't think he was," I said. "Later, yes, but not then."

Even before I was out of college, I had started to travel with him when I could. He paid for most things. That was when we began our life in foreign hotels.

"It was a completely glamorous life," I said. "From where I came from," I explained, "room service was about as decadent as you could get, ordering a plate of French fries in the middle of the night. Ordering a bottle of champagne when there wasn't anything to celebrate—oh, boy. Ordering massages. A second bottle of champagne."

Dean made his pictures. I finished school. We had his apartment, we traveled, and between travels, I worked in a museum store, I worked in a box office, I worked in a gallery. I arranged to quit the day before he was going off somewhere, and usually I went with him.

"Once we got into a big fight," I said. "More than once, it was an ongoing fight, and after it, we split up for a number of months."

"He wanted you to get a life of your own," Helen said.

"He wanted me to tag along, but he wanted me to have my own reason for tagging along," I said. "Made me want to punch him. I think I may have punched him. I did. I meant to hit him in the arm, and I hit him in the jaw. It was ugly."

"So you split up," Helen said.

But I could not live without him. And somehow I found out where he was working, that he had gotten a commission to shoot an archaeological dig in Turkey, and so I went

to Turkey and to that dig, and I got a job on the dig unbeknownst to him.

"One morning, he found me working alone in a pit," I
said, "sifting dirt through a windowscreen. Dean didn't say
anything. He just joined me in the pit. It was hot. We took
off our shirts. He was helping me dig out the corner of this
ancient city that I had been assigned to uncover with a
trowel and a pastry brush. We were using our hands. And
we found something."

"What?" Helen asked.

"We didn't know what," I said. "It was a clay object of
some kind, and we had exposed only a bit of the surface. You
were supposed to report something like this to your team
leader, and then a more experienced excavator would come
in and unearth the artifact. But I didn't say anything and
Dean didn't say anything, and he went off to his trailer and
I went off to mine. The next morning, we met up at the pit
again," I said, "and we got right to work, and we slowly and
carefully brushed away more dirt from around the urn—we
knew it was an urn—and we could see that it was large and
well preserved, an incredible find, an urn with some kind of
painted fretting and a more complex design. A red urn with
black figures dancing. We didn't tell anyone about it and
kept it to ourselves and parted and met up the next day and
that was when we finally were able to remove the urn completely—it had some chips and cracks but was otherwise in
perfect shape—and we showed the section leader and the ar-
chaeologists and we were scolded but mostly praised, and
Dean and I realized that we were holding hands, and we
went off to his trailer or my trailer in the middle of the afternoon and had a memorable reunion, which we referred
to in the years following as the Afternoon of the Urn."

Our life together resumed. I pretended to hold down other
jobs between our travels, but if the truth be told, I was

Dean's assistant, and after a while, when he could afford it, he even paid me a salary. We had an apartment in New York. We traveled and lived in hotel rooms. We dreamed of settling down more permanently somewhere. Our dream house in the country. And then one day, he was having trouble breathing.

"You know the rest," I said.

"I don't know the rest," Helen said.

But what was there to say? That he was someone who was intensely afraid of disease but never went to the doctor. That we had always been safe together, but that was because Dean was afraid I would make him sick, not the other way around. That he had never felt ill before that afternoon when we were out with a broker looking for land, never ill but then he had lethal holes in his lungs. That he did not fight, that he was sick just once and died quickly as if our life were not worth fighting for, stranding me, how could he, how could he.

"Is that selfish?" I asked Helen after telling her all of this.

Her feet were in the pool. I expected her to say, No, Brad, it's quite normal to think those thoughts, healthy even.

She said, "Yes."

"Yes?" I stood. "He stranded me," I said.

"Give him a break," she said. "He wants to be forgiven."

"He wants . . ." I was mad. "He can't want. He's a bunch of ashes knocking up against the side of some tour boat circling the island of Manhattan is what he is," I said. And then I could not believe that I had been so crass.

"I have to say something," Helen said. "You're not going to like it, but—"

"Say it," I said.

"He painted the rooms of your apartment so he would look good in them? I mean, really. He sounds like he was a little, um . . . Given what you've told me about him . . ."

"Say it," I said.

"He sounds like he was a little vain. A little self-involved," she said.

I was shocked. The sun was rising. There were echoes in the canyon. Breakfast conversations, a truck on the coast road, gulls, a piano. I was stunned.

"I am sure he loved you," Helen said. "But I'm not so sure that he was the best person for you."

Absolutely stunned. "So you're saying that it was good in a way that he died—"

"I am saying," Helen said, standing now, facing me, "that your life with him was not all uncovering urns in far-off places. That's all I am saying."

There we were in the unsparing bright of the new day, me wearing pajama bottoms and Helen in a big T-shirt, one of Ethan's shirts. We had talked all night. She was being far too honest with me as far as I was concerned. I wanted to say, How dare you. I wanted to say, Get out of my house. But I laughed instead, I laughed with relief. I laughed and Helen laughed, too.

Still, I had to punish her a little for her bluntness. I pushed her over the edge into the pool, which at that hour had not been warmed by the sun. I dove in after her. We were treading water in the deep end.

I said, "Sometimes I want to drown. I could drown now, I really could."

She said, "So go ahead and drown. Just make sure you come up for air."

I held my breath and sank to the floor of the pool. Once I was wet, my pajama bottoms offered me little modesty. Helen was there with me, holding her breath, almost naked if not naked, too. I remember that we remained submerged in the deep end for a long time. An hour, longer. Of course, I am exaggerating the moment. But that is how I remember it: We remained underwater all morning.

We finished sheathing the exterior of the house and covered all of the walls with a thick brown paper before we began putting up the siding. Installing the siding proved to be exacting work since we could not afford to make any mistakes when we beveled the expensive clear lumber, we could not waste the wood by mismeasuring it, a tedious and glacial enterprise since we had to use sharp and thin nails that would not split the wood and nail sets to drive them in, puttying all abrasions, but rewarding work, too, because we returned to the most basic carpentry, the sawing and the leveling and the hammering, because the house outwardly began to look more and more like a real house. Helen's plans called for a wide fascia running beneath the shallow eave and an abstract frieze running around the entire house and simple trim along the gable ends to create pediments that would rest on the columns we would build. This was going to be a handsome house with handsome lines.

Now the summer heat made us sweat and burn. Now the climate was against us, but we worked at a steady pace to align the clapboard so that the horizontal lines of the house flowed evenly and parallel in spite of the vertical windows that interrupted them. The corners of the house posed the greatest challenge, first because we had to reckon the merging strips of siding—if they did not come together along the same latitude, we had to start over—and second because we had to miter the boards into perfect right angles. The first corner took us a week to get right. But these were the long days of long light, and the ocean breeze tended to cool us off in the late afternoon, which was when we did our best work. And then the sun went down and we watched it set and we returned to my house, where we changed into our swimsuits and dove into the pool.

We swam laps but mostly just floated in the water and cooled off at the end of the day, and sometimes Helen impressed us with a dive. We swam and then Helen helped me make dinner while Ethan played the piano. He became quite serious about his practicing, sight-reading the scores that we had found in a closet and improvising his own jazz, mostly improvising. When he played the printed music, I detected a certain frustration in his repetition of trickier passages; he would go over the same measure again and again until he got the passage right. Let me borrow a metaphor from our carpentry: It was as if he had to keep planing an edge of a board because it was never quite level; Ethan kept running the block plane along the pine, shaving off curls of wood and brushing them away. But I detected a certain satisfaction, too, especially in his extemporaneous music, the jazz that came straight from the heart.

Helen was my sous-chef and I think she knew that I enjoyed myself in the kitchen, so she encouraged me to experiment and to avoid cooking the same dinner twice for the three of us. Some of the dishes I made did not always turn out quite the way I had envisioned them, like the salmon that I tried to curry and grill—the fish did not hold the spice and I overcooked the steaks—although the pear and lime and apple chutney that I made for that meal went well with some game hens that I stuffed with wild rice and currants and glazed with honey and apricots. Some of the dishes that I cooked turned out pretty well, if I do say so myself, the simpler concoctions, the chickens that I roasted and the vegetables that I marinated and grilled and tossed with couscous.

We ate well and what money we had seemed to be going toward these feasts, toward the wine, our dinners during which we discussed the next day's work. And after dinner,

Helen began to draw the interior, first in sketches and then in more detailed drafts, and we talked about what the inside of the house should look like.

"If the outside is stark and white and maybe a little cool," Helen said, "I think the inside should be warm and inviting and cozy."

"There should be a lot of woodworking," I said.

"Which will be hard for us to pull off, not to mention more expensive than your basic drywall," Helen said as she paged through the last chapter of the how-to book, "Interior Finishes."

"There should be a lot of wood," I insisted, "that will be dark at night but light during the day. Wood floors," I said.

"Oh, sure, hardwood floors," Helen said.

"And wood walls," Ethan said.

"Okay," Helen conceded, "there will be warm wood everywhere."

"It should be like the inside of a cello," Ethan said but quickly retracted that description: "Sorry, that's precious."

"No, it's not," I said.

"No, you're right," Helen said. "A cello on the inside." And that became our ambiguous but defined objective, to make the interior when we got around to the interior dreamily and plaintively baritone.

"What about the fireplace?" Ethan said. "How should we finish that off?"

"It has to be a great stone hearth," I said matter-of-factly. And I had an idea. "We can collect stones from the burned-out houses from the glen," I said.

"You mean pieces of other people's houses?" Ethan asked. "That's kind of morbid, Brad."

"No, it's not," Helen said. "We would cut them and fit them together and end up with a black stone mantel."

Ethan was skeptical. "Can we top it off with a plank of dark wood?"

"Definitely," Helen said.

We worked all day and swam at night and dined and talked and swam again. Helen and Ethan seemed to me to be more casually intimate. Picture us out on the lawn staring at the stars. We are lying on our backs. Ethan and Helen are holding each other. I excuse myself, and as soon as I walk away, I see her lying on him, holding herself above him, not kissing, just holding herself there. And for my part . . . I had a plan. Soon I would make them an offer, I would buy the lower lot. I had not and would not mention the idea until the time was right. Soon I would start dating people. It would happen, although I did not know how exactly, it would happen because I wanted it to happen. We went to bed late and sometimes I met up with Helen by the pool. In the morning we ate a hearty breakfast and were eager to get back in the pickup and work our way over to Las Patas Glen.

It was a simple routine, an uncomplicated regimen, an easy commune, work and play and sleep and work and play and sleep—a river of days, one washing into the next, wondrous days that varied only in the shifting tasks that we assigned ourselves as we finished the exterior of the house.

We finished the siding and the fascia that ran beneath the eave, a bordered nine-inch band, and we finished off the gables with matching trim and then we worked on the frieze. The frieze was an abstraction, it told no story; it was a simple extrusion of panels of varying sizes and blocks between the panels and molding around the blocks and panels beneath the fascia and eave and above the clapboard and tall windows. The detail work looked complicated in the plans and sounded complicated when Helen described the lines that she wanted, the symmetrical patterns, the allusive effect she was after—and it was indeed complicated to install, because like the siding, we could not fudge what we were doing, each piece had to be aligned—but in the end, the details were simple and created a quality of simple movement beneath the eave, motion if a house can have motion.

We erected the columns, which involved some clever engineering because we should have built them earlier than we did. Helen had to figure out a way of creating temporary bracing with angled planks shoved beneath the gables so that we could insert a sturdy post and then build a square base around that post and the round unfluted columns, which we had to smooth out with putty so they looked like they were doing the real support work when they were actually more decorative than functional. We left room at the top to affix the moldings of the unfussy capitals, a no-nonsense order.

We installed the skylights. And we installed the windows, too. The trick to which turned out to be the careful leveling of the openings in the frame: We had to plane the frame to the fraction required so that the window and its casing would sit squarely and work right, and in several cases, we had to make a shim out of a shingle scrap in order to build up the sill that we wanted. The windows were heavy, glass was heavy, and both Helen and I had to hold them in place while Ethan secured them with nails. They were long windows, three big panes to a frame, and they opened out. The same windows on both floors, and then we did the doors, which were even trickier to position, heavier and harder to maneuver, and we had to recheck and recheck the plumbness of the hinge sides in order for the doors to fit and then open and close properly. Like good stairs, good doors were supposed to go unnoticed. The upstairs doors opened out onto the porches and looked exactly like the windows, three panes to a panel. The front door, the noble threshold, was a broad door inset with a window that was in effect a miniature three-paned allusion to the rest of the casements in the house.

And then, although it did not seem possible, we had more

or less finished the exterior. And we had run out of money; or I should say Ethan and Helen had run out of money. The Zaynes turned down my offer of a loan; they had stopped paying me at the end of the day. Or they said that they would think about a loan, I think. There was so much more to do, the entire guts of the place—the plumbing, the web of electrical wires to lay in—and the interior that was going to be like the inside of a cello. At least we had the paint, which had been purchased a while back, and so we took our time painting because we did not want to come to the inevitable standstill that we faced. It was July.

We painted the house a shade of white that was pearl and sometimes translucent like alabaster when the sun was bright, a shade of white that tended to gray and age as the day faded. We were not sure what we were going to do when we were done painting, and so we painted with deliberate leisure.

I remember that one afternoon when the sun got the better of us, we had to retreat into the house, and we went inside during a time of the day when the cliff was soaked with light so that the only available shade was under the stairs. The three of us sat under the staircase and closed our eyes and cooled off.

Helen said, "When we were collecting stones from our neighbors' land this morning, I was thinking about how we could hire ourselves out to them. We could build them all new houses."

"We could build different houses all over this side of the canyon," Ethan said.

"But we would paint them all white," I said.

"White houses with gray roofs and a lot of windows," Ethan said.

"And then we would plant trees," Helen said.

"Tall and green and swaying trees," Ethan said.

"And then there are other canyons," I said.

"Other burned-out canyons," Ethan said.

"We'll line these canyons with white houses," I said.

"One canyon at a time," Helen said.

"Okay, one canyon at a time," I said, and I think that I believed that we truly would build other houses eventually. And was that so absurd? We could have formed a house-building company; our craft would have only improved with each house that we put up. Was that so absurd?

Doomed from the get-go. That line echoes in my mind. Who said it, Ethan? No, I think it was Helen, and she said it later in the summer, that fall.

One morning Ethan walked into the house and screamed our names. Helen and I were adding blackened bricks and chunks of concrete from a scorched foundation to our growing heap. We ran into the house, and before we had taken more than a step inside, Ethan was holding us back, telling us that it was not safe, to stand back.

Where the upper floor overlapped with the lower floor, where there was an expanse of long joists, several beams had collapsed during the night. Part of the upstairs flooring had caved in, smashing the staircase railing and damaging the lower floor. Rafters of the lower roof had come down—part of that roof had collapsed as well—and there was a hole through which we could see the sun. There was broken glass everywhere, glass from an upstairs window that came down, too.

At first I thought that the place had been vandalized by some roving gang, but the beams had collapsed because— there was no way around the apparent truth—Helen's design contained a major structural flaw. The span of the beams was simply too long to carry the weight of the upper floor. The joists had held up while we added the roofing and while we had sheathed the walls, but when we built up the exterior with siding and added the windows, they snapped.

Ethan pushed us back and outside. He glared at Helen but

did not say anything. He walked down the hill to the pickup and drove away, out to the canyon road.

And I will say that even then, standing amid the web of sawdust hanging in the air, amid the splintered beams and collapsed roof and sagging floor and broken glass, with Ethan having driven off who knew where, even then I believed that we would build other houses in time, white houses fenced with cypresses all along the Pacific coast.

THREE

Years later I ran into Ethan in San Francisco. I found him sitting alone in the window of a fashionably dingy café at the end of the day, holding his cigarette in front of him like a dart. I walked by and he saw me first and waved. I was so astonished to see him that after our initial handshake and awkward hug, I could barely speak. Ethan, however, hardly seemed fazed. He ordered me coffee and flashed me a grin as if he had been waiting for me for hours and accepted my tacit apology for showing up so late.

Years later he looked the same: Maybe he had more of a beard; he was dressed the same, although it was autumn and he was wearing a bomber jacket and a striped scarf; his eyes were not as blue as when I had known him before. We talked about what we had done and where we had gone during our time apart, and our conversation remained easy as long as we avoided our mutual past. Which became increasingly difficult the longer we sat there and sipped our coffee; which became next to impossible after about twenty minutes. It was getting dark, and so we exchanged phone numbers, but I suspected and perhaps hoped that I would never hear from him.

I glanced at my watch and mumbled something about where I had to be that evening, but instead of leaving, I asked a waiter to refill my mug. It was cold and dank in the café, and Ethan pulled his scarf up higher around his neck.

He said, "If you live in Southern California for any length of time, you are always cold no matter where else you travel."

I had discovered this, too. "The sun just isn't as bright anywhere else," I said.

"No, not nearly as bright," he said.

I was nervous, my hand was shaking, and I spilled coffee on my lap, on the table, everywhere, on the floor. Ethan hopped across the room and grabbed a wad of napkins from the bar. He walked with a trace of a limp.

I watched him soak up the coffee and, unable to hold back any longer, I rambled. I said, "Sometimes I'll be doing something physical, like sweeping out the cellar or raking leaves or even planting flowers, and I'll drift, and then before I know it, I'm back in Encantado Canyon. I can feel a hammer in my hand, and I can see you or Helen holding a board in place while I pound in the nails. Or I'm the one holding the board, and Helen is doing the hammering, and I can feel the vibration of the wood beneath my palms."

Ethan stared at the table.

"I don't even necessarily have to be doing something physical," I said. "I mean, I can be at a concert or waiting for a friend outside a cinema, and I'll float back to the canyon—"

"Why are you telling me this?" Ethan looked up.

"Sometimes I think that if a place ceases to exist in reality," I said, "then it will also cease to exist in your dreams. More than once, I've considered dropping everything and getting in my car and heading for the coast road. I want to go back and burn our house down."

"Like your grandfather," Ethan said.

"I told you about him? Yes, like him. Except that I don't want to wait until I'm old and sick," I said.

Ethan lit another cigarette. "You know, I almost torched the house that morning," he said.

"What morning?"

"That morning when we discovered that those joints had snapped."

"No, I didn't know that," I said.

"I wanted to torch the house and sell the land. I stormed off and drove away and was gone for a while, do you remember? And when I came back, I had those tanks of gas in my truck. You asked what they were for and I don't know what I said, something stupid. I was going to light a spectacular fire."

I did not remember Ethan returning with gas tanks in his pickup that morning, although the more I thought about it, the more I could picture them.

"But you didn't torch the house," I said.

"I couldn't go through with it," Ethan said.

I glanced at my watch. "You're probably going to think I'm crazy," I said, "but if we left now—"

"We'd get there before dawn," Ethan said. He laughed. "You're not serious."

Part of me wanted to see the house in flames, and part of me only wanted to take a drive and see where we ended up.

"You are serious," he said. It was his turn to check his watch. "I'm supposed to be somewhere. In fact, I should probably be on my way."

"Right," I said. "Me, too."

Neither one of us got up to leave.

"Are you hungry?" he asked.

"I could eat something," I said.

"You know, they make great sandwiches here," Ethan said.

I scanned the menu.

"The chicken salad is excellent," he said. "And have some soup. You would like their soup."

"I'm suddenly very hungry," I said.

"I could really go for a bowl of the split-pea soup myself," Ethan said.

"Why don't you order for both of us," I said and settled back in my chair.

Ethan smoked two more cigarettes. We did our best to speak only about inconsequential matters. I think that I even heard myself say something about how all the rain we were having would make for a wonderful cabernet, when in truth I knew nothing about wine.

And then, just as the food came, I asked, "Why didn't you go through with it? That morning, why didn't you torch the house? What stopped you?"

Ethan sat up straight and then slumped in his chair.

I did not mean for my question to sound like an accusation, but his answer seemed urgent to me, urgent and possibly linked to so many other answers that had eluded me. If he could tell me what prevented someone from commiting arson, then I might also understand the opposite, what made someone actually start a fire.

"I came to that turn in the driveway," Ethan said, "and I got out of the pickup. And before I knew it, I was looking over the cliff to see if I could pick out the wreck of the red toy car in the brush. I thought that I saw it, which was pretty unlikely, of course, because the wildfire would have obliterated it. I really did want us to pack up and leave that canyon for good. I had the gas, but—What stopped me?" he asked. "I really don't know."

So we arrived at the house and discovered the snapped beams, and Ethan drove off. Helen and I went back inside and tried to clean up the mess. Once we did sweep up the glass and the splinters of wood and once we did cart off the broken staircase railing, the house did not look so irreparably damaged nor for that matter unsafe. There was the hole in the roof and the sagging floor—there was the looming issue of what other flaws in the design might become dangerously apparent—but the problem at hand seemed fixable.

Helen talked about the support columns that we would construct and how they might actually contribute an architectural element that was missing from the interior of the lower floor. She talked fast and with a manic eagerness to launch right into the repairs while we swept up the wood and glass. But then she sat down on a lower stair and was, with a single deep breath, very quiet. She rubbed her eyes with her fingers.

"Helen?"

She said, "It was a cloudy day that day—"

"What day?" I asked.

"Ethan was working in the garden down in the lower lot."

I stopped sweeping.

"Wes had a red toy car that my parents had sent him for his birthday. It was a handsome little sports car," she said, "a convertible, it ran on rechargeable batteries. He loved it and drove around it everywhere, following Ethan around wherever Ethan went. . . . And so Ethan was planting his herbs and his flowers and Wes was driving his car and bringing his father packets of seeds or stakes or twine. . . . Well, I don't know what he was doing exactly, I wasn't there." She stopped.

"Where were you?" I asked.

"Taking a shower. I would take long, long showers, even during the drought. I used to lie down in the tub with the shower on. Then I would get dressed and take these endless drives. I would go nowhere in particular, I would just drive, and that was where I was headed, nowhere, but I was in a big rush to go nowhere," she said. "I tore down the driveway in my station wagon and I came to the turn in the road down by the lower lot. . . . I saw Ethan. I didn't see Wes."

"Oh, Helen," I said.

"No," she said. "No, I didn't hit him. He had crossed the driveway and gotten out of the way of my car, but it's a narrow road, you know, a blind turn, and he—"

"Oh, Helen," I said again. I was not sure that I needed to hear the rest.

"We figure that he didn't realize that he had gotten out of the way, and so he was still trying to maneuver his little car to the side of the road. There was a guardrail there before the fire, but he must have rolled down the turn to where there was a gap in the rail. . . . Ethan saw it happen. And I knew something was wrong when I had driven beyond the turn and when I could see Ethan in my rearview mirror, Ethan hurdling over the guardrail and running down the side of the hill, slipping in the brush, falling himself." Helen buried her face in her hands. "He was dead when we got to him," she said. "From the fall, from the impact. He was dead under his red car at the bottom of the property."

I was leaning on my broom and could not move. I should have sat down next to Helen on the stairs and put my arm around her, but my first instinct was to blame her in the way that I now understood Ethan blamed her for the accident. If she had not been driving so recklessly down the driveway when she knew full well that the boy was down there . . . I blamed her even though Ethan had been watching their son and he was the one who let him play in the road. But it is a mother who gives her son his life, she is not supposed to take it away, and I cannot deny that I blamed Helen more than I blamed Ethan when I finally heard the story. Which was absurd, I realized moments later, absurd to dispense blame at all. They had lost their son, that was all that mattered. I dropped my broom and hopped over to Helen to sit down next to her and wrap my arm around her and hold her, but she pulled away.

"We had reached a point where we were trying to spend as much time away from each other as possible," she said. "Ethan was gardening and I was cooking or doing a crossword or puttering, anything to avoid him. I would worry that he would finish doing whatever he was doing and come up to the house, and I had to get away from him, so that was where I was going. Nowhere specific, just out of the house because I was sure that he was on his way up the hill."

"People can drift," I said matter-of-factly, stupidly, as if I needed to expound on the nature of love and marriage. However, I was not really thinking about Ethan and Helen as much as I was thinking about myself and Dean. About our house in the country, which, although we never said it in so many words, was a project in which we hoped to immerse ourselves because we needed to do something to recover that astonishing, that evanescent rush of courtship that had long since faded from our lives.

"There was a time," Helen said, "when there were perfect days, one after another, each full of meaningless chores, grocery shopping and washing windows and staking the tomatoes and whatever. Chores that made the day busy and exhausting. And then we would settle into the evening. Wes was a baby. We had an inflatable pool that we would sit him up in out on the deck. We would mix cocktails and watch the sun set. We would put Wes in his crib and make ourselves fish and corn for dinner. We would drink a bottle of cold wine. We read a book to each other, a mystery. We spread a blanket on the deck and looked at the stars and we were very close. But then one day . . ."

"The sound of his voice," I said.

"The way he looked at me," she said. "The way I caught myself looking at him."

"You were tired all the time," I said.

"He would come to bed long after I had already gone to bed," she said.

"You would get up and be gone before he woke up," I said.

"So you can see," she said, looking at the hole in the roof, "how he has been waiting for the next accident to happen," she said. "Expecting it. Maybe counting on it to happen."

"I don't think that's fair," I said.

"It happened, look. And now he's gone and I would not be all that surprised if he went back to your house and packed up his stuff and drove away." Ethan had been gone for over an hour. "I would not be surprised if we never saw him again," she said.

I looked out the window and saw the white pickup parked down the driveway by the lower lot. "He's back," I said.

Helen had a look for herself. She picked up a broom and started sweeping again.

"Let me go down and talk to him," I said.

"Ambassador Brad," she said.

"Let me tell him that it's not as bad as it looks."

"If he can't see that for himself, then . . ." She did not finish her thought.

"Let me talk to him," I said and went outside and down the steep driveway, unsure of what it was precisely that I wanted to broker, what sort of accord.

"Hey," Ethan called out when he saw me. He was looking down the slope of burned-out scrub.

"Hey," I said. I noticed tanks of fuel in the bay of the truck. Five big tanks lined up and reeking of gasoline. "What are those for?" I asked.

Ethan looked back at the truck, then at me, and he said, "Oh, well, you never know when you'll want to take a really long trip." He lit a cigarette but did not smoke it.

The accident had unfolded in a few quick seconds here at

this turn in the road. How could they drive up the mountain each morning without reliving it?

"It's not as bad as it looks up there," I said.

He surprised me with his slow grin. "I know that," he said.

"It's definitely fixable," I said even though he apparently did not need to be convinced.

"We can just rig up some columns or something," he said.

"That was what Helen was saying," I said.

Helen once told me that she was not all that fond of babies. Babies are cute and all, she said, but they are not their own persons until you can talk to them and they can talk to you. So she had looked forward to the conversations that she would have with her son. And he had started talking to her. He worried that the plants on the lower lot would dry out in the summer heat. She could imagine the conversations that they would have in years to come. The stories that she would read to him. The friends whom he would bring home. The lies that he would tell her when he stayed out late; the way she would be a cool mom about it all. And then one day, he would move away from home and only phone when he had a hot date and needed to know how to roast a chicken.

I wondered but never asked whether the Zaynes wanted to have another child. At one point, Helen mentioned that the layout of the lower floor could be divided and renovated to include a child's room, but that was the only real hint that after rebuilding their house they would reconstruct their family. Helen also told me that after Wes died, she could not get used to the idea that there was not a child somewhere who was waiting for her to check up on him. Whenever she left the canyon, she always felt as though she should be phoning her son or her son's baby-sitter to say when she would come home. Once you become a mother, she said, you are always a mother. Or you think like one.

Busy days and then tall drinks on the deck at dusk; the

baby in the inflatable pool; lavender in bloom up and down the bluff, and the ocean rolling in the distance; the prospect of slow passion in the late evening; the prospect of days and nights like this for years to come. It was a life worth reclaiming. That it could be reclaimed was what inspired Helen. That they would try and fail to get it back was what made Ethan want to run away. And what would it mean if they did fail? Would they really sell their land? Where would they live, where would they go? In a certain sense, failure seemed entirely possible; another beam might collapse in the night. But at the same time, the consequences of failure, the various scenarios for what might follow such a defeat, were unfathomable.

"Money is the real problem," Ethan said. "What are we going to do about money?" he asked, not a question that I was obliged to answer.

Although I had not mentioned the idea of my buying the lower lot before, not even to Helen, I blurted out the notion to Ethan.

He listened to my proposal, but he said, "We can't take your money, Brad."

"But I want you to take my—Wait, this isn't some veiled loan," I said, glancing back at the lot, which, I noticed for the first time, was on even more of an incline, a potentially undevelopable incline, than the lot above it. "I want that land," I said.

"I had it all planted one year," he said. "I had roses. I had strawberries. I had a sweet lime tree. I had loads of poppies."

"You don't want to sell it," I said.

"It's not that," he said. "I think that one of us should find work."

He finished his cigarette and walked over to the pickup to snuff it out in the ashtray under the dash.

"She's waiting for you," I said.

"I know," he said.

"It's going to be a great house," I said.

"Yes, Helen designed a great house," he said. "Maybe it's a little ambitious, but we'll work it all out."

We got in the pickup to drive it the short way up the hill.

"One of us should work," he said.

As we pulled up to the house, we could see Helen on the roof. She was ripping out the broken shingles, tearing at them with the claw of a hammer and then chucking them, winging them like skimming stones down the tragic drop of the canyon.

We figured out a way to brace the beams of the floor with temporary columns while we tore up a stretch of underfloor and, returning to a section in the how-to book on load-bearing columns, we sank sturdy posts into concrete under the floor and inserted them beneath new and doubled-up joists—all of which seemed like a complicated surgery at the time but which took us only one day to devise and a fast three to complete. The new columns, once the floor had been rebuilt, once the ceiling was repaired, ended up framing the rear wall of the lower tier of the house quite handsomely; we talked about how the columns could be dressed with wood, how they would carry the motif of the upstairs porch columns into the downstairs.

We fixed the snapped rafters and the torn roof. We replaced the damaged siding, the broken window. That much took us another week. Unbeknownst to Helen and Ethan, I charged the new window on my own credit card, but I did not order the new staircase railing because I knew that they would get suspicious.

Ethan worked alongside Helen and me in making these repairs—in no way did he retreat from the project—but often in the middle of the afternoon, he announced that he had an errand to run. He was never more specific than that, but we knew that he was looking for work. Soon these so-called errands took up a larger part of the afternoon, and soon he barely made it back to the canyon by dusk.

Then one day Ethan met up with us back at my house, it was dark out, and he was all smiles because he had landed a job back at the big white hotel in Santa Monica where he and Helen had sought refuge after the fire. He had loved that hotel. He would be a front desk clerk.

"I got the night shift," he said, the idea being that he would make some money at night but save the days for building. He had agreed to start the next evening. "I'll take messages and deliver faxes and give people their keys and maybe recommend restaurants," he told us as if we did not know what a front desk clerk in a hotel did.

"Congratulations," Helen said without emotion. And then: "Of course, you won't be making much."

"I'll be making something," Ethan said. "We could use something," he said.

"But you won't . . ." Helen did not finish the thought. Instead she went off for a swim, alone.

Ethan got a night job, and that was how Helen and I found ourselves together in the evenings. I do not recall what we did for the first couple of nights without him, during that first week when he would drive my car into the city at dusk and not return until after we had gone to bed. We tried to stick to the routine of a swim after working on the house—we did little more than paint the exterior trim—and then dinner and maybe another swim. We were supposed to be using this time to plan the rest of the project, to read up on plumbing and to draft more drawings of the interior carpentry. We tried to stick to the routine, but these were long nights, empty nights, and we grew restless.

That was when we began taking our epic drives, cruising

the coast road, heading into the valley. We drove halfway across the width of the state and back. Sometimes we ended up in a desert town where we went to whatever movie was showing in the local cinema. Sometimes we stopped off at the café-poolroom and had a sandwich and some lemonade and then turned right around and drove back the way we had come. But mostly we drove without stopping along these dusty and narrow passes, the unpopulated, untrafficked highways that appeared to have been paved for no other purpose than our listless wandering. Some nights we did not drive all that far and ended up back at the Paradise Diner, which was open twenty-four hours, and we ordered coffee and fries and corn muffins and sat in a booth for hours without speaking a word.

And then late one night when we were in the diner, I proposed that we go for a walk on the beach. We waited for the traffic to subside and ran across the highway. We were walking down the road toward the rocks, and we passed the house through which we had taken our shortcut the day we met. We dawdled there.

I said, "It's one thing to say that we had the wrong address during the day, but people shoot prowlers at night and claim self-defense."

Helen tried the outer door to the compound anyway. It was unlocked. My heart thudded with such force that I was sure that this throbbing alone would alert anyone who might be sleeping inside the beach house.

Everything sounded so much louder at night, our sandals on the wood stairs down into the atrium, the potted agave that wobbled and nearly fell over when I brushed against it in the dark. I could not decide whether the fact that there were no outside lights on meant that the owner was away or at home, having turned off all the lights before going to bed. I trotted down the long boarded passageway to the stairs that led down to the beach, but Helen loitered by the sliding glass doors, her hands cupped around her eyes as she peered into the dark house.

"Helen," I called as loudly as I could and still whisper. I waved her toward me.

"There's no one here," she said in her normal speaking voice.

I shushed her.

"I'm telling you no one is home," she insisted. And then she tried the sliding door to see if it, too, might be open.

I leaped over to her. "What do you think you're doing?"

"Didn't you ever go out for an early-evening stroll in your neighborhood just to see what the insides of other people's houses looked like? You know, when the lights were on but curtains not yet drawn for the night?"

Dean and I had a favorite block of brownstones in the Village. You could check out the parlor floors at twilight. You could see what sorts of paintings people collected. Their walls of books, their antique lamps, their patterned upholsteries.

"Let's go down to the beach," I said. "It sounds like low tide. I bet you we could walk all the way to Trancas."

She followed me a few steps but stopped in front of the door, not sliding glass doors but a regular front door with a white life preserver with a surname scribbled across it where someone might tack up a wreath. Helen crouched down to examine the lock.

"Get out of my light," she said, meaning the moonlight, when I pulled at her elbow.

"You can't be serious," I said.

"It's not like we're going to steal anything," Helen said, removing her wallet from her shorts, and from her wallet, a credit card. "We'll just look around," she said. She inserted her credit card above the lock in the door and in one fast move slid it down to the lock. She repeated the maneuver several times until the card finally caught the bolt of the lock, pressing it back, and the door, when Helen turned the knob, opened. She stepped inside the house. She pulled me after her and shut the door.

"We were in luck," she said. "The dead bolt wasn't on. The credit card wouldn't have worked with a dead bolt. Come to think of it, it doesn't work for much of anything these days." Again she spoke in a normal voice.

"Where did you learn that trick?" I whispered.

"Tell me that you never got locked out of your parents' house when you were growing up," she said, "and came home late and had to break in without them finding out."

I was about to say that Ethan was the one who always lost his keys, not me, but Helen had led me inside and now that we were inside . . . You would think that the more houses you stayed in, the more you house-sat, the less you would be interested in how other people live. But the truth is quite the opposite. There is something exciting about the initial probe, that first snoop. Titillating, I admit it. I wanted a look around. And no one was home, I was sure of it when Helen punched a dimmer switch and turned on the lights in the main room, when she pulled back a sliding door to the deck and let in the ocean roar and the salty sea air, when I gasped. I gasped when I could see the decor.

The house was essentially one cavernous two-story room, the upper perimeter of which was lined with a balcony. There were bedrooms off of the balcony upstairs, and downstairs, the kitchen and dining area were tucked under the overhang. But the main feature of the big room and the house, at least at night when the sea was black through the wall of ocean-facing windows, was a chandelier suspended from a beamed ceiling with a thick web of ropes.

It took me a moment to realize that the lights of this chandelier were supposed to resemble lanterns and that these lanterns were mounted on an oversized ship's wheel. The walls were all paneled, but rough-hewn and unfinished and adorned with various swathes of fishing nets and buoys and life preservers like the one we had encountered on the front door. And everywhere we turned, we found nautical bibelots, compasses and miniature signal flags and more lanterns and pieces of rope tied into complicated knots and a score of other objects that seemed to serve a sea-going purpose but whose function I could not determine since I knew nothing about boats. There were jars of shells lined up along the pass-through counter of the kitchen and starfish tacked up to the walls along with framed prints of naval battles and, as a dining table centerpiece, the requisite ship-in-a-bottle.

"Yo, ho, ho," Helen said.

The place did not look inhabited, which should not have come as a surprise since it rarely looked like anyone was home when we walked by on the beach. The couches and chairs in the main room were all covered with white sheets. When I lifted up one of these sheets, I found a blue upholstery patterned with gold anchors.

Upstairs, the same motif, the same netting on the walls and prints of battleships, along with a lot of brass—a brass bed, brass reading lamps, brass railings along the balcony. Again I was struck by how unused the beach house looked; there was no pile of night-table reading, no towels hanging in the bathroom, and few clothes in the closet. The bathroom off the master bedroom turned out to be my favorite and Helen's favorite room. It was essentially undecorated except for a pink conch by the sink. There was a sauna room beyond the sink and the wide tub, and the tub was placed against a picture window. A shower with an ocean view. More than an ocean view, because the beach had eroded to the point that the high tide came in under the stilts of the houses here, and I imagined that when it did, if you were in the tub, it would feel like you were at sea. Indeed the entire house began to feel like a houseboat, which made the nautical scheme somewhat bearable.

Helen stepped in the tub. "I could soak here for days," she said. She eyed the faucets.

"Don't even think about it," I said.

"I wasn't going to take a bath," she said, stepping out of the tub. "Besides," she said, teasing, "a tub that big needs two people in it."

"Rub-a-dub-dub," I said.

Downstairs again, we stood out on the deck and watched the waves or what we could see of the waves illuminated by the lights of a neighbor's house. Watching the waves made me sleepy, so instead of heading out the door like a sensible person, I stepped back inside and plopped down on the couch in the main room, pulling up some of the sheet that covered it. Helen sat down next to me. She stretched out with her head on my lap and closed her eyes. The ocean lapped against the piers of the house. I stroked her dark hair, she fell asleep, and I guess that I dozed off, too.

We woke up at the same time, in a panic. How much time had passed, an hour, an hour and a half?

We fluffed up the couch cushions and spread the sheet over the furniture and checked the entire house in a quick scan to be certain that we had covered our tracks. We exchanged a nod, the place looked the same as how we'd found it (I was an expert in such matters: When you house-sit for people and they return, they want to believe that you never truly lived in their house, that you never slept in their bed), and then, even though we both knew that no one was about to show up at that house, a house that did not even have a bar of soap or bottle of shampoo in its regal tub, we ran outside and shut the door and tore up the steps and bolted across the highway, almost darting into the passing traffic, back across the highway to the Paradise Diner.

We were breathing hard and laughing hard, and I was very glad to see the white pickup in the parking lot where we had left it. The pickup was parked next to my car.

Ethan sat alone in the booth and was the only customer in the diner. "Helen," he said. "Brad." He had seen the truck in the lot on his way home from his night shift. It was an astonishing four in the morning. "Did you guys go for a walk on the beach?"

"A walk," I said.

"A lovely walk," Helen said, "yes."

She and I exchanged a conspiratorial wink.

"It was a nice night for a walk on the beach," he said. "You guys must have walked far, it's late."

"All the way to Trancas," Helen said.

"To Trancas and back," I said.

Once you keep one secret from someone, you can keep any secret from him, and chances are that you will. Helen was blushing. This was much more of a betrayal than any we would later commit because it is the secrecy, after all, that corrodes any union, any friendship or marriage, the secrecy more than the actual assignations that constitute an affair. I thought her blushing would give us up, but Ethan did not appear to believe anything other than what we had told him.

I was starving and ordered myself a full meal, since we were only a few hours away from breakfast. Eggs-over-easy and bacon and toast and muffins. And coffee, which pretty much insured that I would not sleep or that I would fall asleep late enough to miss most of the next day. Helen ordered breakfast, too.

"I'm so glad that I found you two," Ethan said, "because I have incredible news."

"What?" I asked.

"Guess," he said.

"You gave someone the wrong key when he came back from a night out," Helen said, "and he walked into the wrong room and there was a scene and you got fired."

Ethan smirked. "I got a new job at the hotel."

From the way he was beaming, from the way he looked wide awake at this hour, I knew what he was going to tell us. "You're kidding," I said.

"No," he said. "It's a total lark."

"That's wonderful," I said and shook his hand.

Helen had not caught on. "What new job?" she asked.

"When I took my break," Ethan said, "I went into the hotel bar for some coffee, and as it turned out, they had just lost their pianist, a guy who signed up to go on somebody's concert tour. I asked the manager there if I could just mess around on the piano a bit—I knew that I was auditioning, I'm not going to pretend like I didn't know that I was auditioning—and I played quite well, as well as I can, anyway."

"What did you play?" I asked.

"The usual standards, the usual blues. They liked the blues, they said. They want more of a jazz-age feel to the place. And they hired me on the spot. I start tomorrow. I have to find a tux or something decent to—"

"Ethan," Helen said. She was sitting across the table from him and leaned over it so that she could kiss him. She looked genuinely thrilled for him, and while she had been nasty and resentful before about his leaving the canyon and spending the nights away from her, away from us, she was warm now, she was loving.

"I couldn't believe it when they said they wanted me to play, and it's basically the same hours," he said, pausing to yawn, "as the desk shift, and I'll get paid a little more and then maybe I'll get tips, too, I'm not really sure."

We ate our food in silence. I imagined that Ethan was thinking about his new gig and what he would play and wondering if he was good enough to pull it off because above all else a piano player in a hotel bar had to exude a kind of nonchalance and unflappable confidence when he rambled from one melody into the next. Helen, I thought, had to be thinking what I was thinking. That we had gotten inside that house so easily. That there were houses all along the beach that no one used during the week. There were weekend houses all over the canyon, empty houses at every bend.

We never planned to break into a particular house. We never staked it out ahead of time. We drove out into the desert and back, we drove up and down the coast—we drove until we could drive no farther. And then we spotted a place where it looked like no one was home. We trespassed. We broke in. That was the season when we would borrow a house for an evening and return it as good as new.

In hindsight I ask myself why we did what we did that summer, and I know that we were driven by more than boredom and restlessness and more than a curiosity about how other people lived in these dark houses which we could try on the way you might go to a car dealership and test-drive a car when you have no intention of buying it. I do not have an answer except to say that whenever we cross a threshold of danger, of risk, and discover that the enemy is not at hand, we feel safe—maybe falsely safe because who can say when the enemy will return, but safe just the same. It is a kind of safety that makes you drowsy with relief. It is an addictive rush. But the high wears off, and you need to seek it out again, you need a fix.

Eventually we would have to return to the lives that we had postponed before building the house in the canyon, that was our problem. We could not build that house forever.

A week later we set out from the diner to take a midnight walk on the beach. Helen led the way, and she headed east along the coast road, the long way. But when we reached the easternmost of the grouping of houses across from the diner, when we came up to a taller and whiter and better-kept house than those adjacent to it—by better-kept I mean that we had noticed that there were no barnacles on the stilts of this house when we passed it on the beach, that its siding was not wind-chapped and peeling, that its windows were not stained by the ocean spray—we tried the outer door on the street. It was locked.

I would have kept on walking down the road, but Helen, who waited for a break in the traffic before jumping up to try and grab hold of the top of the compound, was determined to get inside. I was positive that she would land on a cactus on the other side, or worse, plunge to the patio below, but when she asked for a leg up, I made a stirrup with my hands and lifted her—she was light—with a muffled groan and whatever strength I could summon. She grabbed the top of the wall, she had a leg over, and then slowly, with gymnastic grace, as if she had been performing such feats all of her life, she straddled the wall and eased herself over to the other side.

"Wow," I heard her say. And then, when she opened the street door for me: "Brad, what a surprise, I wasn't expecting you."

What had wowed her was the atrium. All of these beach houses were built according to the same basic layout with an outer wall and garage and then patio and finally the house pressed up right to the water. But unlike the one other beach house we had visited, the front garden of this one—or rear garden, depending upon how you looked at the property—was lavishly and extravagantly planted in bougainvillea and ivies and fragrant jasmine and all manner of flowering plants beyond my botanical learning. There were garlands of vines along the railings of the steps leading down to the house and trellises everywhere, but most noticeable was a gazebo that occupied the central part of the patio, a gazebo with gingerbread trim and a verdigris vane, a folly that belonged at the edge of a great lawn; it was all wrong here. Unlike the innocuous beach-side of the house, this side of the house was heavily ornamented with extravagant trim, more gingerbreading and latticework, a decidedly fussy and turn-of-the-century frivolity that was carried into the interior design as well.

Helen located a downstairs window that was open a crack, a window into a bathroom, which she shoved open wide and through which we climbed inside.

What foof. Each room of this house was wallpapered with a different bright floral pattern, several patterns: one for the wainscoting and one for above the wainscoting and one for the border of the ceiling and sometimes the ceiling itself. The furniture was as ornate as the walls—the chairs were skirted and upholstered with flower-print fabrics, and if they were not upholstered, the wood was scrolled and molded into animal claws. The place made me dizzy. I am talking lace. I am talking pillows embroidered with HOME SWEET HOME and scraps of Psalms. And the house smelled sweet, sickeningly sweet and nothing like the ocean, like cinnamon, like jams were being stewed on the stove. The only modern-looking objects in the house besides the microwave and coffeemaker in the kitchen and a television were a slide projector on a table in the main parlor—this was a house of parlors, not rooms— and a screen that had been folded up in the corner. We sat down on a hideous love seat.

"Did you see the silver?" Helen asked. "There's a fortune in silver in the sideboard," she said.

"Should we take it?" I asked jokingly.

Helen did not laugh.

"No, no, no," I said.

"We could really use the money," she said. "I know of a good pawnshop in Beverly Hills, very discreet. I hocked a watch there once."

I stared at her.

"I thought you said that you were a thief."

"That was just a rumor you started," I said.

She did not say anything.

"Helen," I said.

"Okay, okay. We won't take the silver. Or the cash that's in a jar next to the cereal in the cupboard."

"Helen," I said again.

"Hey," she said, "set up that screen."

I obeyed her and pulled open the screen and dragged it out into the center of the room. Helen flipped on the slide projector. A carousel was already in place. I returned to the love seat, and she advanced the carousel to the first slide. It was a landscape. Somewhere very green and hilly with old stone walls following the swells of the hills. Dean would have been thrilled, I thought. Although he would have shot the wall quite differently, framing it at an angle and moving in for a closer shot—with much more mystery and in black-and-white. The second slide was a shot of a country abbey. A woman had her arm around a priest who was holding a bunch of flowers. Another landscape like the first followed, and then a slide of a cottage with a thatched roof.

"That was a marvelous trip," Helen said.

"A marvelous trip? Which trip?" I asked. For a moment I thought that she might be referring to my life with Dean.

"This trip, our trip," she said. "Silly," and she kissed my cheek. A quick spousal peck. "You must remember the first week of this trip."

I had no idea what she was talking about.

"You must remember the first week of our trip," she said again.

She had lost her mind.

"Surely you have not forgotten about this trip. The one that we are looking at slides of. Our trip."

And the rules of her game became clear to me in a flash.

"Surely you remember—"

"I do, I do," I said. "What a trip. Let's see . . . Did it rain?" I asked.

"Did it ever," she said. "We had never seen such rain."

"No," I said, "never. But then the sun came out."

"We had never seen such sun," Helen said and advanced the carousel of slides. Now we were looking at a friendly elderly couple who were standing amid a garden of tomatoes and other staked vegetables. The woman had a basket on her arm, a basket full of eggplant and squash.

"They were good to us," I said. "Putting us up and all."

"Putting up with us," Helen said. "I still have dreams of her plum pudding."

"And her pork roast," I said.

"Although I did not much care for her dandelion wine."

"The wine made us woozy," I said.

"You were wild when you were woozy," Helen said.

"How was I wild?" I asked.

We were looking at a shot of a pub on a country lane.

"If you don't remember, I am certainly not going to tell you," Helen said.

We were looking at a barn that could have been several hundred years old. A barn and then more landscapes of green hills and stone walls. Suddenly the screen went white; we had come to the end of the carousel.

"Well, that was a good trip," I said.

"We don't travel anymore," Helen said.

"We should travel more often," I agreed.

We were driving back up the canyon road when Helen said, "You didn't really think I was serious about stealing the silver, did you? You did."

"Maybe," I said.

"And you really believed that I had found a jar of money—"

"Okay, okay," I said. She teased me, but I suspected that if I had said, Yes, grab all the silver, she would have done it.

We were home before Ethan. Helen yawned and kissed me good night.

"So in the future, we will travel more," she said.

"Definitely," I said.

"We'll travel very far away for several months at a time," she said.

"Where would you like to go?" I asked but she did not have an answer.

I nodded off in a chaise by the pool and woke up when Ethan dove in hours later. I counted laps for him and lost count. He was manic from his night at the piano. It was the kind of hotel bar where people came in quite late for a nightcap, to wind down, to make the evening last and last. He had played well, he reported, hours and hours of his own jazz, one moody set gliding into the next. His own jazz sprinkled with a few requests. He swam laps so that he could tire himself out enough to sleep, and he was still swimming when I left him and went upstairs to bed.

Eventually Ethan had made enough money—he was paid under the table and patrons of the piano bar indeed gave him tips when he played requests, they tipped generously—so that we could make a trip into Ventura to a store where we bought pipes and pipe fittings, elbows and tees and Y-branches and other joints in alphabetic shapes, and faucets and valves and all of the tools that we needed and did not have, like a propane torch, like a hacksaw, a decent chisel. Eventually we got back to work.

Helen's plans for the framing and the exterior had been

meticulously rendered on broad blueprint pages and detailed further on pages and pages of graph paper, but her plans for the plumbing that we were supposed to install looked like doodles on cocktail napkins by comparison. She had come up with a sketch that looked like a family tree with most of the names of relatives left out. Like a subway map for a congested city, the stations unlabeled. With this crude outline, we were supposed to chalk-mark where the pipes would be inserted into the frame and then cut the pipes appropriately and fit them together to test the assembly and then prepare the walls and then finally install the assembled plumbing.

Since we were working with new materials, iron and copper and plastic, we decided to practice on a few sample pieces, and right away I knew that we were in trouble. None of us took to the new technique required by our new tools, the chiseling and hacksawing of the pipes—the cacophonous scrape of metal against metal, of the sawteeth against the piping, sent chills up my spine—and our work was sloppy and we knew it. When we tried to cut a pipe, we always ended up hacksawing and chiseling it enough so that we could then break it with brute force, which meant denting and damaging the thinner tubings and which meant that we ended up with crudely sliced pieces that we then needed to file down in order to remove burrs and chinks that would interfere with the flow of water. And when we tried to fit these pipes together, forget it. The spigot-end of a pipe never quite fit snugly into the bell-end; there were gaps in our joints, there were holes that would make for splendid leaks.

Helen was the first to admit that her drawings were inadequate, a rush job she said, and Ethan became visibly unhappy at the prospect of having to cut out the necessary notches and drill the necessary holes in the studs and joists for the plumbing. He did not want to touch the framing. The house looked like a house on the outside, that was the irony, it more or less looked ready to be moved into. Yet we were spending our days in the raw interior, and from that perspective, from the inside looking out, it did not look like our months of labor had amounted to much. It got hot in the canyon and very dry. Our tempers were just waiting to blossom.

And then we could not find the water source, the well, which was actually a well that was shared with some of the other properties on this particular bend of Las Patas Glen, the properties where no one was rebuilding and therefore where nobody was restoring what by now were clogged and possibly fume-hazardous mains. It was possible that we would hook up the new pipes to the well and sewage drainage and only discover that we could get no water up to the house because it was pouring out underneath some-body's unrazed ruins and that we could not unload the drainage without flooding Helen and Ethan's property with muck. After some exploring, we did find the well at the bot-tom of a neighbor's land down the slope, a well and its com-plex array of shut-off valves encased in a metal shed, and we found the remnants of the building drain from Ethan and Helen's old house. The drain was gnarled and would need to be replaced, and some of it had run underground, which would mean digging out the old to insert the new, and what had been described in Chapter 9, "Plumbing," as a fairly straightforward process now became an overwhelming pro-ject in its own right, which led Helen to suggest that profes-sionals be brought in. And paid their big-time salaries, their by-the-hour wages. She was the first to shoot down her own suggestion, but the fact that she even suggested it sig-nified a defeat in itself.

Ethan flipped ahead in the chapter on plumbing to see if we could skip some steps and move on, which was what we decided to do. Somehow we managed to rough in the principal trunks of the plumbing, the soil stack that ran the vertical height of the house, the aorta off of which all other pipes and vents would branch, and the main house drain, which we would insert beneath the lower floor and pitch at a downward slant and hopefully connect with the main sewage line someday. Ethan was really the driving force behind this latest push, and when he was tired, we all lost momentum and made mistakes. And he was tired often since he worked all night and since he was the kind of person who did not function well with less than eight hours of magnificent sleep. He was tired and he kept tripping over the piping that was strewn all around the house, inside and outside; he was tired and had no patience for our latest gaffe.

We had to lift up some of the underfloor to drill holes in the joists and insert the drainage pipe that we had assembled, and after we drilled the hole in the center of the joist, at the weak point in the span of the beam, instead of drilling it on the side where the load of the iron could be carried, the misdrilled floor joist snapped in two when we put in the pipe. Needless to say, we were reminded of other beams that had splintered under stress.

Ethan's face became a sunburned red, his arms and chest red, too. He shouted at Helen and at me, too—he had never lost his temper with me before—and he exaggerated the situation—all we would have to do would be to brace the broken joist and learn from our mistake—and he claimed that the structural integrity of the whole house had once again been compromised. Ethan said that this was not a house in which he would feel safe living and drove off as was his wont. He returned an hour later and apologized and blamed his mood on sleep deficiency, but I did not believe that he had gotten over his anger because he still looked sunburned. The next day, we drove separate cars to the house and Ethan came later than Helen and I did and left earlier, well before sundown. He had stopped spending the nights with us and bit by bit he was giving up the days.

So Helen and I were more or less working on the plumbing by ourselves, and I became the one who cradled the textbook in my arm and read the instructions and did not understand the words on the page as I read them. I think that the authors of our guidebook, like us, preferred the pure and basic carpentry of house-building to all other tasks and consequently did not explain themselves as well as they had in earlier chapters. But I should point out that the plumbing in this house was not terribly complicated as far as plumbing goes because there was the kitchen upstairs along with a half-bathroom and then the main bathroom downstairs, and all of the pipes were supposed to be carried in the framing that Ethan and Helen had built against the rear retaining wall. And still, we could not seem to figure out where exactly we needed to branch out from the main stack and where we needed to add air chambers or vents or various valves. Then there was the issue of hot-water and cold-water pipes and how far apart they needed to be placed, and the issue of iron pipes versus copper pipes, copper versus plastic, when we should use which. And then there was the hot-water heater and its own caution-packed instructions to follow. And the traps under sinks for which we had not procured the right fittings. And so on and so on.

I had known Helen long enough now to know that she loved puzzles of any kind, Helen who as a girl had reportedly taken apart her mother's radio, the family television, and numerous phones. And I could tell that her heart was not in figuring out the puzzle of the plumbing. The house was littered with tubes that looked like colossal pieces of uncooked pasta. Her heart was not in it, and she and I had become restless again.

House number three on our grand tour that summer was a classic California bungalow halfway up Encantado Canyon Road, not a beach house but a secluded hillside home at the end of a private drive and nestled amid a close of eucalyptus.

It was August. The days were slow and the nights slower. We were going to drive out into the desert and find a movie to see, but then we decided instead to fix ourselves a simple feast. We went to the market in Trancas, and it was when we driving back up the canyon that Helen instructed me to veer off the main road.

It was a wonderful house, shingled green and with a cedar roof and cedar trim and wraparound eaves that cast long embracing shadows in the moonlight of the early evening. Screened gabled porches buttressed the main one-story square of the house, and if you squinted, the place blended into the woods that surrounded it. It was an old house.

"We need ideas for our interior," Helen said to me as we pulled up to the house, as if suddenly we needed to justify our unjustifiable intrusions.

"Gee, it looks like no one's home," I said.

"Too bad," Helen said. "I'd hate to have to come back another night, since we've come this far. . . ."

Helen got in through a door in the back which looked as though it had warped with the years and would never lock properly. She greeted me at the front door.

"You left the groceries in the truck," she said. "The ice cream will melt. We can put it in the refrigerator while we look around."

I retrieved the grocery bags and headed straight for the kitchen, but unfortunately the refrigerator had been unplugged and defrosted, which on the one hand meant that we did not have to worry about anyone coming home and finding us—the owners of this house were probably away—but which also meant that our perishables were doomed in this heat. Even the fresh raspberries that I had picked up to sprinkle on the chocolate ice cream were getting mushy.

Helen looked around the kitchen; the doors of the cabinets were glassed, so she had no trouble finding bowls, and then she doled out the ice cream, a half-pint per person, and dumped the raspberries on top. She located some spoons for us. We marched off to the foyer with our bowls in hand, careful not to drip any ice cream on the dark hardwood floors or on the dark rugs, green rugs bordered with blue and red flowers.

This would not be my favorite house—my favorite would be the last one that we broke into, a glass house—but it would be a close runner-up. Whereas the interiors of the beach houses were gaudy and overdone, a premium had been placed on quality here, and good taste prevailed in this house with its paneled wainscoting and quiet cream walls, with its square brass lamps and bulky but expertly made, polished wood furniture. Wood, wood, and more wood, inside and out. We had found a model decor for ourselves after all, and what Ethan had meant when he said that he wanted the inside of our house to look like a cello was exemplified here by the different kinds of wood that had been used around the bungalow, dark and light and grainy and smooth, a palette of browns and blacks, of oak and ebony. This was a tactile house, you wanted to run your hand along every wall, along every tabletop; you wanted to open and shut all of the kitchen cabinets and drawers with their neat brass pulls. We were foolish, looking back, leaving our paw prints everywhere in that canyon bungalow. We touched everything.

The twin porches were dreamy rooms, one off the living

room, one off the master bedroom. They were drenched with cricket chirps, although I did not recall hearing crickets anywhere else in the canyon. The trees around the house were old and tall, and they blocked the ocean view. There was a hammock strung up in one corner of the porch off the living room, and I stretched out in it and finished my ice cream and would have fallen asleep there had I not heard Helen back in the kitchen banging around. She had decided that we would eat dinner here, and why not? We would clean the place thoroughly when we left, we would wash and dry our dishes. We would eat a feast in this tree house of a house and then make it look like we had never been there.

"I've got the fish," Helen said, preparing the trout. She was going to cook it in a big cast-iron skillet. "You do the salad."

I cleaned the lettuce and began slicing up an avocado and some plum tomatoes and a crisp cucumber. I got the couscous going, too, and when I wanted to sauté a red pepper and a zucchini to mix in with the couscous, I bumped Helen's elbow as she was flipping the fish in the skillet. She looked bothered even after I apologized.

"What's wrong?" I asked.

"You know perfectly well what's wrong," she said.

A mood, I kept my distance. But I should have guessed what she was up to from the pitch of her voice, deeper than usual, a certain drawl.

A short while later, she said, "I want the house. You can have first dibs on anything in the house, but I want the house."

I played along. "I want the hammock on the porch," I said.

"Fine," Helen said. Her eyes were red, and she looked like she had been crying for hours. She had been chopping shallots. "I'm going to claim the pottery if—"

"Not so fast," I said. "I want some of the pottery."

"What and break up the collection? Fine," she said. "You can have the pottery."

She dished out the fish and poured the shallot sauce over it. I opened the bottle of merlot that we had bought and tossed the salad with a vinaigrette. We sat down to dinner at the long table in the formal dining room with an empty fruit bowl as its centerpiece.

"The fish is splendid," I said.

"Ditto the couscous and salad," she said. "I want the furniture in the bedroom."

I sipped my wine and was not really enjoying our game, it was too mean.

"I said that I want—"

"You know what?" I said. "You take whatever you want. Leave me what you don't want, and I'll be happy with that. Good choice of wine, by the way."

"This is odd," Helen said. "Here we are in the middle of a messy divorce, but we can meet in the old house and be so civil. We can cook a dinner together like we used to."

I picked up my wineglass and moved down to Helen's end of the table. "What would it take to get you back?" I asked.

"You can have the books. I've read all the books," she said.

"I want the car," I said.

"Take the car," she said.

"So it's over?" I asked. "It's really over?"

"It's never over," she said, not looking me in the eye. "How can it ever be over?"

I thought that was the end of it. We were back to eating our dinner and cleaning up the kitchen—it would be cleaner than when we found it—and opening windows to air out the fish smell. Helen—the real Helen, the pretend Helen: Tell me where to draw the line—was in a visibly better mood. She whistled while she made us espresso with an old filter pot-contraption with long handles that she figured out how to use. We took our coffee out on the porch. I heard an owl. We sat close together on a wicker settee, my bare leg brushing against hers.

"Of course," Helen said, "we could put off selling the house for a while. . . ."

I was not in the mood to start in again, so I did not respond.

"Do you really want to sell this place?" she asked. "I don't. Do you?"

"No," I said, giving in. "We had so many good days here," I said.

"Perfect days," Helen said, "one after another."

She spilled a bit of coffee on my thigh and was quick to dab it with a napkin, although my shorts were stained. She tried to rub the stain out and made it worse, and that was how her hand ended up on my thigh. I felt my leg tense to her touch. I leaned back, and she did not remove her hand. Her palm was against my leg, and I reached behind her and massaged the back of her neck with my thumb and fingers. What was happening seemed tender enough, friendly enough, but at some point, one game ended and another began.

Helen slid her hand under my shorts and discovered that I was hard.

I stopped massaging her neck.

She removed her hand and sat up straight.

"I'm sorry," I apologized first.

"No, I'm the one who is sorry," she said.

"The wine," I said.

"The heat," she said.

"The hot wine," I said with a forced chuckle.

"I'm lonely," she said.

"I know," I said. That was really my first understanding of the canyon that lay between her and Ethan. "Me, too. You don't need to explain."

I made a dumb joke about how our how-to book had warned us to space the hot-water and cold-water pipes at least eight inches apart but we had clearly not heeded that warning. I did not get my own punch line, but Helen laughed.

"Okay," she said. "We got carried away," she said. "It happens."

"I love you," I said. It sort of popped out, but I meant it. I meant that I needed her and was glad to know her as well as I did. I gave her a kiss, a decidedly friendly kiss, on the cheek.

She said, "You're a cool friend, Brad Gray. A very cool friend."

Later, after we had cleaned up the bungalow and returned to the house at the top of the canyon road, I heard Ethan come home and swim his laps. I closed myself off in a bathroom and masturbated and took a long bath.

The next night we went to see him play at the hotel bar. We drove the pickup into the city at dusk, driving away from the setting sun, and I realized that it was the first time that the three of us had traveled in this direction together. We had dressed up as much as we could manage. I was wearing my one blazer and my best white trousers; I borrowed a silver and green rep tie from Ethan. Helen wore a white cotton dress that buttoned all the way down the front, down to her ankles, and black sandals that reached up her ankles to the hem of her dress. She wore a choker made from a white ribbon. And Ethan wore what he wore every night, a white dinner jacket that was big in the shoulders, a semi-pressed white shirt, baggy black trousers, and a thin black bow tie. He wore loafers and went sockless. We looked silly, valet-parking the pickup. We looked swank going into the hotel. Tanned, worldly.

It was a big white Deco hotel with steep rounded corners and ribboned windows bending around these corners. Punctuating the stretches of glass on each floor, there were black panels and inverted silver triangles set into the panels, silver arrows which as the night fell turned out to be lights that illuminated the facade and made the hotel look like it was a ship afloat at sea. A long silver and black canopy reached across the wide width of the sidewalk and a doorman saluted Ethan as if he were a big-tipping guest.

We cut through the lobby, a dark wood and red-velveted lobby bordered with tall potted ferns, and Helen and I took a booth at the back of the hotel bar—I should say we disappeared into the deep den of that booth, a curve of green fabric and more dark wood around a small black marble table—while Ethan said something to the two bartenders who glanced our way. Ethan stepped over to the piano behind the bar, almost beyond our view even though it was a small room, and he began playing right away.

A bartender served us complimentary drinks, and Ethan warmed up with a zippy singsongy treatment of a normally downbeat ballad. I got drunk fast, drunk more on the mood of the place, the nostalgia in the air, than on the sloe gin I found unquenching. Drunk on Ethan's playing, which was as potable as ever, and then drunk, too, on the subsequent bourbon I ordered, on the mix of distillations. I did not even like gin or bourbon, but I thought that I should be drinking gin and bourbon in a place like this. Helen rested her chin on her palm and leaned on her elbow. She was not watching Ethan as far as I could tell, and not looking at me. The hotel bar was about as classic as a hotel bar could get, and I wondered if she was remembering all of the other hotel bars that she had visited with Ethan. Her eyes were glazed.

The predinner crowd trickled in. People meeting each

other at the bar. People retreating to the L of booths for more intimate rendezvous. Ethan played without a break. We kept drinking. I could not really see him, but I could see his legs beneath the piano, and I noticed that he had slipped out of his loafers, that he was depressing the piano pedals and keeping his tempo barefoot. He had a cigarette going but rarely puffed on it. He used a demitasse saucer for an ash-tray.

He dutifully played the requests that were passed on to him by the bartenders, and I have to admit that while I was enjoying myself and enjoying Ethan's jazz, something both-ered me. Maybe I did not like sharing him and his piano with a bar packed with well-dressed strangers, and I wondered if sharing Ethan with strangers was what made Helen wrinkle her nose and grimace.

I said, "Ethan has a public now."

And Helen did not respond, or she misheard me because she said, "Straight up, no ice, thank you," and handed me her glass.

I went up to the bar and got her a new whiskey.

The predinner crowd dropped off and there was an hour when no one came in. Ethan talked to us for a stretch, or he talked to me; Helen did not say anything other than to com-pliment his playing.

The after-dinner crowd, the into-the-night crowd, came in next, and they were loud and collectively giddy, their chatter running counterpoint to Ethan's blues. And then out of the blue, out of the blues as it were, Ethan began to sing. He sang scat.

Helen sat up straight. Like me, I did not think that she had ever heard him sing like this before, not beyond the private confines of a shower. Ethan sang, and while he did not have a memorable voice, he had a sweet voice, a friendly voice that really was not suited to the melancholic music with which he accompanied himself. Soon his scat evolved into fragments of song, and I began to suspect that the reason he intermittently sang nonsense phrases was because he did not know all the words to these songs. The effect was nevertheless endearing, the intercutting between lyrics and babble. He was charming.

Ethan in front of an audience. He became animated in a way that I had never seen him come alive before. He had put gel in his hair and slicked it back, and from where I sat, he looked like a different person, like a man of the world who had wandered in from the street and just started playing, a performer who longed for a stage.

Helen summed it up, and this comment probably explained her silence that evening. She said, "He belongs here." Emphasis on the word here. As opposed to there, and by there, read the canyon. "He always has belonged here," she went on, lying down on the cushion of the booth, "and it kind of makes me crazy that he took so long getting here. Doesn't it make you crazy?"

She lay there for a while and then excused herself and went to the ladies' room, emerging fifteen minutes later looking rather green. She had gotten sick, she did not have to tell me. She wanted to be in bed, so I crossed the room to Ethan and discussed the matter with him, and I had the bartender call a cab and then we—the bartender and me—walked Helen to the taxi, Ethan playing the piano all the while, never abandoning his post.

Helen and I took a very expensive ride back to the canyon.

Eventually we gave up on the plumbing. We agreed that we would return to it at a later date and tried to neaten up the house by collecting the uninstalled pipes in tidy piles downstairs. On to the next chapter in the how-to book. But the chapter on heating seemed even more insurmountable than the one on plumbing. Helen had made no drawings of the heating system, not even a doodle of a schematic, and she and Ethan had never really decided on what kind of system they wanted in their house in the first place. Plus we were back to the issue of hooking up to the outside world. Helen and Ethan's previous house had been gas-heated, and none of us looked forward to scouting out the gas lines and determining what kind of shape they were in, not to mention the fact that in order to get gas running through the house, we would have to deal with the local gas company, which was a problem because Helen, I learned, had decided to ignore the process of securing building permits and only adhere to the various codes recommended in the how-to book, rather than the ones the county had ordained.

I was the one who suggested that we skip ahead to the chapter on electricity.

We all assumed that we would breeze through the wiring of the house because Helen understood the basics of circuitry and currents. She led the charge, so to speak. And we recovered our momentum and did not even consider hooking up the house to a power source or what that would entail by way of dealing with the world beyond the canyon; this was a house that could be connected to the rest of the planet in time, we decided, when everything was completely installed and ready to be switched on or flushed out or warmed up. First we would lay in the wiring. First we would test it with batteries to see if our circuits worked. We had plenty to do for now.

So once again the three of us drove to Ventura, and with the hard-earned crisp cash that Ethan had brought home, we purchased spools of cable and all kinds of outlets for switches and lights and a main service panel (which came with a set of instructions, a how-to book unto itself). We bought more tools, pliers mostly, electrician's pliers and long-nose pliers. We were glad that we were not going to have to cut out as many chunks of our framing as we were supposed to cut out for the plumbing; wires were much easier to snake through a house than pipes, we discovered, much more malleable. And as soon as we got back from the store, we taught ourselves whatever new techniques we needed to master, how to cut a cable and apply a protective bushing. We learned one more language when we spliced these wires: There were pigtail splices and western-union splices and bunch splices and solderless splices. Wires came together in about as many ways as ropes were tied into knots.

But then we got bogged down with rules of electrical systems; that was when we began to stray. The cables were color-coded, no problem, and white wires connected to white wires, black to black. But were we supposed to connect white wires to chrome screws or black wires to chrome screws? No, black wires were connected to brass screws, and two-way switches had to be connected to black wires. No, to white wires. And two-way switches only came with brass screws, which meant that, um, black wires had to be connected to them, right, yet if the switch was at the end of a circuit, then you ended up with one black wire in that particular case only and had to connect it to . . . You could connect it to a white wire . . . Even though white wires were connected to white wires in the understood segregation of wiring among the fellowship of electricians.

Soon there were tangles of wires littered all over the house, and soon it was hot and Ethan was tired and took a nap in the bay of the pickup and then burned his chest and went home in a snit because no one had woken him up to prevent him from baking. Helen and I tried to install the service panel, but we got nowhere. There were wires everywhere, insidious wires poking out of the framing, wires like spiderwebs. We slowed down, we dragged, we gave up and went for a swim.

House number four was a famous house, an Italianate mini-villa in a pale rose stucco designed by a well-known architect, a house that I had seen written up in a magazine. I would not have recognized it if we had come upon it at night.

Ethan had offered to work a double shift at the hotel, sitting in for the pianist who entertained the teatime crowd and then playing his usual gig. When he left in the middle of the afternoon, we knew that we were not going to see him until the next morning. So Helen and I began our drive much earlier than usual, working our way east, in and out of neighboring canyons, east and south along the coast. I spotted the famous house set into the hillside, its terraces stepping down toward the ocean. From the higher road, we could squint at the series of interior courts around which the rooms of the house were laid out. The lowest terrace looked out on a long pool, a pool that appeared to bring the ocean closer to the mountain.

We parked under an empty carport at the top of the hill and had to walk down a trellised set of stairs to get to the entrance, a grand door between two short columns. Right away, I noticed some kind of video camera angled down at us from the lintel above the door, and I pushed Helen back a step so that we were out of its scope. A red light beneath the camera pulsed.

Chances were that in a house with a security system presumably as sophisticated as this one, there would be cameras positioned all around the exterior, and anyone with half a mind would have returned to his car and driven off. Chances were that the camera over the front door had already caught a glimpse of us.

Helen looked at me with raised eyebrows: What should we do?

I had liked what I had seen of this house when I read about it in the magazine and I did not want to leave so hastily without a little more of a look around. I figured that by the time the police were summoned by the silent alarm that we would probably trigger, we would be gone; we would only walk around the perimeter of the house and then drive away. To answer Helen's question, I nodded toward the wooden gate to the right of the house.

Which we climbed over. We jumped down onto a walkway that wended through a grove of pomegranate trees—there were lumps of smashed and rotten fruit everywhere—and then emerged on a patio with a table beneath a trellis of wisteria. The path led down more stairs to another patio, and another, and so on, following the descent of the house down the bluff. Each patio was lined with potted shrubs and banked with beds of jasmine that in turn spilled into the disorderly chaparral. The path led all the way down to the pool, which we had seen from the road. But we did not go down to the pool just yet.

All along each patio, there were locked glass doors which afforded us a decent peek inside. There was a bedroom with a broad white bed and white pillows and white armchairs around a blue stone fireplace. There was a grand salon with pale yellow walls and sisal rugs and more white furniture and polished wood and several large landscape paintings by the same artist, wheat fields distilled down to bands of maize and blue. There was a kitchen with copper pots hanging from a ceiling rack and neat green cabinets and a vast industrial stove. But it was the room off a middle patio that made us both a little crazy to get inside. The study, and not just any study. The study of an architect.

The study was the only room capped with a square cupola, a bell tower that rose a floor above the rest of the tiled roof, and the clerestory of that cupola washed the room with sunlight. The walls were decorated by more of the landscape painter's work, smaller works which were propped up on the tops of the steep bookcases, bookcases crammed with big art books. And then there was the broad drafting table around which there were all manner of triangles and jars of pencils and scales and compasses. . . . There was something taped down to the table, plans, but we could not see them from our vantage.

I did not notice when Helen slipped away from me, and I was rather startled when she appeared inside, once again opening a door for me.

"People are so careless," she said.

"What about the alarm?" I asked. "Aren't there motion detectors?"

She explained that she had noticed an open door off the next patio, and since it was open, she reasoned that an alarm could not be on.

"People are careless," I agreed, heading for the drafting table, "aren't they?"

We slid the T square up to the top of the board and studied the plans. They were for a library—I do not recall where—and both of us were in heaven. The architect was apparently also designing furniture for the library, and we found rough sketches for tables and chairs of a delicate taper and curve. We must have studied these plans for an hour, an hour of intense scrutiny during which we had to fill in certain details ourselves—the hue of the limestone facade, the way the recessed lighting dripped down the walls of the reading room, and so on—and when I finally looked up, I realized that Helen, leaning on an elbow, was not examining the blueprints at all but staring at my face instead. She was smiling.

"What?" I asked.

"Nothing," she said.

"No, what?"

She was leaving the room, leading me into another room. The living room. The dining room and kitchen.

"Helen," I said, catching up with her in the bedroom, at the foot of the bed.

When I stepped toward her, she grabbed my hands and pulled me close. Then she pressed both of her hands flat against my chest and, turning her head to a slight angle and inhaling, breathing me in as it were, she rested her head on my shoulder and breathed out as if she were exhaling a fine plume of smoke.

I do not know how long we stood like that. Her breath was a light breeze against my neck; it was a sensation that was at once familiar and alien. Eventually I held her hips and pushed away from her just far enough so that I could kiss her. And then kiss her neck. And pull her shirt away from her collar, her shoulder.

Years later, I was breaking up with a man whom I had been seeing for close to two years. The man was hurt and wanted to hurt me back. Words were his weapon of choice, and he said, I just want you to know that I never believed a word you said about you and that woman. Unfortunately, I could not offer an adequate self-defense because my affair with Helen was as incredible to me then, too, as it was when it happened. I said, It was very unexpected, and left it at that.

I had unbuttoned her blouse and pulled it over her shoulders and I was kissing her breast and the side of her chest and she fell back on the bed, working at my belt with fast fingers. We were mostly naked then, her hands flat against my chest again, holding me above her. I wanted to explore her more, I wanted to go slower, but she flipped me over and opened a night table drawer and tore at something with her teeth. She rolled a condom over me and I thought I would burst, and then we were fast, then we were in a hungry hurry.

I should say that whenever I thought about my life and how I wanted to spend it, taking the long view, I imagined myself in the company of a man. When I thought about women, I thought in terms of moments and evenings and single seasons of passion, finite vistas of time; but I did crave their affections, I always have. And I should also say that I can see how a man could have played the role that Helen did, that a man could have been the one to usher me back to the land of the living. But the fact remains that it was Helen who performed that feat.

Spent and lying next to me, me on my back and her on her side, watching me as she had watched me examine the blueprints, she said, "You look surprised."

"I am surprised," I said, "you don't know how surprised."

She touched my face. She ran her fingertips along my brow, my jaw, my ear. That was when I knew that I no longer wanted to be alone, not by choice.

I think I wanted to surprise her back, if surprising was the game, and so I pinned her and I started in again, setting the pace, and eventually I rolled on my back and I had her ride me, and outside the sun was setting.

The more improbable our lovemaking, the more—what is the right word? transcendent? pure?—the more honest it was. There was always something stripped-down about our sex. I mean sex on a white bed, the blankets thrown off. I mean sex in the afternoon, the windows open, the curtain catching the breeze. That was the way it was at first. Later, when it was expected, when it was routine, that was when we began to fail each other. She needed me in the same way that I needed her, I knew that. She needed to hold as much as she needed to be held. I do not know, however, if I ever truly made her feel less lonesome. Maybe I did, but only for a time.

But let me linger there in that first bed. Helen lay on her stomach. I formed a brush with my first two fingers and pretended to paint her body with the colors of the canyon. The slope of her thigh in magenta bougainvillea. The side of her ribs and breast in green chaparral. Her cheek blue like the sky. I never wanted to be alone again.

We showered. We dried off. I brushed Helen's hair, she combed mine. We had made a terrible mess of this house, in the bathroom, in the bedroom. We did not want to be tawdry and rude—nor did we want to leave so much evidence of our breaking and entering—and so we gathered up the sheets and pillowcases and towels and found the laundry room and figured out how to use the washer.

While we were waiting for the sheets and towels to wash, we could not resist the pool, and, still naked, dove in and swam over to two twin white rafts floating in the deep end. We each stretched out on one and napped for a while.

The days were shorter now and the sun was gone from the sky. What light there was came from the outside lamps that had ignited in a startling flash. Helen paddled her raft over to mine and then slipped aboard so that the two of us were tenuously balanced in the center of the deep end.

"I want to live on an island," she said.

"To tell you the truth," I said, "I've never really been all that into this game—"

"I'm serious," she said. "I want to live on an island."

"An island where?" I asked.

"It doesn't really matter where. I want to buy the whole island and build a house on the highest ground."

"An island," I said. "What about the canyon house?" I asked.

"What about the canyon house?" I asked again when she did not answer me.

"It was just a thought," she said. "Don't get so upset."

"I'm not upset, I'm . . ." I was upset, there was no hiding it. "It's just that I don't want to be living all alone on the lower lot," I said.

"The lower lot?"

"Never mind," I said.

I rolled off the raft, which meant that Helen tipped over and fell into the water, too, and she tried to grab my ankle at the bottom of the pool, but I surfaced, and she tried to grab my arm as I pulled myself out of the water. She chased me inside.

We put the sheets and towels in the dryer, and later, when we took them out to fold them, we noticed that we had inadvertently dried a load of white clothes, some shirts and T-shirts and bras that must have been left in the washer. We folded them and left them on top of the dryer, but when we were making the bed and began to consider what it meant that there had been laundry in the washing machine, we realized that whoever lived here probably had not gone all that far away and might, now that it was evening, just be returning at any moment. We left right away, with the bed only half-made.

We saw little of Ethan in the days that followed. He continued to work double shifts at the hotel bar. When we did see him, we talked about the house and what work needed to be done, but this was idle chat. The smallest talk.

I always assumed, even then, that he somehow knew about my affair with Helen from the very moment it began.

Miles away, he could feel a hand on his hip the way my hand had rested on Helen's hip. Miles away, he knew and he did not try to stop it. He was, in his way, leaving us, and we were just making it easier for him.

He had to have known because I was then and am now a minor-league liar. I cannot look at someone when I bend the truth; I had trouble looking him in the eye.

He left in the afternoon, earlier and earlier, and I waited until he was gone and I watched his car—my car, that is— descend the canyon road—the telescope came in handy— and I had to see the car racing east on the coast road before I found Helen wherever she was, by the pool, in bed. I found her and I made love as if I was thirsty, and I was thirsty for her. These days blended into each other, and I just remember them as one long romp. A white bed, the blanket pulled back, pillows tossed on the floor. The windows open to the afternoon breeze.

This was our routine. Ethan left. We fooled around. Then we tried to build.

Helen had managed to install the service panel of the electrical system while I more or less mastered the language of the wires and screws, what connected to what, while I learned what needed to be learned about grounding wires. With the service panel in place, the hardest part of the wiring was behind us—that was the claim made in the how-to book—and yet as we tried to install the various circuits branching out from the fuse box, we ran into trouble. We tried to run a cable upstairs and connect it to another cable that ran to an outlet and then a switch and then a ceiling outlet; we tried to close the loop to insure a happy continuum of electricity, but when we inserted a circuit-tester, its gauge indicated that the circuit would not work. We looked for a faulty strip of cabling or a damaged outlet box, some gap in the circle of wiring, but we found nothing wrong. We replaced all of the cables to no avail. We man-

aged to get one circuit in, however, only one over the course
of a morning, but we kept running into the same problem
when we began to lay in another cable. . . .

Back to my house. A nap, a swim. Maybe we fooled
around again. Maybe we went for a drive. Back to the
canyon again, and we drank something cold and strong,
vodka, bourbon.

One day, Helen and I did not bother crossing the canyon.
We complained that it was too hot and too dry to work. And
the day after that, we did not go across the canyon to work
either. Nor the day after that.

The white house in the distance looked like it was made
of white sand. Sand that we had carried up from the shore.
And sooner or later the tide would come in and wash our
castle away, and then we would not have to feel so guilty
about abandoning it.

Then one afternoon we drove around and could not find a
house to break into. Helen drove us back to Encantado
Canyon Road. We stripped and went to bed together, although we did not make love. We were too hot to move, we
only napped.

In the early evening, I got up to take a swim before dinner. I slipped on my bathing suit and went down to the
pool, which was where I found Ethan stretched out on a
towel and staring at the sky.

"How long have you been home?" I asked.

"A while," he said.

I was a light enough sleeper that I would have heard him
open the door to my bedroom if he had tried to find us; I
was fairly certain that he had not seen us together, which
was not to say that he had not, however, noticed that all of

the other bedrooms were empty and then deduced that Helen and I were together in the same room with the door closed.

"I have the night off," he said. He stood and walked over to me. He swallowed hard. He said, "I thought you were my friend."

That was my cue to say, I am your friend, Ethan. That was when I was supposed to say, I have no idea what you're talking about. And he waited for me to make my defense. I said nothing. I sighed. Guilty as charged.

"I would not have done this to you," he said.

"Ethan," Helen said. I had not heard her come downstairs. "Come talk to me," she said.

Ethan stepped around me, and I thought he was going to shove me in the pool. I wish that he had done something, that he had at the very least punched me squarely in the jaw. He went inside with Helen. I wanted to follow him in, but I swam laps instead.

I caught bits and pieces of what they said whenever I stopped swimming and caught my breath.

"We're not getting the house built," Ethan said. "Where are all the drawings for the interior that you said you would do?"

"This is strange coming from you," Helen said. "I don't exactly see you picking up the old hammer and banging away—"

Ethan: "I am the one who went and got a job so we could finish. I am the one who is working while you . . ."

Helen: "While I what?"

"While you . . ."

"While I what? While I what, Ethan?"

"While you know perfectly well what, Helen," Ethan said. "Whatever," he said.

"No," Helen said.

"No what?" he asked. "No, you haven't been fooling around with our friend the thief?"

"No," Helen said, "I have not."

If I could hear the lie in her voice all the way out in the pool, I did not expect that he would believe her.

"Our friend the thief is our only friend," she said. "I wouldn't. We haven't."

Why not just tell him? It was what he wanted to hear.

Ethan: "Well, I'm sorry if I—"

Helen: "Don't be sorry."

Silence again, and I had to swim or my eavesdropping would have become obvious. When I came up for air again, I heard Helen:

"At least you're finally doing what you always wanted to do," she said.

"This is true," Ethan said.

"And I'm proud of you."

"Please don't condescend," he said.

"I'm not condescending," Helen said. "You'll know when I'm condescending."

"If you're so proud," Ethan said, "then why have you only come to see me play once? And when you did come, you got sick."

Silence again. But I did not swim, I listened and I did not care if they knew that I was listening.

Her: "I'm not sure I want to live in the canyon."

Him: "Now you decide this. Where would you rather live?"

Her: "On an island somewhere. An island anywhere, you can choose where."

Him, perking up: "An island, really? You haven't mentioned an island before."

Her, getting excited, too: "A whole island to ourselves. And we'd build the house on the highest ground."

"It would have to be a house with at least three floors and a single tower rising over the house like a lighthouse," Ethan said.

"And porches everywhere, big wide porches," Helen said.

"And the only way to get to the island would be by boat."

"Even once you had docked, you would still have to climb a trail of hundreds of steps up the rock."

"Would there be fireplaces?" Ethan asked.

"In every room," Helen said.

"It would have to be somewhere where it rains a lot."

"You can only get to this island by boat," Helen said, "but when it rains, you can't even take a boat there."

"We would be alone on the island in the rain," Ethan said. "Stranded."

"A white house on an island in the rain," Helen said, and then they were quiet again.

More laps. When I surfaced they were still quiet, and their silence began to make me nuts. They were not talking, which meant that, after all had been admitted or not admitted, as was the case, they were together once again, reunited in a long marriage of rifts and reunions, that they were making love on the rug. Ethan was doing her, I was sure of it, and why not? She was his, he was hers. Ethan half-dressed, Helen half-dressed. They were boffing in the living room and it made me nuts and I hopped out of the water. If she was not going to confirm for him what he already knew, I would, and I dashed into the house, dripping wet.

I found them sitting on opposite couches on opposite sides of the room, not even holding hands. They were only staring at each other.

Ethan looked at me standing in the doorway dripping; Helen turned around and looked, too. When she turned back toward Ethan, she sank in the couch. He looked at me and waited for me to say something, glancing at me, then back to Helen, at me again. I stood there dripping and waiting for someone to make a move.

"I'm late for work," he said.

"I thought you said that you had the night off," Helen said.

Ethan did not answer her. He went upstairs and Helen did not follow him. He came down a short while later with a duffel bag slung over his shoulder. In a blink, he was gone. He drove off in my car.

He did not return to the canyon that night. He did not return to the canyon the next day.

And the day after that when he did not return, Helen looked glum.

"He took my car," I said. "Not that I care, he can have it. But if we wanted to find him," I said, "we could call the police—"

"Don't call the police," Helen said.

"He left you before," I said, "and he came back. He'll come back again."

But she did not want to be consoled. She said, "We've known each other too long. I honestly hope that he doesn't come back, if you must know. Fuck him, the fucker, I don't give a fuck what he does," she said in a perfectly calm voice.

"Okay," I said, "if that's the way you feel about it."

"That's the way I feel about it," she said.

I will confess that at that moment I did not care whether we ever saw Ethan again, such were my delusions that Helen and I could live happily ever after without him.

It was September and it was very hot, the air mysteriously still, and we spent that day lounging around the pool waiting for the cool reprieve of the ocean breeze that always began brushing by at one-thirty in the afternoon and gusting in earnest by two. We waited and we waited, but the ocean breeze never blew inland that afternoon because it was pushed back by a stronger current, by a ruthless wind out of the Mojave that swept west across the city and the mountain range.

The Santa Anas had begun.

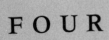

FOUR

That was the season of record winds when wildfires destroyed canyon after canyon along the Pacific coast. These were migrant currents born far to the east that heated up when they traveled the span of the desert, winds that folded in on themselves, that compressed when they rushed down the leeward slopes of mountains, accelerating much like a truck descending a canyon without braking. These were reckless winds, drunk-driven winds. The Santa Anas usually blew for a stretch of three or four days, but that was the autumn when they lasted an unbearable ten days before subsiding for a mere seventy-two hours, before starting up again in a second wave that went on for another two weeks. And it was during the second long siege of the Santa Anas when the fires began to storm out of control, when firefighters were flown in from all over the continent, storms of wind and flame that made the previous year's devastating fire season seem mild by comparison.

The air became thick with dust and eventually with smoke, which filtered the sunlight into an amber wash that jaundiced all things white in our white world, the beaches and the stucco and the cotton we wore. These were deceptive winds because on the one hand, clouds of smoke stampeded west, clouds racing and colliding with one another, and yet at the same time, all of the trees rustled in a stutter, their boughs dancing in slow motion. The ocean looked frozen, as if it had been pressed flat with a thin layer of glass, as if the water had in fact turned to glass and the entire Pacific could be shattered by one angry fist. And when the fires began, it did not matter how far from them we fled because we could still smell what we could not necessarily see; we could never get away from the burning timber, the vaporized sap, the exploding chaparral. We could never escape the ash, the thin ash hanging in the dry air, the flaking ash drifting down from branches, a queer snow that smeared black when we brushed it from our skin.

Houses creaked and walls cracked and roof shingles curled. Plants gave up, they wizened, they yellowed, they crumbled to the touch. Trees collapsed. Great oaks lay in repose across empty streets, cypresses toppled left and right. It was a miracle that any species survived such stultifying heat, a deep-searing heat that soaked through our flesh right down to the bone, that exposed our skulls to the sun, that made us thirsty beyond any possible quenching, a driving heat that reddened our eyes and left us bleary and squinting. Heat that made us stupid. Forget about trying to calm babies who cried themselves tearless that September, that October. Forget about the companionship of dogs; pet them and they growled at you. You were lucky if you had a cat, because cats knew how to scout out the coolest spot in any house, and if you followed your cat, say, to the back of a closet, you were likely to find the only place to curl up and take a nap or, for that matter, sleep at night.

To say that tempers ignited easily would be a gross understatement. I could not count the number of times I saw motorists screaming at each other, getting out of their cars to fight, jamming traffic for blocks and blocks behind them. Countless arguments drifting out of houses and apartments—arguments broadcast on the radio or so it seemed—arguments drowned out only by distant sirens, which were always approaching but never quite arriving. We became incendiary creatures, we combusted when we sighed. We ranted, we shouted, and then we had to lie down. When our tempers were not flaring up, we were napping, and when we were not napping, we found ourselves wandering the city, robbed of speech, lurching toward the occasional mirage of easy swaying palm trees and afternoon rain. Alas, only a mirage.

The history of these winds was a history of desperation. There was the defense attorney who went berserk with a machete. There was the woman who left her twin infants in a station wagon with the windows closed. There was the family that drove off of the bridge of a freeway interchange. There were the kids who went around dropping homemade bombs into mailboxes, who blew themselves up by accident one afternoon. There was the college student who held a radio host at knifepoint and rambled on air for an evening about the imminent apocalypse; he talked for hours and the city listened. And while one heard about similar madness elsewhere in the world, which occurred during similar fronts of malevolent winds, the foehn winds in the Alps or chinook winds in the Rockies, for example, or the sirocco of Northern Africa and the Mediterranean, indeed while there was an entire canon of dreaded hot winds that included the simoom of the Asian desert and the khamsin blowing south out of Egypt and the harmattan on the Atlantic coast of Africa, our own locally grown Santa Anas were distinguished by the natural disasters that they inevitably spawned each year. There were other mean winds in the world, but the Santa Anas inspired true and justified fear.

Often the wildfires began with acts of arson or negligence,

but sometimes they were set off by wind-downed power lines or a hot car engine passing over dried leaves and sometimes simply because resins in the chaparral boiled and boiled and exploded into flame. And when the winter was as rainy and wet as the previous winter had been, when the brush therefore flourished in the spring, and then when the summer air was so hot that all of this brand-new brush dried to a crisp, well, there was fuel and there was more fuel for fires of such velocity and wind that they did not need the Santa Anas to fan them after a while; these were self-sustaining fires that came into their own. That was the season of statistics, of people murdered and divorced, of petty theft and random assaults, of firemen who died when they were ambushed by shifting drafts, of homes destroyed and acres burned. Nine firefighters and two thousand one hundred and fifty-six homes, to be precise, two hundred and ten thousand acres scorched black and bare.

We felt isolated from the rest of the world and isolated from one another, quarantined to the shade of our separate houses and separated from one another within our houses. Helen and I spent entire days in that stucco mansion at the top of Encantado Canyon without seeing each other, and I have no idea what we did, no recollection. These were lost days, a blur. Ethan was gone and I knew that Helen missed him, although she never admitted it. I missed him and did admit it; I would say something benign like, "I wish Ethan were here to play the piano, that would cheer us up," and Helen would not respond.

She and I both traipsed around the house in various states of undress, and we met up in one bedroom or another, or the living room or dining room or wherever there was the least amount of sunlight, and fooled around. We avoided the side of the house that looked across the canyon to the house that we had stopped building. When I did catch a glimpse of the Las Patas Glen peak and when I did see that house, I tried to convince myself that it belonged to someone I did not know. I did not know who was building that house or what kind of a house it would be, nor did I care. I tried but failed to separate us from the white house in the distance, and so I went to great lengths to block it out, drawing curtains and pulling down shades. But then I would peel the curtain back, and there it was, our house; it would not go away.

Like any weather front, the Santa Ana windstorms had their tantrums and their kinder moods—these were capricious and fast-shifting winds—and so now and then when we least expected it, the Santa Anas died down and we enjoyed an hour of still air and sometimes, if we were lucky, a lazy zephyr, a bise from the ocean. Usually this moment of stasis came at the end of the day, and sometimes Helen and I did look across the canyon and discuss the house that we were building and all that needed to be done. And there were dusks when Helen actually sat down at her drafting board with its T square that had warped a bit in the heat, when she sat down with the specific ambition of at long last drawing up plans for the rest of the interior; she would go back and make the plumbing and electrical systems work and then map out the finishes, all of the paneling and shelving and cabinetry and the fireplace of blackened stones and the floors and every last detail of molding.

Except when Helen sat down at her drafting board, she did not work on the canyon house and returned instead to her how-to book and skimmed an early chapter and then thought about the new house that she had in mind, the island house that she had talked about. Not that she had any specific island in mind. She began to design a house in the way that I drew houses when I was fourteen, for fictional, for wholly imagined sites. A big house on an island with wide porches and a tower and windows everywhere.

I did not ask her why she was drawing an island house as

opposed to getting real work done on our real canyon house, but I did ask if I could see what she was working on, to take a look at her sketches, and she refused to show them to me. "Get away," she said and became mean. Once when I did sneak a peek at one drawing and she caught me in the act, she grabbed the page from me and then held it over the kitchen sink and lit it with a match and burned it. She became childish, I thought, juvenile, and I did not like her in these moods, so I left her alone and never asked about the island house again.

During those three days when the Santa Anas altogether ceased, I proposed that we go back to work on the house, but Helen, who seemed certain that the winds would return, that it was only a matter of time, spent her time drawing the island house instead. And then the Santa Anas began again, and I just wanted to cry, except crying was the last thing you wanted to do when these winds blew; crying dried you out, crying made you even more miserable.

We never got dressed and rarely went out during the first wave of Santa Anas, and we did not talk much, talk was tiring. At first we had air conditioning, but then the system broke down from overuse. I called the real-estate agent in charge of selling the house and told her and she was furious. She said that it was my fault that it had broken—What do you mean you have been running it all day every day? What, do you think you own the place?—and she said that she wanted the house to be nice and cool when she brought clients around, which I doubted would happen because she had not shown the house in months. I did try to locate someone to fix the air conditioning, but to no avail; air-conditioner repairmen were basically booked until the end of the millennium, such was the demand that season. I did not want to pay for the repair anyway because I would have had to reach deeper into my bank account, into which I was already reaching deeply and feeling unhappy about it.

Helen scraped together some cash, which she squeezed from her tapped-out credit cards and from some insane credit company, three companies actually, which offered her new charge cards, the fools. That was the money we lived on.

We messed around in every room but our lovemaking changed. It was becoming sex as something to do, sex in place of conversation. We were affectionate at the outset. Helen would lie on the floor in one room or another—heat rises and so we would stay low—and I propped myself up on my elbow next to her, and I formed a paintbrush with my fingers and painted her body in the saturated colors of the dried-out canyon, her breast in the pale green of the flammable chaparral, her stomach in the transparent orange of the withered bougainvillea, her hip in the bleached blue of the foamless tide, and she would roll me over and kiss my upper back with her lips, her miraculously cool, cool lips, my middle back, my lower back. We began with affection and all the time in the world to dispense it. But somewhere along the way, maybe when we moved from the floor to a couch or a bed, the pace picked up and I felt trapped, if you can feel trapped when you are the top-person, and our sex was like driving somewhere on the highway and being late and having to speed up to make up for lost time.

I remember that once—more than once—that often I caught our reflection in the gray mirror of a turned-off television. I watched my back and buttocks rise and fall, and this was far from a turn-on because I drifted away from myself and felt as though I were watching two strangers go at it. And I had to close my eyes in order to fall back into the rhythm of the moment, and closing my eyes, to be very honest, to be blunt, meant that I could have been fucking anyone.

Finally we could not stand that house at the top of Encantado Canyon. We had to get out, and we went for a drive. And we both came alive for a while once we got out of the house. I drove with one arm and held Helen's hand with my shifting hand. We were happy driving because we achieved a false sense of motion. But it was hot, forever hot, and we both craved an evening of air conditioning. . . .

We got through the gate of a ranch far to the east and north of our canyon and discovered that there was a big log cabin of a house at the center, highest point of a meadow and then several cute cottages, also log-faced, tucked into the hills that bordered the stead. The guest house we drove up to did not appear to be occupied—nor did the big house, not at all lit up at night—but the door was locked, its knob unworkable.

Helen said, "Stand back," and then, with three quick kicks, bashed the door in.

"Nice," I said.

"Hey," she said, stepping inside and flipping on a light, "you said that you just wanted to get a good night's sleep in a cool house, and so . . ."

It was a one-room cottage with a bathroom and kitchenette and two twin beds on one side of the room, a couch and two armchairs on the other side positioned around a free-standing woodstove. And it was a cottage with an air conditioner in one of its three windows. We turned it on, it was loud. We stripped and stood in front of it. We were lucky, because most people in this part of the world did not need air conditioners for most of the year, and no one ever installed them in small houses. The host who owned this guest cabin took good care of his visitors. I imagined that the main house was an arctic refuge compared to the cabin, but I was content to stay where we were.

The furniture upholstery and the bedspreads were done up in a green floral pattern, and everything else in the cabin was veneer. I felt as though we had stopped off at a motel for the night. The small refrigerator was amply stocked with bottled ale; we helped ourselves. The one closet was packed with board games, and so we were set, we had all we needed, except maybe a pizza, and Helen picked up a phone to order a delivery, but I pulled the wire from the wall before she had a chance to make the call. We stuck to the beer and got drunk. We played games, we fell asleep.

Later in the night, however, we woke up hungry. Helen decided that we should check out the main house and see what was in the refrigerator. We scampered across a stone terrace behind the house and happily discovered a door to the kitchen that was open. There was half a yellow cake with chocolate icing in the large and humming refrigerator along with a bowl of potato salad and another of cole slaw and roast beef and rolls in a bread box, the fixings for a splendid midnight supper. But then we heard some noises, human stirrings, someone flushing a toilet, and we tore out of the house, leaving the refrigerator door wide open and half-eaten sandwiches on the counter, half-eaten wedges of cake, and sprinted back to the cottage—looking back over my shoulder, I noticed a light on upstairs in the house—and hopped in the pickup and drove off with a screech that echoed for what seemed like miles.

I yelled at Helen when we cleared the gate of the ranch, I really let her have it. We had been so careless. Did we want to get caught? In retrospect, I think we did; that is the only explanation for our recklessness. And then to top it all off, when we were driving down the coast road, Helen showed me a black wallet that she had found lying on a plate on the kitchen table along with car keys. She had meant to take the cash from the wallet, some fifty dollars, and then put the wallet back. She removed the cash now and winged the wallet out the window.

"Good, very good," I said. "Now we really are thieves."

"We need the cash," Helen said, showing no remorse.

"If you want to get caught," I said, "that's swell by me, but leave me out of it."

I was ready to apologize to her when we got back to the canyon, but I did not have a chance because she wandered off to take a cold bath, and then we were sticking to opposite sides of the house the next day, avoiding each other.

I had no idea where Helen was when the real-estate agent came by that morning, and between showing her client the kitchen and the deck beyond the kitchen, the agent pulled me aside and berated me for not getting the air conditioner fixed and for not keeping the place tidy. The house was not terribly messy, but there were couch cushions all over the floor in the living room and cereal boxes out in the kitchen along with unwashed dishes in the sink. The chaises and outdoor furniture around the pool were admittedly in disarray, and the beds, all of the beds, had not been made in weeks. Duvets and blankets lay in puddles of white fabric at every turn.

While I was being taken to task, the real-estate agent's client, a frizzy-haired once-famous rock star whose music I sort of knew—he was famous for his mindless dance tracks—wandered off to the pool. We found him there, mesmerized, watching Helen swim laps. Helen seemed completely unaware of the fact that she was performing. All three of us, the real-estate agent and the rock star and I, watched her swim. For some reason the rock star mistook me for the man selling the house and said that it was too bad about my wife and me splitting up but I had not done so badly in the end, wink, wink, had I? He watched Helen swim back and forth and bit his lip appreciatively. Helen had to have known that we were all watching her because she began to show off her various strokes. She swam a butterfly, a strong breaststroke.

I think that it was later that same day or maybe the day after that when we saw the local news and learned that the sheriff was investigating the rash of burglaries that had been reported in the western reaches of Los Angeles County. Upon first hearing this story, I assumed that the burglaries were unconnected to our trespassing. Indeed there was footage of the burgled homes and they were not the houses that we had broken into. But then there was a quick glimpse of the ranch house where we had fixed ourselves a snack, and so we had all the proof we needed that our luck had run out and there was no way we could chance another break-in. I said that we had to stop and fortunately Helen agreed with me.

But we did not stop—I blamed the winds for our lack of caution—and we got inside the homes that we happened upon during our random drives any way we could, breaking down doors or smashing windows to crawl in. Our premise was always that we needed an air-conditioned respite. Your Honor, we were hot. We were going crazy because we were so hot, and that was not far from the truth. Your Honor, forgive us, we will never do it again. And even though I did not condone it, I did nothing to stop Helen from looking for and taking whatever petty cash she found lying around. She said we needed the money and we did, and so she took twenty dollars here, ten there.

There was the house in the hills to the northwest, a house with wide porches and swings on the porches, a house amid a citrus grove; there were oranges and lemons rotting on the browned lawn. There was the house with cats in it—which meant that someone would show up to feed the cats, and yet we hung around all night—that was when I learned how to follow a cat into a closet to find the coolest floor—cats in every room, long-haired and short-haired cats who were friendly and careened into our calves despite the heat. Helen was great with the cats, I will never forget. She had a way of looking them in the eye and speaking to them like old friends.

There was the house with the eerie stuffed owls. The house with the collection of rare books. There was the house that was under construction, a brashly modern metal-and-glass job with an unfinished interior that made us feel guilty about our own unfinished work, and while I was checking out the craftsmanship, as if I were qualified to judge it, Helen wandered outside. I could not find her until she called to me from the blue-green deep end of the empty pool. She just was sitting there, her knees pulled close to her chest; she looked so small.

She said, "Look, I drowned."

"Do you want me to rescue you?" I asked.

She said something I did not quite hear.

"What?" I asked.

"Doomed from the get-go," she said. That was when she said it. I did not know what she meant. I did not want to know what she meant.

And then there was the house back on the beach in the strip of homes across from the Paradise Diner. A house much like the first we broke into, and we were back late at night again, and as we were hitting the locked knob with an iron pipe we found on the side of the road, as we crossed the outer threshold into the compound of this beach house and entered the atrium, we set off an alarm. A deafening siren of an alarm.

It was a good thing we had set off the alarm and run back to the diner and hopped in the pickup and escaped up the canyon road because people were home at that house on the coast road. A man in pajama bottoms tore out of the house after us, waving a cleaver. If we had not parked across the highway, he would have caught up with us, and we could not be sure that he did not get our license plate. We could not be sure that after we drove off, he did not ask around in the diner to see if we could be identified by the one waitress or the cook in the kitchen. A man and a woman in a white pickup. We were fairly sure that we were safe, but we had come close to being nabbed, and having come close to arrest, having heard further reports on the news about the unsolved burglaries, we promised each other to stop breaking into houses, and we almost did stop. Almost.

Now the fires had begun to the east and to the south, still far away. Yet we could smell them and the smoke blew in along with the dust and there was the ash everywhere. The ash on the surface of the pool. The ash on our skin. We had to blow it away because when we rubbed it off, our arms and legs became all sooty and gray. Now the Southland was on fire, and the local news crews reported nonstop, and we watched the television coverage with maps open on our laps.

We never turned on the lights at night because we did not want to make the house any warmer than it was, not even with the mild incandescence of a single lamp—the television was our only concession to radiant illumination—and so we sat in the dark. The smoke and dust obscured the sun. Night spilled into day, day into night.

And one night, we were going through the motions of getting hot and bothered, we slowed down, and I remember rolling off of Helen and launching into an apology. I blamed the winds, but I knew that there was something that she wanted from me that I could not give her. But she made it clear that she was the one who wanted to apologize. She needed to tell me something, but she needed to get drunk first, she said. We got smashed on cheap wine; then we moved on to the hard stuff. She said that she missed Ethan. I told her that she hardly needed to explain herself.

"He'll come back," I said.

"Not this time. Pass the . . . what are we drinking now?"

"Vodka. He will come back, he has to come back—"

"You don't get it," she said. "He already would be back if he was coming back. I have to tell you something," she said.

I thought that she had already told me what she needed to tell me, that she missed Ethan.

"I'm a monster," she said.

"How are you a monster?" I asked.

"I'm a beast," she said.

"It's so hot," I said.

"Listen," she said.

I did not want to hear whatever it was she was going to say. "Let's go for another swim," I said.

"Listen to me," she said. "I set our house on fire."

I did not know what she meant. I walked across the room to look across the canyon.

"No, the first house," she said. "The one that burned down in the wildfire . . . I set it on fire before the wildfire came."

"You what? You set it on fire?" I did not believe her.

"That is what I am telling you."

"Why? It would have burned anyway," I said. "Right? It would have—"

"Maybe," Helen said. "Maybe not. It is possible that the firemen would have saved our place, it is possible, but I did not want that to happen."

I slumped down a wall and stayed on the opposite side of the room from her.

"Ethan was gone and I was crazy," she said. "The fire was coming and that was when I decided to pour a tank of gasoline all around the house and light a match. And then I got out. And then the big fire met up with my fire. And by the time the firemen got to the canyon, there was nothing they could do but let the Las Patas Glen side burn out and make a stand to save the Encantado Canyon Road side. If I had not set the—"

"Okay," I said. I did not want her to go on.

"Then they may have been able to save Las Patas Glen and all of the houses—"

"Okay!" I screamed. "Shut up, just shut up."

The television was on without the sound. Fires on the screen. I could close my eyes and imagine Helen dousing the furniture with fuel, but I could not envision her tossing a match.

"I was crazy," she said. "I lost it that day. I wanted to make sure that my house burned down, and I did not even think about the rest of the glen."

"The glen would have burned anyway," I said.

"I have to take part of the blame," she said. "I never told Ethan."

"Why did you—"

"You know why," she said.

And I did. She had to destroy her home so that Ethan would have to find her and so that they could start over. They would comb the ruins and find keys. They would retire to a hotel and sob and make love. Then they would be together again. They would plan, they would rebuild. That was all she wanted, and so she had to make sure that her house burned down, and I knew that, but I disliked her at that moment for her frantic selfishness, for jeopardizing the rest of the canyon. I disliked her for telling me this and I was not even entirely certain that what she told me was true. But I believed her, hard as I tried not to, and I sat on the floor and stared at her and did not dare close my eyes because then I might have been able to imagine her lighting the match, I would picture it.

Helen said, "But now I don't have anything to burn. If I torched the house that we're building, it would not bring Ethan back, would it?"

Somehow through my anger and my disgust, I understood that Helen had been carrying around the secret of that mad afternoon for a long time, and I realized that she had confessed it to me not because she wanted to push me away but because she simply could not carry it around any longer; the secret had become too heavy.

"Helen," I said. I crawled across the room to her. Her crime, if she was indeed responsible for fueling the fire in the glen, was not an offense for me to pardon or not pardon, and I did not think that she expected me to forgive her. What I could do was hold her. "Helen." I took her into my arms and let her rest her head in my lap.

She said, "I was so crazy that afternoon."

"I know," I said.

"I want another child," she said.

I stroked her hair. A child was the something that I could not give her. "Ethan will come back," I said. The life that came with a child.

"Late in the afternoons we would take these naps, the three of us. Wes was a baby and he only slept in the afternoons. Ethan and I would lay him down between us. It was hot and we were all naked. A breeze cooled us off," she said. "I want that again."

"Ethan will come—"

"Brad," she said. "Don't say anything. You don't have to say anything."

I wanted to be drunker then than I had ever been, and toward that end I made excellent progress. We watched the fires and fell asleep.

The phone woke me up early the next morning. It was the real-estate agent calling. The rock star wanted the house and had made an offer. Even with the fires burning out of control, perhaps because the fires were burning out of control, the real-estate agent claimed that she was closing deals left and right. Was I by any chance looking for a place to live?

Helen and I would have to move out of the Encantado Canyon house very soon.

That news was all the incentive we needed to get back to work. We had to make the Las Patas Glen house immediately inhabitable, which meant once and for all mastering the plumbing and electricity, and yet what we both really wanted to do more than anything else was to return to our most basic carpentry, to the glory days of our sawing and leveling and hammering. We should have laid in the guts and vital organs of the house and then stuffed the walls with insulation and closed in the interior with some kind of boarding before even contemplating the finish work, that was what our text instructed us to do, and to change the order of these culminating chapters in any way was impractical and wasteful since we would have to rip up the vast majority of whatever we installed in order to insert what we had left out.

We made a trip to the lumberyard in Ventura and used whatever was left of our cash and credit to purchase wood for the floorboards, which, except for the baseboards, was supposed to be the very last element to attend to when building a house. We bought wide boards of a fine and sturdy white oak with a straight and silvery grain. These boards had been milled with a tongued edge and a grooved edge, and after we laid in the first strip of several boards along the length of the upstairs, we fit the tongue of the second lengthwise strip into the groove of the first, designating a scrap of a floorboard as a driving board and hammering it in turn to make sure the parallel lengths of oak were flush and straight. Then we used nail sets to hammer nails into the tongue at an angle. And we fit in the next boards and the next, and so on and so on—this was a straightforward task, just what the doctor ordered.

Despite the heat and the fact that what little bit of clothing we wore soon became soaked with sweat, despite our dizziness from the dust in the air and our queasiness from being hung over, despite the fact that we were not actually making real progress toward making the house functional and despite the fact that we would need to remove much of this flooring to finish the plumbing, we worked well and in a steady rhythm, measuring the oak and cutting it and fitting it, driving it into place and nailing it down, measuring, cutting, driving, nailing, and it was good work: The floors looked solid, the wood dark and mature. The old hammer felt comfortable in my grip, and my arm strong, and I think that we regained a sense of confidence and mission.

We bought the wood very early in the morning and started laying in the floorboards as soon as we got back to the canyon with it and worked into the afternoon without stopping for lunch. I was certain that we would have the entire floor in by the end of the day, so sure was our stride. And while there was no escaping the wind and the heat and the ash hanging in the air, it was possible for a while to go on with our day as if the disastrous fires swallowing canyons whole were nations away.

We worked and worked and worked, and the work in itself was inebriating, easier and easier, but somehow, in a single minute it seemed, we slowed down again. Our rhythm became erratic. I do not know when it was exactly because the smoke and dust in the air obscured the true position of the sun in the afternoon sky, if there even was a sun in that sky. We began to drag and what had become an automatic task became a labor. Each nail that we drove in seemed to need its own negotiation. I wanted to go back across the canyon and sleep until the fires had been extinguished.

There were fires raging to the south and east, and while some of them had been checked after only eating up a few hundred homes, new hot spots flared up, new fires were born, to the west now in our county, to the north.

Helen said that she wanted to call it a day and I concurred, but we kept working, working slowly, nailing and then measuring. Cutting. Hammering. Nailing and making mistakes and renailing.

We had not given up, but we might as well have given up when, in the late afternoon, on the day-side of dusk, a blondish figure wearing white clothing appeared in the downstairs doorway.

I think that part of my shock in seeing Ethan came from having accepted Helen's assurances that he was gone for good. He did not say anything. He greeted Helen with a long meaningful kiss and he shook my hand firmly and then he spelled Helen, taking her hammer from her.

Ethan and I knocked a floorboard into place—he followed my lead when he drove the nails in at the proper angle—and then because this gesture seemed so obviously symbolic in the way that elected officials will pass off a shovel at a groundbreaking, Helen took my hammer from me and worked with him, too. Then Ethan lit a cigarette and took a deep drag on it and Helen massaged his shoulders, and we sat on the edge of the bald rock of Las Patas Glen and watched the sun set, or I should say that we pretended to watch the sun set since we could not actually see it through the graying web of cinders hanging over the ocean, through the ashes falling like a light rain.

Ethan had stayed in the city. He had been given a discounted room at the hotel where he had taken over the afternoon slot and held on to his nighttime gig, and so he had in effect been playing the piano nonstop for the better part of a month. He had taken the weekend off. He told us that the hotel bar had become a hot spot (although one did not speak of hot spots during the fire season, it was in poor taste), and Ethan could take some of the credit—word of mouth had it that the kid could play, and some record producers had even stopped by one night—but he was the first to acknowledge that the air conditioning was what lured people into the bar at all hours, tense Angelinos who sought to relieve their stress with a little cool air and drink.

At first, Ethan indicated that he had just come out to the canyon to visit us—he announced that he would not be spending the night—but he did stay, he stayed the entire weekend, and we went through the paces of our old routine, swimming and dining and drinking wine and swimming again, mostly lounging around the dark house, which, in Ethan's honor, we brightened up a bit with candles. I did not really know whether he and Helen were back together in an intimate sense, but I suspected that they were and that did not bother me; I may have been a tad jealous, but mostly I was relieved.

We did not talk much, it was too hot, but Ethan did regale us with tales of the hotel bar and who came and went, and it seemed to me as though he had returned from a long sojourn abroad, from years of travel on foot. It hardly seemed possible to me that he had remained so close because the weather did not appear to have taken any noticeable toll on him; Helen and I had both lost weight. His presence was refreshing, I felt rejuvenated, although I could not say that Helen experienced the same renewal.

She listened to Ethan and smiled as she had smiled when she saw him, a pleased, relieved, glad-to-be-wrong kind of smile. But that smile disappeared quickly, and soon enough, she was sitting on the opposite side of the room from him. She floated in and out of our conversation, what talk there was, and sometimes she went for an hour without saying anything at all.

"How's the house?" Ethan asked at one point. "The floor is looking good."

"It's oak," I said, "and the house is . . . coming along. We just have to go back and take care of a few things. . . ."

"Such as?" Ethan asked.

"Oh, you know, the plumbing, the electricity," I said.

"Cool," Ethan said, and he did not appear too concerned to have found us more or less in the same place where he had left us. "We have to get the house done and move on to the next one," he said cheerfully.

"Another white house," I said, "further down the canyon."

"And then another one after that," he said.

"Up and down the canyon road," I said.

"Helen," Ethan said. "Helen?"

"Ethan," she replied.

"I have a surprise for us tomorrow," he said.

"I don't like surprises," she said.

"You love surprises," he said.

"Maybe I've changed," she said. "You never know," she said.

"What kind of a surprise?" I asked Ethan.

"We're going to take a trip," he said, "a short drive."

"Great," I said.

"It has to do with the house," he said to Helen.

She nodded. Had she heard him?

"It's for the house," he tried again.

"Cool," I said, and Helen announced that she was sleepy and went off to bed.

The next morning we ate a substantial breakfast of eggs and toast and muffins and coffee which Ethan prepared. Helen had perked up by her third cup of coffee. Suddenly she was excited to get going wherever we were going; Ethan was not going to reveal our destination or the purpose of this day trip until we had arrived wherever.

And I remember that this was the last great day that the three of us spent together, one final outing. We piled in the pickup and Ethan headed west up the coast road, west of Ventura and Oxnard and north toward Santa Barbara, then north off the coast road toward Ojai. Helen had lapsed into a genuine good mood—that alone made the day worthwhile—and although I doubted that it was geographically possible, it seemed as though we had entered a range of hills beyond the view of the ocean which was free of ash and smoke, indeed entirely cut off from the Santa Anas. The air was cool and the sky blue with hope. We veered off the rural route and Ethan steered down an empty country lane. We passed farms and orchards.

"Come on," Helen said, squeezing Ethan's knee, "tell us where we're going."

"Nope," he said, grinning.

Finally, checking an address that he had scribbled on a cocktail napkin and matching that address to the one stenciled on a red mailbox, he turned off the road and onto a private unpaved drive that wended toward a small yellow house in the distance.

Before we made it as far as the house, however, we could see that it neither had a roof nor windows, and when we parked by the front door and greeted an older man in overalls and wire-rimmed glasses, we could see that much of the inside of this house had been gutted. Or not so much gutted, we soon discovered, as dismantled piece by piece.

A crew of three men was busy ripping away a wall of paneling in a front parlor—I say ripping when in truth they were carefully and methodically removing molding and then nails and then the broad dark paneling and making an obvious effort to do as little damage as possible to the woodworking—while two other men watched and occasionally appraised the polished wood as it was removed. After these two men approved the paneling, the crew carried a stack of it out to another pickup, a bigger, newer model than our truck, and the older man in the overalls measured the stack with a folding ruler and scribbled notations on a clipboard. One of the two men who was buying the wood—that was the apparent transaction in progress—said something to the effect of, Their loss, our gain.

Ethan explained what he meant. The man was referring to another couple, not present, who had purchased the farmland and who had decided to tear down the yellow house in order to build a much larger and freshly designed house in its place. But these were savvy and fiscally-minded folk, and they knew that all of the wood in the house that they were going to destroy was worth something to someone. Old wood, extraordinary wood, wood with stories to tell. It was a pity to see it torn apart, but like the two men who told us that they were renovating their house back in Los Angeles, we could salvage it and save it and reuse it for our own interior. That was Ethan's surprise. The hotel bar bartender had heard about the house that Ethan had been working on in Encantado Canyon—that Ethan had apparently talked about the house made Helen glow with delight—and as Ethan described the cellolike interior he had imagined for it, the bartender remembered something that he had heard from a regular patron who was also building a new house west of the city, building a new house but ripping another one down first. And maybe that was the reason that Ethan had come back when he did, if he required a reason, because he knew where we could get ahold of some really fine old wood at a good price since the couple building the new house had instructed their contractor, the man in the overalls, to get rid of what he could but not to haggle.

The house—semistripped down to the studs, with cloud-shaped patches of walls still intact, with gaping holes, with certain key elements already gone, all the stairs save a few bottom risers, the hearth, even structural components like ceiling joists and rafters, which made me wonder how safe the house was from sudden collapse—was a tough old house determined to preserve a certain dignity and grace of proportions until the very end. This was a house that would not go easily, not without a struggle. And with the anatomy of this house laid bare, we could see how the place had been constructed however many decades ago. We could compare and contrast the framing with that of our own project, and our house and this dying house had more in common than not in the way they had been put together. We arrived at a certain kinship with the unknown carpenters who had made this place. Now we had to take something away and use it, we were morally obligated.

We climbed a ladder to the second floor, and there was a vast variety of wood to choose from. Wood that was smooth and warmly polished but rubbed of gloss, cracked here and there, stained by human hands in places, some of it faded from exposure to the sun, some of it as rich and dark as freshly brewed java. Once the two men had left, we had the place to ourselves and the contractor, followed by his crew, joined us upstairs. Without him, we would not have been able to identify all of the types of wood. He knew his wood, wood was his life, he told us. And he bounced back and forth among us as we split up and drifted into various bedrooms and back downstairs.

"I found some amazing paneling," Helen shouted from one room. It turned out to be American walnut.

"Hey, come take a look at this medicine cabinet," Ethan called from the bathroom. A cabinet and some shelves that were also walnut but stained to look like yew.

I had wandered down to the kitchen, where there was an entire chattering discourse of dark woods under way among the cabinets and counters and paneling and molding and window frames. Rosewood cabinets and more walnut— prized black walnut for a banquette in a recessed niche—and cherrywood and oak and teak and even some mahogany. Wood grains resembling all manner of landscapes, flat prairies and eroded canyons and languid bays.

"Helen," I shouted, "Ethan."

The kitchen was inspiring, it was exactly what we were after. Helen had to touch every surface. Ethan kept licking his lips as if he wanted to eat this wood. Indeed it looked edible, like cinnamon, like nutmeg, like chocolate, like coffee. The longer I studied these hardwoods in a hundred hues of brown, the more other colors emerged, reds in the oak and blues in the rosewood and greens in the walnut. When I rubbed a windowsill or a cabinet door, a metallic dust seemed to blush to the surface, silver and copper and gold. Combining all of these woods, orchestrating them as if this was exactly what we were after—it could be done.

The crew of deconstructing carpenters began to remove the closet frames and closet doors that we picked out, the built-in bookcases, the various cabinet doors and drawers. There was quite a bit of old furniture lying around as well, three pearwood chairs that were a steal, a chestnut dresser with ebony handles, a must. An old oak table, another chair. We wanted more than we could haul back, we would have to come back for seconds. We wanted it all, even if we did not know how we would incorporate the various fragments into our interior just yet. We wanted it all and loaded what we could into our truck hours later, baseboards and ceiling trim and two big doors of an armoire, and Ethan paid for the wood with his hard-earned cash, most if not all of his cash, I suspected. He unfolded crisp bills into the open palm of the smiling contractor. We promised to return. We said that we might even be back later that afternoon. We never did make it back.

Driving back to the canyon, we headed into the winds. The windshield clouded with a thick film of dust. We had covered the wood in the bay with a tarp, but even so, it, too, was dusty when we unloaded it at the house, and we spent the rest of the day cleaning it up. By the time we made it back to my house, the recently sold house, we each had to take a long shower because these winds had a way of making you feel as though you were never quite clean. There was always more desert dust in your hair.

That night Ethan gave Helen a present, a pocket-sized book on how to finish wood. It was a fascinating and comprehensive guide to manufactured stains and treatments that we could apply to our wood to bring out the natural grain or through prescribed alchemies make one wood look like another wood or color it or give the lumber a look, a style, a texture all its own. Some of these treatments involved rubbing pigments into the grain, rubbing in lime or latex or gold powder or graphite. Some treatments required wire-brushing or singeing the wood. One technique involved applying the blended pulp of rhubarb leaves. And then there were the various combinations of dyes and stains and processes and appliqués which invited experimentation.

"I want to try the graphite powder rubbing on the rosewood-stained cherry," Ethan said.

"I'm into the wire-brushed, white-lime-treated singed walnut, myself," I said.

"This is incredible," Helen said. "This gets me excited to start in again," she said to Ethan, "thank you." She flipped back and forth through the guide, turning the pages faster and faster.

Ethan oohed, I ahed.

"If I had to choose," Helen said, "if I had to choose between the walnut family or the oak family for the study—"

"The study?" Ethan asked. "You mean the downstairs?"

"The walnut or the oak or the rosewood," she said, "I would choose . . ." Back and forth through the pages.

"What study?" I asked.

"The study in the tower," Helen stated matter-of-factly, still flipping through the book. "I mean, that's what will be up there, a study. Unless you'd like the tower to be a bedroom. But I think it should be a kind of meditation room, a lookout."

"The tower," Ethan said.

"You were the one who said the house had to have a tower," Helen said. "Like a lighthouse on the island?"

"The island," Ethan said.

"The island house," I told him. "Helen's been working on a house for an island," I said, all gung-ho even if I was as annoyed as Ethan appeared to be by Helen's drift. "She's been drawing up plans," I said.

"I see," he said.

"A white house on an island in the rain," Helen said.

"A white house on an island in the rain," Ethan said as if he were learning the words to a song.

The evening heat weighed us down, regret was in the wind. Ethan regretting that he had come back, I thought, me regretting the way I had treated Helen's talk of an island house as if it were a happening project. We had the television on and the pictures of the approaching fires cast a hot orange glow over the room.

Helen startled me when she bolted up and headed for the pool. Ethan and I stared at the television instead of at each other, and then we heard a splash. When we turned around, we saw Helen, fully dressed, bouncing off the diving board into the pool. Up and up, her arms back, her back arched, and then straight in. She got out of the water and dove off the board again. She practiced her dives and meanwhile the world burned down.

Fires raged out of control everywhere in the Southland, and
the fires to the north and east gradually moved toward us—
which meant that they were traveling south and west—
closing in on us now and closing off our path to the city.
Ethan was not sure whether the coast road was open all the
way into Santa Monica, but he needed and wanted to get
back to work, and so as foolish as it was, he headed out early
in the afternoon. He put on his white jacket and thin tie and
loafers and he left us. If the fires did cut off the coast road
later in the day, he would not be able to get back to us.

Before he left, he pulled me aside. He said, "You know
where I'll be."

"Yes, but don't worry about us," I said.

"The weather will get better soon," he said.

"It has to," I said. "It will."

Ethan left and Helen and I tried to remain cool, which
proved impossible. We went so far as to lie down on the
floor in the darkest corner of the darkest bedroom; we did
not move except to breathe, but we were still unbearably
hot and dehydrated and depressed by the prospect of the
even greater swells of heat that would soon drift our way
as the firestorms approached. We decided that the only way
to ride out this latest heat wave would be to locate some air
conditioning.

I would like to say that I put up an argument, that I refused to get in the pickup with her at the end of the day, but
I issued no protest whatsoever and was a full partner in our
final crime. I was the one who suggested that we take the
mountain road west away from the worst fires.

There are two principal roads that follow the east-west latitude of the mountain range, the coast road that I have men-

tioned again and again, the easy-bending route on which it was impossible to get lost—you always knew where you were headed, what with the ocean on one side of you, the hills on the other—and that road on which we had traveled less and drove along now, the two-lane highway that ran along the spine of the range, a road prone to wild turns and coiling narrows, a road of fast drops and ear-popping ascents, a perplexing road on which even those of us with a honed sense of direction became disoriented. East was south and north west, and you never knew quite which way you were facing or turning toward. Overall the road took us west, but when we spotted an isolated, rectangular glass house riding a hill in a vale below us, I had no idea where we were in relation to the ocean or the city or the fires.

We veered off the mountain road and traveled down a dirt road toward the glass house but soon found that the house once beneath us was suddenly above us. To reach it, we had to follow another dirt road up the hill, but that second road was blocked off by a locked gate. So we parked the car at the bottom of the hill down the dirt road, far beyond the gate, and then walked back up and climbed a tall chain-link fence and dropped over and onto the property. We headed up to the house. It was a sweaty trek up steep ground, all clay and brush and slippery beneath our sandals, and when we finally reached the house, we were desperate to get inside at any cost. All of the walls were glass, glass from the floor to the ceiling, and so we could easily determine that no one was home; there was no garage to hide a car. Together we kicked in a tall wood door and closed it behind us.

The house was a simple glass box and the only house of the ones that we had illicitly explored that made me want to move in immediately and never leave. It was a stark cottage with a flat roof, just a living room and a bedroom divided by a narrow kitchen upstairs; there was a second bedroom in the basement. The fireplace and chimney, which poked through the center of the box, appeared to have been fashioned from the same rock on which the house was situated—picture a house impaled on a tall boulder—and because the walls were all glass and because the place had been furnished by someone with an ascetic bent, I knew that this was not a house in which I would accumulate unnecessary possessions, not a house in which I would be tempted to play games or talk around what I was thinking. There would be no place to hide, nowhere to stash secrets; everything would be out in the open in such a house.

We did not do much in the way of looking around. We found the central air conditioner and turned it on and then collapsed on the broad low bed of the upstairs bedroom, where we lay on our backs and stared at the blank ceiling. We cooled off. The sun went down and it became very dark. We fell asleep.

Hours later, I awoke and saw Helen lying on her side next to me, propped up on her elbow, blinking, watching me. She spoke as if she were continuing a conversation that she had been having with me while I slept.

She said, "Ethan did not have to tell me what he was thinking, I knew what he was thinking. Why talk about some made-up island when we have a whole canyon to ourselves? But the island is what's keeping me going. I have been holding on for so long now, and I just don't know how much longer I can keep going. I just don't know. I don't know how much longer. I don't—"

I shushed her and I pulled her to me. I told her to blame the winds for how she felt, to blame everything on the winds, and she pulled away from me as if I was not taking her seriously, as if I was writing off her confession, which I can now see all too clearly in hindsight was her cry for help. I stretched out and drew her toward me again and calmed her by kissing her neck and shoulders and holding her with as much strength as I had in my arms so that she would know that I would catch her if she ever fell. Soon we were asleep again.

I did not know what time it was when I woke up again, still holding Helen, who was fast asleep, or why I knew to wake when I did. I suppose I awoke because I heard the boy enter the room. I heard him breathing.

I did not know what time it was when I woke up and saw a boy standing at the foot of the bed and holding a gun. A boy pointing a gun at me, at us. He must have been about twelve or thirteen, a boy at that awkward age when his hands are too big for his arms and his arms too long for his body. The gun was too big for his hands, a square black gun with a long square barrel. He was holding the gun with both hands and he was frozen, speechless, but smiling a bit. I noticed that the drawer of the night table next to me had been pulled open.

A boy at that awkward age with a gun too big for his hands and a smile that was growing with idiotic confidence. Helen was still asleep, and my fear was that she would wake up and either scream, which would scare the boy into pulling the trigger, or try something foolish, which would bring about the same end.

I convinced myself that I was only having a nightmare and closed my eyes and opened them to see a boy standing at the foot of the bed, a boy with a gun in his hands, and Helen stirring, waking in my arms.

What happened next happened in the space of two minutes at most.

These are the moments we replay in our minds. We relive them and we relive them. These are the moments that happen too fast for us to recall with accuracy. They become fiction as soon as we live them, but they remain vivid. Two minutes, less.

The boy called for his father. He yelled, Father. He yelled, Hey, Dad.

A car door slammed outside. I heard a man call back and say something in an irritated voice, Just a minute, just a minute. Something like that.

The boy yelled again and the father yelled back, and needless to say, Helen had woken up with the first scream, and I held her tightly in my arms so that she would not move and scare the boy into thinking that we wanted to chance a struggle for the gun.

Now we were both staring at the boy, who was waiting for his father and getting nervous, shifting his weight from foot to foot, losing his cool. He had brown hair and a round face. He looked intelligent.

I looked him in the eye and pleaded with him to remain calm as we in turn would remain calm. He had a look about him, however, as if he wanted to show me that he was a man and not a boy. He was not very good at sports, but he could be a hero when he needed to be a hero.

The boy was shifting his weight and clutching the gun and swallowing hard, and when Helen and I took our eyes off of him for a brief second to conspire some sort of way out, he called for his father again.

Again his father told him to wait, and I almost suggested to the boy that he explain to his father that he was holding a man and a woman at gunpoint. Then his father might come at once. I said nothing.

I thought about how when he shot us, if he shot us, the bullets would fly every which way and probably shatter the walls of the bedroom, of the entire glass house.

I felt Helen easing away from me. Slowly, slowly. And I let go of her.

The boy aimed the gun at her. He meant business. He took a step back, but he meant business.

What was she doing? What was she trying to do?

I tried to meet her glance so that she could tell me what she planned to do and what my role would be, and because I could not figure out what she was doing—she had eased herself over to the edge of the bed and the boy shifted his aim back and forth, at me, at her, at me, at her—I had to come up with my own plan, which was actually a lot more dangerous than Helen's as it turned out.

I would have pounced on the boy and tried to wrest the gun from his grip. He would have shot me in the stomach.

Helen bolted up from the bed. The boy aimed the gun at her. Her gamble was that he would not be able to shoot right away, and her gamble paid off. She picked up the night table on her side of the bed and raised this table—a tiny bookcase really—over her head, letting the lamp crash to the floor.

The boy was too scared to shoot and he shouted for his father, who had to have heard the lamp break.

Helen threw the night table with all of her might at a broad pane of the glass wall, and the window smashed into a thousand glittering pieces, the hot dry evening air rushing inside. She jumped out of the house through the broken window and I followed her.

The father had to have heard his glass house break.

And still the boy did not shoot. He was shouting. I did not look back, so I do not know if he even aimed the gun at us. I cut my shin on the edge of the window frame.

We ran. We ran and ran.

I followed Helen straight down the slope of the property. Down the hill that we had climbed up, sliding, and losing our footing, and falling. Falling and running and falling.

I heard the boy screaming behind us. I heard the father's

screams of confusion. I heard a gunshot reverberate throughout the canyon. The boy must have fired at us. Or was he just trying to make it look as if he had scared us off? No, he was chasing us, that became apparent soon enough.

We did not look back and we fell and shuffled down the rocky slope, and we made it back to the chain-link fence, which we climbed and threw ourselves over, and landed on the dirt road and rolled a ways until we were able to stop rolling and get up and hop in the pickup, Helen behind the wheel, fumbling for her keys, me trying to close the passenger-side door as she started up the engine, which thankfully turned over with only one wheeze.

Another shot.

The father calling after the boy.

Helen shifting into gear. Headlights on, high beams on. She swung the pickup into a U-turn and headed up the narrow dirt road.

I saw the father running out the driveway, running toward us. A tall man, a big paunch. He was in our lights, running at the pickup. Shouting what? No idea. He was in our way, in our path. There was no way around him. Some of what happened next was his fault, his doing. Did he want to show his son how to be a hero? What was he doing?

Helen shifted into reverse. It was very dark.

Where was the boy, behind his father?

The father's face in our high beams: I remember confusion more than fear or anger. Wait, hold on, just wait a minute.

Helen shot back in reverse and that was when we hit something.

The boy.

He had chased us, fired once, chased us down the slope, fired again, climbed over the fence. Maybe the father was trying to head him off and stop him from trying to be a hero. What was the boy going to do, jump into the bay of the trunk?

The boy had chased us down the slope of the property and climbed the fence and dropped over to the road and run at us, and when Helen shifted into reverse and accelerated backward to escape the approaching father, she hit the boy, she backed right into him and we heard a terrifying slam and crunch in the darkness.

Each side of the pickup was equipped with a side-view mirror. I had looked into the side-view mirror on my side, and I had seen something. I had seen the boy, I was sure of it. I had a second to stop Helen. I had two seconds at the most during which I shouted nothing, said nothing. We replay these moments again and again. The boy lived, I know that now, but that was not the point. We hit him and we hit him hard and we thought that we had killed him, that we had run him over. We were certain that we had killed him.

Helen shifted back into drive and lurched toward the father, who had seen what had happened and dove out of the way in time for us to drive up the hill again, and this time, we kept driving.

In my mirror, I could see the boy lying on the dark road, a fast-dimming image. A boy all broken and lifeless. I was sure, Helen was sure, that he was dead.

I wanted her to stop, I screamed at her to stop and go back.

Helen kept driving back the way we had come. She drove way too fast down the center of the road. She was not going back. There was no going back.

"I killed him," she said when we had reached the mountain road. No, not the mountain road, but some other canyon road that took us toward the ocean, I realized. A road that would spill into the coast road. I was all turned around.

"I killed him," she said again.

I said, "No, we just hit him, and he'll be okay," although

I did not believe what I was saying because I was certain that he was dead. Now it was too late to go back; I doubted that we would have found our way back.

"It's happening all over again," she said. "I killed him. He fell over the edge. I killed him."

"Helen, quiet. Quiet. Calm down," I said, "slow down."

At the coast road, there was a pay phone, and we stopped and called an ambulance. Where was the scene of the accident? We did not know. Where are you calling from? We did not know how far west we had driven. Who are you? We did not say.

"Will you just send a fucking ambulance over there?" Helen screamed into the phone.

We were informed that an ambulance had been dispatched to a home a few miles away from where we were calling from, and we were instructed to stay where we were so that a policeman could come by and escort us back to the scene of the accident.

We got back in the pickup and I wanted to drive, but Helen insisted that she take the wheel. She drove east on the coast road. We headed home, convinced that we had killed a boy. Our recklessness had caught up with us. We were to blame. There were radio reports about the fires moving south, closer now, but no mention of a boy who had been run over by a white pickup in a hit-and-run. We drove east on the coast road and came to our canyon but Helen kept going. I did not know where we were headed.

Weeks later I did some calling around and learned that the boy had been taken to a hospital and remained there for a time; he had been seriously injured, but he was treated and ultimately released and taken home. We were to blame for his injuries but not his death. That night as we drove toward the city, however, we both thought that we had killed a boy, and Helen believed that she had killed two.

Ethan was playing to a mostly empty bar when we showed up after one in the morning, but with fires pushing the fringes of the basin, there was quite a buzz in the room, and his rolling medley of blues provided the needed calming antidote to this nervous chatter. He acknowledged us with a wink and did not look surprised to see us when we retreated to a booth in the rear of the bar, the same one we had hung out in the only other time that we had come here. We were conspicuously underdressed. Our arms were black with smeared ash, and I wondered if anyone thought that we were refugees from the fires.

Ethan sent over some drinks. I was far too nauseous even to take one sip, but Helen knocked back the highball in a single gulp as if the gin and soda were spring water. Ethan took a break from the piano and joined us in the booth. It was not until he asked what had happened to my shin, all bruised and swollen around the wine-colored gash which had clotted and looked much worse than it probably was, that I remembered cutting myself during our escape. I did not have a ready explanation.

"What happened?" Ethan asked again, concerned.

"Nothing happened," Helen said and mimed to the bartender to pour her another drink. One more time we kept Ethan in the dark, or I should say Helen had decided to lie to him because I wanted to tell him everything. I wanted to tell someone.

"Tell me what happened," Ethan said. "Did the fire—"

Helen cut him off by reaching across the small table and clutching his arm, his hand. Nothing, she told him with a stare, nothing happened. But she had to say something to shut him up, so she said, "It's this ash," brushing some from her shirt, smearing her arms. "It's getting to me."

"I heard that the winds are supposed to die down," Ethan said.

"Then they'll put out all of the fires," I said.

"And we'll have some nice cool breezes and even some rain," Helen said.

"I still have a room upstairs," Ethan said. "I mean, if you two want to take a shower or lie down. We don't even have to go back to the canyon tonight. We can stay here until the fires are out and—"

"Ethan," Helen said, "please. We're fine. Really, we're okay." And as she drank another gin and soda in a single gulp, despite her thirst, she looked fine and okay. And when she said, "This is almost over," in a calm and sane voice, I believed that everything would be over by morning. The boy would not die. The fires would indeed be extinguished. The sun would rise as it always rose. "But you know, I do think I would like a shower," Helen added, "just to cool off and get rid this ash."

Ethan told her to go to the front desk across the lobby and explain who she was and ask for the key to his room upstairs; he had misplaced the key that he had been given, it was not in his jacket or trousers.

"I'll come with you," I said to her.

"You stay here," she said, and so I remained seated. It is the great crime of my life that I let her go off alone. I will never stop wondering what would have happened if I had insisted upon going upstairs with her.

But I let her go and part of the reason that I let her go was because I did think that she had killed the boy. And I did believe her when she said that she had set her own house on fire and possibly caused a glen to burn when it might not have burned. And I believed her, too, when she said that it was happening all over again, that some great wheel of tragedy had turned one full spin and that this wheel would turn and turn; there was no stopping it.

Helen gave me a kiss, an intense and long kiss that embarrassed me, what with Ethan across the table, and then she kissed him, too, and stepped around him so that she stood beside him and so that she could press his head against her stomach and hold him there for a while. When she let go, she walked away and she did not look back at us.

I ordered another drink, and Ethan had one, too. We did not say anything to each other, but I did look at him and when I was drunk enough, I did say, "We killed a boy."

These were cruel words to speak to him, of course, and I was so obviously drunk that Ethan replied, "Sure, you did," before he stood abruptly and returned to the piano.

Ethan played and I drank as much as I could. One hour went by. Two hours. I fell asleep with my head on the table.

Three hours later, Ethan returned to the booth and sat down and was ready to call it an evening, a morning, whatever—no one was left in the bar but me—and that was when I told him everything. I told Ethan about all of the break-ins and about the glass house and about the boy with the gun, the boy whom Helen had hit.

"We killed a boy," I said.

Ethan squinted at me. He tried to say something but looked at his watch instead. "Where's Helen now?" he asked.

"Upstairs," I said.

"We should go to the police," he said. "Right away," standing. "We have to get Helen and go to the police."

We went upstairs to Ethan's room on the seventh floor and knocked on the door. Helen did not answer. We knocked harder, and still no Helen.

We went back downstairs. In the elevator, Ethan grabbed my shirt and shoved me against the wall, knocking the wind from me, scaring me. Ethan with a wild, frightened look in his eyes. He slammed me against the elevator doors.

"You stupid fuck," he screamed. "You stupid, stupid fuck."

I collapsed into the lobby when the doors opened and he let go of me. I stumbled off to the side of the room and coughed and threw up.

Ethan helped me to my feet. He was sobbing. He was sorry and sobbing and I wished that he would finish beating me up because I deserved it. I was crying, too.

The night manager of the hotel hopped over to us, and Ethan explained that we were locked out of his room, that his wife was locked in his room.

Ethan covered his eyes with his hand. "Oh, no," he said, "oh, no." It was as if he knew what we would find before we even got in the room. "She talked about doing this before," he said. "After Wes died. She talked about doing something like this."

"Oh, no," I said.

The night manager took us upstairs and opened the door to Ethan's room. We found Helen in the bathtub.

Beautiful in death. One arm hanging over the side of the tub. Her head tipped back. A marble statue by a reflecting pool, a statue that had slipped into that pool.

No, I am remembering it all wrong. Her death was clumsy and gruesome. I could not connect that lifeless pale body with the dark and beautiful woman whom I had known.

I believe that she meant to do what she did, she had swallowed so many pills. We found seven empty vials, over-the-counter junk which, from the paper bag we also found, we assumed she had gone out and purchased at the twenty-four-hour pharmacy down the street from the hotel. She had taken the pills and washed them down with a bottle and a half of rum and then drawn a warm bath—the water was not even tepid by the time we got to her—and she had to have known that from the mix of a few pills and one or two drinks alone, she would lapse into a fatal slumber; she had meant to do it.

And naturally I always wonder whether she intended to fail, if we were supposed to figure out what she was doing sooner, if we were supposed to find her in time to bring her back to life. Her true motive would always remain uncertain because she had chosen a method of suicide that some people survive. She had not, for example, pulled a plastic bag over her head as advertised in the various how-to books available to the browsing public. Although there was a plastic bag on the floor of the bathroom by the tub. Perhaps she had conked out before she had a chance to use it.

Her skin was amber, it looked petrified. It was not Helen, I kept telling myself, not her in the tub. And slowly it sank in. These are the moments that plague us. We go back. We play them out differently than the way they happened. We revive her, she lives. Soon we are building a house again.

Ethan passed out. I threw up again in the bathroom sink. The night manager called an ambulance, although Helen was dead and beyond resuscitation.

Ethan and I sat on the edge of the bed in the hotel room, each of us wrapped in blankets provided by members of the emergency medical team, who kindly informed us that we were in shock and asked us politely to go to the hospital. Ethan refused and so I refused to go, too. He kept sighing. I was angry at Helen for doing this to him and to me, but mostly to him, because I transferred whatever I was feeling to Ethan. She was the love of his life. How dare she become a statistic in this season of statistics, how dare she.

I found some hotel stationery on the desk in the room, and I thought at first that Helen had left us a note. But she had not. Or maybe it was a letter of a sort. There were three sheets of stationery, each covered with what looked like hasty doodles. The doodles were sketches of a house, and I quickly recognized that these rough drawings matched the plans for the island house that she had been working on; I had gotten enough of a glimpse of those plans to connect them. There was no way that Ethan could know that these sketches had any meaning, so I told him. There was the tower rising above the rest of the tall house. There were the porches with vistas of the sound. A white house on an island in the rain.

Ethan crumpled the pages into a wad, but then he flattened them on the bed and ironed them with his hand and studied them for a while. Three views of a house. He traced and retraced the uneven lines on one page with his finger, smearing the ink, blotting the drawings with his tears.

Ethan and I sat on the edge of the bed for about a half-hour and waited for the police to arrive, but because there was no one who could be saved in this hotel room and there were people who needed to be evacuated from approaching fires, the police were taking their time getting to us. At some point, Ethan began to pace. And then he dashed out the door of the suite and ran off to the elevator, and when the elevator did not come right away, he went down the stairs.

"Ethan? Ethan," I shouted and chased after him.

I caught up with him in the lobby. I grabbed his arm out on the street. He took my hand, he held my hand. His eyes were bluer than I had ever seen them. He pulled me down the sidewalk after him. We walked fast up the street and to my car. He had the keys in the ignition before I could ask him where we were going.

"West," he said.

"Back to the canyon?" I asked.

"West," was all he would say.

But when it became apparent that the coast road ahead of us had been closed because the fires had already swept down into several of the canyons west of the city, he drove up the first canyon road that we came to in the Palisades and eventually turned onto the main mountain road. Ethan drove like a maniac. He was swerving all over the lane.

I said, "Slow down, will you?"

He did slow down for a while. I turned on the radio and we heard a report that indicated that we would run into a fire and the blockade around the fire zone before we reached our canyon.

"Well, we'll just drive into the fire," Ethan said, and I began to think, Fine with me, let's drive right into the fire, why not?

Now the wind was behind us and we were driving very fast again. Now I did not care what happened to us. We were heading into the fire, and compared to everything else that had happened in the last half-day that made no sense—the accident at the glass house, losing Helen—this plan to drive into the fire actually seemed like the logical thing to do. We would drive into the fire and go up in flames. I was thinking, They slip away from me, anyone I love to any degree. Dean. Helen. Sand through my fingers.

We passed some traffic, a stream of cars coming in the opposite direction, but the traffic thinned until ours was the only car on the road. We followed the twists of the road along the spine of the range, and we drove faster and faster, and strangely enough when we came to a red light at the intersection with a major canyon road that was closed off both to the north and south, meaning that we did not need to stop, we came to a screeching halt.

I was lost. I was not sure how far west we had gone. Ethan switched off the radio. He looked at me and took a deep breath and then he pressed his pedal foot to the floor and charged through the intersection before the light had changed, and my old car picked up speed, and I braced myself in the passenger seat, and we went faster, and the wind was behind us, pushing us, and the fires were somewhere in front of us, and we followed the sharp curves of the narrower road west of the intersection, narrowing and curving in on itself, the road banked on one side by rock and a cliff and steep drop on the right. Now I saw the ocean beyond the canyons, and then with another turn, the ocean was out of view. Another turn, faster, another turn, faster.

We shot down a straight stretch of road and suddenly approached a barrier that had been set up to prevent people from entering the fire zone—if there were signs, we were going too fast for me to read them—but it was an unmonitored roadblock—if there were police there, we did not see them—a temporary fence of wood and pylons, and so we barreled right through it, and the wood barrier splintered apart into a hundred splinters and the pylons flew up in the air and the dust from the road enveloped us.

We would either dive off a cliff or smash into the bank of the road. One way or another, we were going to crash. That was what Ethan wanted to do, he wanted to crash my car and kill us both.

But then through a parting cloud of dust, he saw what I saw, that there was a patch of wet road ahead of us. I did not know, do not know why the road was wet along that straightaway of the mountain road—if I had to guess, I would say that the water came from a nearby helicopter drop of seawater on a hot spot of a fire being fought in the canyon below us—and that was when Ethan braked the way he would brake if he was not trying to get us killed. I mean he braked on instinct. His instinct was not to speed through a watery, slippery patch of road, but to take that stretch at a slower speed to avoid wiping out. His instinct was to survive.

We were traveling too fast not to wipe out, and so while Ethan did pump the brakes, we did spin around when we hit the wet road. And then we crashed into the rocks and bounced across the road to the railing along the cliff and bounced back against the rocks. Ethan managed to turn the steering wheel back and forth against these swerves and we stayed on the road to turn left down a sharp bend and then right along another curve. Except that Ethan could not make that last turn, and so we plowed head-on into the side of the mountain.

We crashed and I heard Ethan groan and then I leaned back in my seat and sighed myself into a black sleep.

FIVE

One evening not too long ago, I drove through a valley of vineyards, which contrary to my expectations was not fragrant with the pungency of the harvest, of grapes ripe on the vine, but redolent instead of that strange blend of scents that I associated with a canyon so many years to the south of me. The lemon tint of the citrus trees; the wash of the rosemary thriving beneath a dry white sun; the school-paste smell of the eucalyptus in bloom; the salt of the ocean. By the time I reached the home of a friend at the edge of that valley of vineyards, I was lost in bittersweet recollection, I was full of regret, and I ended up walking around the pale yellow house and around it again without ringing the doorbell, without going inside to the dinner party that this friend whom I did not know all that well was ostensibly throwing in my honor.

The house had turned out well, cozy like my friend wanted it, but durable and solid with its terra-cotta terraces and its ever so slightly tapered stucco walls and its numerous French doors and grids of windows and its high clerestory beneath a broad flat eave, an eave supported by long brackets reaching up from a second-floor loggia, these brackets and all of the trim in a timber painted green to match the landscape. The skin of this house had faded well during its first summer so that the place looked as old as the tall sycamores that canopied the terrace.

After my third or fourth tour of the exterior, I could not really claim that I was admiring my architecture. Dusk had fallen softly over the valley and so the quiet gray and dark wood interior of this house glowed warmly. The big kitchen was where the action was because that was where my apron-clad friend was holding court, stirring a tall pot of a no doubt splendid stew at the same time that he told his guests, each outfitted with a goblet of local wine, a story that was making them all laugh. I did not think that anyone huddled around the stove saw me as I crept around the house, no one waved or came out to the terrace to usher me in, and because I had not been detected, I got back in my car and drove awhile to the nearest pay phone and called my friend, the client for whom I had built my first major project, the host of a tranquil gathering on the first chilly night of the year, and I apologized for my tardiness, my sudden illness on the way over, my decision to turn around and go home and go right to bed, which was in fact what I did.

I knew that I was responsible for every detail of that wine country house, from its antiqued pallor and clean symmetry down to the way the light moved about the house over the course of a day to match the rustle of the surrounding trees, and I knew that my client had become a friend because he appreciated what I had accomplished for him. He believed that he owed me a certain debt. And yet I hardly felt responsible at all for the way the place turned out, I mean the way that it was lived in. The way my client hosted his dinner party from the throne of his stove. The way he would draw his circle of friends around a long table and later to the hearth and a pinyon fire. I had everything to do with the shell but nothing to do with the species that inhabited that shell, and that was the case with the projects to which I had contributed in the past and to my houses-in-progress at the

moment, the houses that I would build in time if I sustained
my practice. That night walking around outside my first sig-
nificant commission, I began to understand that my life as
a house-builder would in many ways resemble my life as a
house-sitter, continuing the restless roaming of those years,
that nomad trance. And what I realized was that I had probably become an architect precisely because I was and always
would be attracted to a mapless way of life.

And then I ran into Ethan in the city a few days later. I
had not seen him since that sorry stone-cold affair back East
that was Helen's memorial service. I remember Ethan in his
various fiberglass casts and gauze bandages, high as a kite on
painkillers—an inappropriately bright and breezy day spent
with the stunned family with whom Helen had lost touch—
they wanted to remember a little girl who had been good at
math and diving—a day that provided nothing of the closure
that we always hear funerals will provide and only fed my
anger at Helen for having given up on Ethan, for abandoning me, for succumbing to the desert winds and the winds
that had engulfed her long before I ever met her. I found
Ethan—in my heart, I had long ago forgiven him for trying
to kill us both—and during our awkward exchange in the
café all these years later, I began to see a way for us both to
escape our nagging grief, the chill that surprised us at least
once a late afternoon no matter the climate or weather, and
that way out would involve our returning to the canyon and
setting the house that we had built on fire, assuming that
the house was still there for us to burn down. I talked about
how I wanted to take the coast road south and return to Encantado Canyon, but Ethan and I ended up ordering dinner
instead. And when we were done eating, I thought that we
would drift back into our separate lives.

But then instead of saying good-bye in front of the café,
Ethan surprised me and walked me to my car. We walked
several blocks. Ethan was shivering, and so I opened the pas-

senger-side door for him and told him to get in the car and warm up before he headed back to the café or wherever. Eventually I turned on the ignition, but Ethan did not get out of my car. I asked him if I could drop him off somewhere, but he had gone totally mute on me. He said nothing when I pulled out into the street and headed south in the city, south toward the highway. I asked him two more times if I could take him anywhere before I left town, and still, nothing. So I followed the signs for the interstate.

Ethan tuned in a station on the car radio and pulled his jacket collar up around his ears. He rested his head against the window. It was night when we reached the coast road; the ocean was black. I headed south.

I did all of the driving, and the farther south we went, the faster my heart beat. The faster my pulse, the faster I drove. Ethan slept.

When he woke up, his voice was weak. He said, "I was dreaming about the time when Helen and I were living in our first apartment. That was in Boston when she was helping her friend start up the company in the corner of our living room. We were painting the apartment. It took us a week, and we were exhausted. But the thing that I realize now is that we painted it too fast. No one ever realizes that marriage does not get much better than when you paint your first apartment together," he said.

He asked me to pull over to the side of the road. He was feeling queasy. I was driving so fast that it took me a while to decelerate and steer onto the shoulder. By the time I stopped, Ethan was pale, and he got out of the car quickly and headed down the bluff.

He bolted away from the car, but he did not come back. Ten minutes went by. Fifteen, and I panicked. I had to dig out a flashlight from the trunk. I headed down the bluff after him, and I called out his name and shined my light everywhere. Then I tripped over his shoes.

"Ethan," I yelled. "Ethan?"

Years later, I had found him only to lose him one more time. I called out to him again, and he still did not respond, not that I would have heard him over the rising tide. I found his jacket lying on the wet sand. I picked up his scarf. I aimed the flashlight at the ocean and thought the worst.

Then I noticed a figure down the beach, a man sitting on the edge of a natural jetty of rocks. I jogged over to the jetty and climbed out the rocks, twice nearly slipping into the agitated tide.

I sat down next to Ethan and had to shout above the roar of the waves. "I'm sorry. I didn't mean to make you miserable," I said.

"I'm not miserable," he said. "Not really."

"Well, I am," I said. I figured that we were about ninety miles north of the canyon.

The tide coming in meant that waves engulfed more of the rocks. I was getting wet, and Ethan was shivering again, so I nodded toward the shore.

Back on the beach, Ethan said, "We can't just go there and burn it down."

"Why not?" I asked.

"Well, for one thing," he said, "someone might be living in it."

In my mind, the house was always empty.

"And for another, it's all that's left of Helen."

And then Ethan told me what he had done with the money that he made from the sale of the canyon property. The sale itself was not terribly surprising news to me because Ethan had vowed to get rid of the land as soon as he got out of the hospital. First he had paid off his considerable debts, he said, and then he had traveled around until he found some land on a wonderful island to the north, which he purchased for a good price. An island just like Helen had wanted, although he could not afford the entire island, but he had been able to stake out a decent lot on high ground. Ethan grinned his infectious grin and I smiled stupidly.

I told him that I had floated around the state for a while and then gone to school and apprenticed with a designer of great houses and that I had become the architect whom Helen should have become. Then I revealed that I had held on to whatever plans Helen had drawn for an island house, that I had held on to them all these years. I had the knowledge now to expand these plans and adapt them to a specific site. And Ethan immediately said that he owned the land for these plans, land he had not visited since signing the papers for the deed.

"You should see the view," he said. "Especially when it rains."

We climbed back up to the highway and to my car. He asked me whether I wanted to see the property on the island.

"We could go there now," he said. "It would take us most of the day."

Here was my choice: to travel north toward an island or to continue the drive south and set a house on fire in the middle of the night.

Ethan offered to drive, and I told him that he had to be kidding. I had forgiven him, as I say, for crashing that day when fires burned everywhere and approached our canyon, the day we lost Helen, but that did not mean that I trusted him now. He promised me that he would not crash, not intentionally at any rate, and he formed a catcher's mitt with his hands, anticipating my pitch, my car keys.

He had crashed my car into a mound of rock dressed with scrub and I heard him moan before I passed out. When I came to minutes later, I discovered that I could open the passenger-side door and, even more miraculous, walk away from the wreck.

My legs were tense and my arms scraped, my knee cut right above where I had gashed my shin the night before, but that was the extent of my injuries, probably because Ethan had been trying to maneuver the car to the right when we crashed and therefore had taken the brunt of the collision. He was a mess, unconscious now, and the shock of seeing his blood-soaked face, his bloody arms, was almost enough to knock me out again. I ran around to his side but could not open or pry open his door, and there was a moment when I believed that he had died. But with his head resting on the steering wheel, he was breathing and breathing easily at that, as if he had decided to nap until someone came along to rescue us. I pulled the beach blanket out from the backseat and draped it over his slumped shoulders, and although I worried that the car would blow up at any moment, I somehow retained enough common sense to leave him where he was rather than move him and do him further harm. He looked broken, and I decided to stay with him until someone found us. Then I decided that I had to run for help.

I screamed for help first and screamed again as I started jogging down the mountain road, around the bend that we had not quite made it around in the car, but we had ended up along one of those unpopulated stretches of park preserve that can separate the canyons of the range the farther west you drive, and unless some other suicidal fool had breached the barrier that we had smashed through, no one would hear me. I spotted a far-off sign for the next canyon road, what looked like an epic distance away, and I ran toward it, I ran as fast as I could. I ran west, I soon realized when I caught a glimpse of the ocean through the smoke and haze, west toward the light of the breaking day. Which was impossible since the sun should have been rising behind me.

The orange horizon toward which I sprinted was in fact the approaching wildfire.

I made it to the canyon and my shins ached, my ribs ached, and I passed another unmanned roadblock, which I took to mean that the steep canyon road that I now dashed down had been evacuated, and there was nothing so strange as a canyon at dawn without any murmurs in the morning fog, without the echoes of breakfast conversations or dogs barking at one another across the ravine, without the hum of trucks passing by on the coast road, and without the gossip of gulls or piano arpeggios. Without the sawing and hammering of a house being framed. It was as if the canyon had been forgotten once it was emptied by whomever was charged with the door-to-door clearing-out of neighborhoods threatened by fire. There was nothing so disconcertingly still as an emptied canyon because even the wind had left the vale at that hour, taking the rustle from the oaks, the sway from the palms.

I made it to the first driveway, a narrow rise off the western side of the canyon road—at first glance it did not look as though this canyon was one of the more populated passes—and I ran up toward the first house at the top of that driveway, and now my legs were giving into the grade, now I was slowing down. I collapsed on the front lawn—also disconcerting was the heat of the earth as the fire closed in, the warm ground cracking beneath me like the ice of a frozen pond—but I picked myself up, gasping, and stumbled to the front door and rang the bell even though I knew that no one would answer.

It was a plain white house, your basic split-level, with white shingles and black shutters and a stone foundation and slate paths around the house and a coiffed complement of boxwood and laurel bushes and beds of bright red geraniums that had held up that season, bright red like the front door, which I rammed with my shoulder, which I rammed several times, which I kicked in. And so there I was breaking into one more house.

I headed straight for the kitchen in the back and a phone with a long cord mounted on a wall and I dialed for help, still breathless as I tried to figure out where I was, where to tell the dispatcher to send the ambulance. A few turns past the blockade that we barreled through, I had to say, but I do not know how far west. West toward the fire, I said, I can see the fire. And not too long after I reluctantly hung up, I heard a siren far away, which I wanted to believe was the siren of Ethan's rescuers.

I would have gone back to him myself, except I had to lie down, I had to catch my breath. I did not make it back to the front lawn, I only made it as far as the living room, and that was where I collapsed, not onto the inviting corduroy couch but onto a soft beige carpet where I may have blacked out again, I do not recall. What I do remember is that at some point I rolled onto my back and that I was staring up at a black and polished grand piano on which a dozen framed photographs had been collected.

Pictures of the people who lived in this white house, I assumed. The largest photo was of a family, a mother with two sons who looked like her, they had her chin, her angled jaw, a photo of the three of them on a beach, maybe the beach at the mouth of the canyon—no, probably another beach of whiter sand and clearer water—a woman with a clever smile and long dark hair with a few handsome streaks of gray and sunglasses slipping off her nose, a woman with an arm around each boy, one blond and one blonder, giggling boys, the younger of which clutched a noble Labrador who knew his best angle, a dog who offered his profile to the camera. A happy day, a great day. These were all pictures of great days amassed on the grand piano, the smiling school portraits, the shots of the boys fishing off a dock by a house on a lake, the tanned mother wearing a cowl of neon leis. Black-

and-white grandparents beaming proudly. And no father, as far as I could tell, unless the father was the author of every photo, which I doubted because I would have found at least one glimpse of him if he were a part of the present household, one shot at least. Here was a woman raising two children by herself, two boys and a Labrador partial to green bandannas, and having a fine and easy time of it, if I were to take the framed album of ski trips and holiday mornings as the complete history of this family.

Now a fire would swallow up the white house with its roll of lawn and ocean view, and I began to wonder, did the woman and the boys flee willingly or did they have to be forced out by the sheriff? They had gotten the dog out, but did they have time to take what was most important with them? What about these photographs on the piano? You would think that when a fire was on its way that you would reach for whatever mementos you could gather to help you remember the place you were about to lose. Maybe there was not enough room in their station wagon for anything unessential. And it occurred to me that the least I could do was to salvage something for them, these photos if nothing else, which I could carry to whatever shelter had been set up at the police station or at a school. I could present them with these few things and say, Your house is gone, but I got these out for you. That seemed like a worthy and doable deed. That much I could do, and all I needed was a tote bag or backpack, a piece of luggage to carry the photographs in. In search of a backpack, I went upstairs.

There were three bedrooms off a central hall. A room with the constellations stenciled on the ceiling, with models of airplanes everywhere, some suspended from curtain rods. A room with posters of rock stars along with art posters and heaps of magazines on the rug. And a big white room with an unmade white bed and a rattan rocker, a rattan chest, a room with beeswax candles and rice paper–shaded lamps. The top of the dresser in this room was covered with inches of dangle earrings and bead necklaces and silver bangle bracelets, and I thought that the woman might like to have some of these things, too. She had stuck photos into the frame of a mirror over the dresser, loose photos of the boys, except these were different photos from the photos of the family downstairs. These were moody pictures. Here were the boys caught candidly, with their hair windblown and in their eyes, lying on the lawn, standing with their pants rolled up on the edge of the shore. Here were the boys as seen by their mother at various moments in their youth, how she wanted to remember them, unposed and wistful, and I plucked the photos from the mirror and gathered them along with the jewelry and dropped everything onto a cotton shawl draped over the rattan chest so that I could wrap them up. And then it occurred to me that the younger boy would want at least one of his model airplanes, and so I dashed back into his room but could not decide whether to take the futuristic jet or the vintage bomber—I took them both—and what about the mitt, the iconic mitt, I had to take the mitt with the ball in it. And then I bounced into the other boy's room and pulled open his top desk drawer and found a cigar box and, once I scanned its contents, knew to take this, too, a cigar box with a roach clip inside and some coins from beyond the border and a local restaurant matchbook and more photos, photos of him with his arm slung over the shoulder of another boy, and the real prize of the box, a harmonica. The mitt, the harmonica, the photos of the boys in the mirror . . . I was fairly certain now that the family had run out of time and grabbed the dog and nothing else and fled. I wondered if they had been away on a trip and not even made it back to the house. Maybe they had gone for a walk on the beach but gone too far before turning around, and at that very moment, all three of them with the dog were in tears as they argued with a cop at the base of the canyon and begged, Please, let us just run in and grab a few things and run out, please.

Sure, they would run inside fast enough, but then what do you grab when you know that what you do not take with you will be destroyed? It was not as easy to condemn inanimate objects as it might seem. That rocker, for instance. Once upon a time, the woman had soothed a boy with a stomachache in that rocker. Once upon a time she had rocked herself to sleep, the night after her divorce came through. The boys were off with their grandparents and she was foolishly alone and very lonely and could not sleep. That rocker had saved her and it in turn should be saved. How did you appraise what was contained in a house and know what mattered, because everything mattered, the worn rug of the upstairs hall and the little television on which you watched a man walk on the moon, on which you watched a cop-serial late at night after the kids had gone to bed and you yourself were tucked in with the man who made that year a good year. What about the sweater that you could put on to feel good-looking. What about the skillet in the kitchen that was like no other skillet, the heavy iron pan in which you scrambled eggs and cooked coq au vin. And then there were the books that lined the shelves on one wall of the woman's bedroom and a wall downstairs in the den, the books of leafy afternoons and nights of rain. And the binoculars on the windowsill. For bird-watching? For spying on the neighbors down the canyon road? I would like this woman, if I knew her, I thought, we would amuse ourselves well together.

I hopped back and forth among the bedrooms of the white house and grabbed a pocket watch that had stopped and a stamp collection and a school tie slung over a desk chair and an archery bow and a tennis racquet and a crocheted afghan, and downstairs I grabbed a camcorder and place mats on the kitchen table and a ceramic teapot, and I was running out of time—I realized that the low roar that I heard could not have been the ocean and that it had to be the fire getting closer—and I would not be able to carry all of this stuff even if I did find some luggage, the one item that I could not seem to locate, and so I bolted out the back door of the house and to the patio there, where I reached for the garden hose uncoiled on the lawn at the same time that I turned on the outside faucet all the way and heaved the hose onto the modest eave of the back of the house, the eave with a bird-feeder hanging by the kitchen window, and the hose slid off, and I kept slinging the hose up to the roof until it stayed there and then I jumped up and grabbed hold of the gutter, a length of which came down on me when I tried to pull myself up, and so I had to drag the picnic table over to the side of the patio and place a bench on the table and climb up to the roof that way.

I told myself not to look to the west but looked west anyway. The orange horizon was brighter now—picture the widening rim of an angry volcano—but I had no idea how long it would take for the fire to get to this canyon. That roar that I had been hearing, that low rumble, was definitely the fire, but I had no idea how fast a fire moved.

I straddled the ridge and I squeezed the spray nozzle of the hose and I aimed it everywhere, all over the dry shingles of the roof, wetting down every inch, and then I sprayed the shrubs around the house, and the lawn and then the roof again and the shrubs and the lawn once more and whatever trees I could reach, the tall shade trees that seemed to come to life when I hosed them down, they glistened, they rustled again, the roof of the white house, the lawn, the trees, drenching everything again and again as I made my stand. I was going to save this house, this home. The fire would come and it would spit embers, but these embers would be impotent when they fell on wet leaves and wet grass and wet shingles. These embers would sputter and lose their glow.

The tall fire would pass around this house and burn everything around it but not anything that I had hosed down, and then I would go back inside and take a bath if I had not emptied the well, and I would borrow a bed and sleep for a very long time.

Deep into the morning, then, I was still standing on the roof and watering everything in sight, and the geranium beds were saturated and the roof shingles soaked and there were puddles on the patio and slate paths and miniature lakes on the lawn and the branches of the trees were dripping as if it had just rained. When I stopped spraying for a while, I could see that some of the smoke below me had blown out to sea, and now I could look down on the canyon—one by one the houses appeared to me—and now I could also see that a fleet of fire trucks had moved up the canyon road, red trucks stationed all along the middle of the glen. I could not be sure, but it looked like the firefighters were going to use the road as a break against the fire, keeping it from spreading to one side of the canyon but not necessarily defending the side that I was on.

Now the fire loomed and what had been a band of flames beneath blankets of smoke before was now a wall, a moving, growing wall of luminous heat. My legs were wet from the hose, my shorts sopping, but as the fire came nearer, the radiant heat of that blaze evaporated everything dry, the patio, the trees, the lawn, my legs and my shorts, everything so that I began to worry that my hours of watering had been pointless. This was a consuming heat, a heat that ate air. The world in front of me was turning to a glassy ripple and I was beginning to have trouble breathing. I felt something stinging against my thigh, and when I reached into the pocket of my shorts, I burned my hand as I removed a tissue that I had stuffed in there, a tissue that had become a glowing ember.

My hours of watering were coming to nothing and I realized that the only way to fight off the fire was to keep hos-

ing down the house even as the flames crept closer and
closer. And I was having to take shallower breaths and there
was so much ash everywhere I looked, the thin ash hanging in the dry air. The fire was loud now and I could not hear
my own voice—I had not even realized that I was shouting
for help—and the wind that preceded the fire was a mean
and reckless wind that turned over lawn chairs and blew
leaves from the trees and stirred up enough dust so that I
could not see what I was doing as I sprayed the hose every
which way, so that I did not see the squad of firefighters at
first, the men and some women in their bulky yellow slick-
ers and knee-high rubber boots and yellow hoods and goggles as they marched up the driveway. There were ten of
them with tanks strapped to their backs, tanks with hoses,
and a truck negotiating the narrow road behind them, two
trucks. They were a faceless bunch who started spraying
their far more powerful hoses in the direction of the fire,
faceless with their goggles and masks. One of them who
looked like he was in charge, the one who directed his troops
to stand at the edge of the property and water the slope
below them, that man motioned me down from the roof.

He was the only one whose face I saw and it was not a
pleased face, not a friendly face. I did not hear what he said
to me, this man with a mustache, what he shouted, but
given the way he pointed and the way he tapped my chest
firmly with his gloved forefinger, I was fairly certain that he
was telling me that I was insane to try to save my house and
that I should run away before he threw me into the fire. I
could not understand him, but I suspected that he was telling
me that I had jeopardized the master plan because the firefighters had determined that the only way to keep the fire
from destroying most of the homes in the canyon was to sac-
rifice the few homes on this side of the main road, homes
that backed up against a nature conservancy, a park that was
thick with chaparral and trees, and they were going to let

all of that brush burn itself out and use the paved road for their break. Now they would try to save my house and the whole canyon, but at what risk, at what risk, a risk not worth it, fuck you, you fool.

Or maybe that was not what the fireman was trying to tell me at all. Because suddenly he was all smiles and oddly jolly at a time like this and pointing every which way and pushing me back toward the house and the roof and slapping me on the back, Good job, good job, as if I had saved the day so far and now he was counting on me to keep at it. I did not know what he had said, but it seemed to me he had been warning me of the dangers of the fire-containment business at the same time that he deputized me and invited me to the fight because a goggled, slickered firefighter came up behind the man in charge and handed me one of the heavy yellow jackets to put on along with gloves. And then following the example of the man in charge, I pulled a hood over my head as he recovered his own head, and donned the goggles and the mask, which, once I was wearing it, made the air as easy and light to breathe as on any blustery autumn day.

Now I was one of them, except for the fact that I was wearing shorts and sneakers instead of yellow pants and rubber boots—my legs were black with soot—and I took the garden hose and followed the chief and fell into rank with the rest of the crew and sprayed the canyon below me, below us. There were big hoses from the trucks being dragged in now, pulled across the lawn, much more powerful hoses of water that appeared to generate their own gust and wind to push back the fire.

Now the fire came over a ridge and it was in full view and bright and as tall as the oldest trees, stories taller than these trees, and I knew that if I had been alone, I would have run, but the men alongside me were not fleeing, some of them had staggered forward a bit, and if they were afraid, I did not know it. It was an amazing sight, the creeping wall of flame,

the trees and brush in the distance becoming black silhou-
ettes and then mere lines and then nothing, the fire leaning
down the slope, a terrifying sight but beautiful, too, that brilliant rolling lava, that sun on the earth, and breathtaking,
literally breathtaking, even with the mask.

I did not know then what I know now, that if the fire had
descended the slope beneath us and come up at us, we
would have been in serious trouble, because a heat-rising
fire moves much more swiftly uphill than down. I did not
know that every firefighter who works a forest or who pa-
trols the Pacific coast has a reckless streak. They all take
chances, they thrive on risk. I did not know really what
kind of chance they were taking or what they would have
done that morning if the helicopters that they had been
promised had not come when they did.

Out of the smoke behind us, two choppers appeared, high
in the air, dangling what looked like balloons of water. In
quick succession, they each flew over the fire now a mere
hundred-yard dash in front of us and dropped their deliv-
eries of ocean water with a splash, and the fire sizzled a bit
and folded back and looked wounded when it lurched forward again, not quite as strong, not quite as determined.
Two other helicopters came in soon after and the firemen
who had stepped forward before raced down the slope now
and I hung back with the second line, which moved forward
slowly as well.

The garden hose would not stretch any farther, and one
man-in-yellow indicated that I should join the guys who
were dragging the hose from the truck, and so I fell in behind them as if I were the anchor-man on a tug-of-war team
and grabbed hold of the hose, and the force of the water
shooting through that hose almost knocked me over. But I
grabbed hold and helped to aim the hose at the ebbing fire—
it felt as if I was wrangling the slippery and mighty dorsal of
an angry aquatic beast.

And the wind was behind us now, blowing west and at the fire, and another three helicopters came in and dropped balloons of water, and the fire was folding back on itself and the fire was in retreat, and I could not help but shout hallelujah because we were winning the skirmish, and we charged the ground that had burned, which could not burn again—that was the guiding principle of fire fighting, what burned once would not burn again—and we dowsed the remaining hot spots, whatever brush had not gone up in flame.

The fire was retreating to the west, but heading south at the same time, and we had kept it away from the house belonging to the woman and the two boys—I had helped saved that house—but the fire was wily, the fire was still strong, and it could crest its way into the canyon again to the south of our position. We had to prepare for another skirmish. We had to head it off at the next pass. We had to outthink it, and we had no time for complex strategies.

Through the muffle of his mask, I heard the man-in-charge say that we had to set a backfire along the ridge beneath us in the lower canyon, we had to do it right away, and the trucks were already down there to back us up, and so move, move, move.

And we ran down the slopes in one fast sweep, through backyards and over a hill and into the preserve of dry brush, and we ran and ran and joined up with another crew that had already started the backfire that would burn out enough brush to create a no-man's-land where the fire, outsmarted, ha-ha, would face a sudden and unexpected deficit of fuel, where we would be able to control it and contain it and beat it back and once and for all protect the canyon.

The backfire was burning itself out and the only reason it might work, it should be said, was because the winds had shifted—half the game was a game of luck—and so this strategic fire did not blow back at us and it did not meet up with the bigger fire and only fuel it, although that could happen, it had already happened earlier that day when the wind changed directions just a few canyons over, I heard someone say.

Now we broke up into different groups with specific tasks all designed to shore up the break that we had established with the backfire, the crew of men with chainsaws who cut away the remaining thicker brush and tossed it into the remaining backfire or carried it back to the road, and then the second crew who came in with shovels and tossed dirt onto the lingering flames, and then the crew that I joined, who were charged with cutting away whatever vegetation was left—there were about five of us, each armed with a pulaski, a chimeric tool that was half-hoe and half-axe, and although I knew that it was for the cause, this ripping out of roots, because the fire could spread underground if we were not careful, that did not make it feel right somehow, not even moral to be tugging away at decades of life—and then finally behind us, a last clean-up crew with rake-hoes who insured that we had made a clean and clear firebreak. If the backfire somehow failed to keep the fire from entering the lower canyon, or if the fire jumped our break either with the embers that it spat forward or through some other gymnastic vault, the trucks back on the road behind us were loaded with water and we could call in the helicopters as long as it was day and the smoke was not too thick for them to fly, and if that still did not work, well . . . A backfire had failed once that morning and two canyons to the immediate west had already been lost, two canyons lined with houses. I heard someone say that the fire had jumped the coast road and burned out the homes along the beach and that the only break that held off that arm of the fire, the same fire that we were fighting now, was the big blue break itself, as it was known, the Pacific.

So the fire had folded back on itself and was burning and burning strong in that century of chaparral beyond us, and when the wind was right, when the wind was again in its favor as it inevitably would be, the fire would launch south and our break would be tested. Deep into the afternoon, then, we were waiting and waiting and going over and over what we had done with our shovels and hoe-axes and rake-hoes, and the hoses were ready and we were tired but poised. There I stood on the front line of the fight, goggled and masked and suited in a yellow flame-retardant uniform, and that was when I realized that I had at long last fallen into the sweep of time that had always eluded me, the cause of the moment, the struggle that I had longed to fight, any larger struggle that might carry me along in its swift stride. For the hour of the fire, my loss was the larger loss, my hope the larger hope.

The fire loomed over us once again, the wall of flames came our way. Now was our chance to fly closer to the sun.

The fire came again, a loud fire, a steep fire, and it swelled and bowed toward our break. And the break worked, it held at first. But then somehow the fire seemed to reach over our clearing; the fire reached as far as the road along one flank, and so there we were again, three men to a hose and spraying the flames and now was our chance to make a run or make a stand, and we made our stand and sprayed and sprayed and the helicopters came in with their drops and then, like a gull that you did not see on a cloudy day until it flew right above you, a small white plane emerged from the smoke with another drop over the heart of the fire, an enormous cascade of water—a movable waterfall, that was what it looked like—and we all cheered as the plane flew out over the sea, and we were soaking wet now, from the plane drop and the several helicopter drops and from the mist of the hoses. And still the fire came at us, although with less fervor now, and we kept washing it down and then, with a last sigh of flame that came quite close to us, within a foot, it lapsed back and scattered into a hundred lesser fires which we attacked with the hoses and with the shovels and whatever tools were within our reach to squelch it, amen.

The smoke cleared and thinned out. We had saved the canyon and all of the houses in it. By dusk, we had won.

Another crew came in behind us, a refreshed and rested group, although they looked pretty beat themselves, and now I saw the faces of the men and women whom I had joined as they removed their hoods and goggles and masks. Now I could know them, and I wanted to thank them. I knew that the fight would go on for them, that there would be days and weeks to come of fighting the other fires in the Southland, but I wanted them to celebrate now, to celebrate whatever battle we had won, which was why when I realized how close we had come to the coast road and the beach, I waved my arm and indicated that they all should follow me down to the shore. And a good ten to fifteen of them did follow my lead down the last bluff to the coast road and down the rocks to the sand.

But once we reached the sand, we had to stop and take a deep breath, and then we drifted down the shore and looked back at the smoldering hills above the coast road. Ten of us wandered down the beach a good quarter-mile, a good half-mile with our mouths agape and our hearts pounding because here was the other side of the fire. The sky was no longer gray with smoke, but it was still quite white and bleached, and beneath that whitened sky was the blackened divide of park preserve and then the canyon of homes that the fire had wasted. The occasional thicket of brush still flared with flames. We drifted farther west along the beach and eventually reached the second canyon that had burned; this was where the fire had jumped the coast road and sacked the houses on the beach. Nothing survived, not a single home. It was a sight that made the firefighters gasp and sigh even though most of them knew all too well what an unsparing wildfire could do. It was a sight that they never got used to, the lingering smoke licking the lone chimneys and stray walls, the last of the smoke hanging low to the ground, a scavenger fog.

We passed some fellow firefighters up on the highway, and I was unsure why they were watching a few palm trees burn out, but that seemed to be what they were doing, washing the road down while the palms dripped bright embers on the pavement. These canyons had been lost, but then again, we also knew that we had saved a canyon to the east and therefore saved the canyons to the east of that one. And so I waved the minyan behind me down toward the water and finally led the charge, discarding my gear on the wet sand and shrugging off the heavy jacket that I had been given, and they all followed me, stepping out of their boots and yellow pants, and we ran into the big blue break, the cold blue break, and hurdled the crashing waves and dove into the tide going out. We stripped and swam in the ocean.

And then I saw where we were, how far west we had wandered. I had waded out far enough into the waves to get a better look at the black hills, and that was when I understood which canyon this was because I recognized the twisted hull up on the mountain side of the road. It was the Paradise Diner and it looked like a wrecked ship.

One by one, I could pick out the ruins in the hills of the once hidden, now naked gulch above the diner, the ruins of houses that I had spied upon from above and houses that I had illicitly explored, houses that I had known intimately, and when I swam out a little farther into the ocean, I could see that the house at the top of that steep rise that had been my palace and my domain was gone, too, it was rubble now, a heap of black stones. Anything that I owned, not that I had owned much, was ash in that rubble. All that did survive up and down the canyon were the swimming pools, odd shapes of water, puddles from my vantage now, queer blue-green puddles. Encantado Canyon Road met up with Las Patas Glen and now the entire vale was black.

And then I followed the Las Patas Glen slope up to its highest peak and I looked for our house but I could not find it. A wave knocked me farther from the shore and I treaded water and stared at the black hills and I still could not find our house and I began to panic. The fire must have jumped across the canyon. The flames must have caught whatever meager tufts of scrub they could and used them as stepping-stones to reach our house. I panicked and looked for the house and could not find it, and I drifted farther out to sea. What a savage twist. Because Helen was gone and Ethan was gone, for all I knew—their absence sank in my gut and nearly pulled me under—and now their house, our unfinished house, Helen's single legacy, all that she had willed a world that she had given up on, had burned into ash.

I had drifted dangerously far into the waves, beyond the reach or call of the firefighters frolicking in the surf, and I gave into the tow and allowed myself to be carried out even farther, and I was cold and my arms and legs were numb, and I backstroked away from the beach. I swam farther from the shore because I thought, Why not, why not, why hold on, what for? I could drown, I could sleep.

I thought about Dean. We were in a hotel room in a country of sunlight and heat, sprawled out on the bed during the hottest part of the day. I lay my head on his chest. I could always sleep with my head on his chest.

We can lead charmed lives, but then one morning we discover that we cannot breathe so well. Our child falls. Then we fumble and we falter and that charm, taken for granted for too long, eludes us. We get lost, we make wrong turns. We think we find our way only to get lost again. We are trapped in a cycle we cannot break—that was what Helen Zayne knew all too well—we are doomed.

No. I do not believe that. Once upon a time I did. I had wandered and I had drifted, but then I came to a western canyon where two people were sculpting a house from the ash. And they rescued me. Helen rescued me, but I could not save her in turn.

I had swum far from the shore but I had not quite given up, and I was still staring at the blackened glen, and then the clouds shifted, they broke, and a certain amount of afternoon sun splashed across the mountains, and I realized that I had been mistaken, dead wrong, because there was the house after all, there was a house in the distance, a white house that I had been unable to pick out against a white sky.

A house in the distance, the only house still standing, the house that we had built, look. Look, Helen, look. And I was mad at her, I shouted at her. I screamed, You gave up too soon, you gave up too soon. Look, it lasted. Look at the house in the distance. If only you had waited out the fire. Oh, Helen, oh, Helen. Look.

And it was a fine and luminous house with sharp edges and an appealing symmetry, an ordered and serene temple rising from and reigning over the gray fate of the canyon. A temple. I had looked at the house from a distance before but not from enough distance to understand that the tall windows arranged along its long flank gave the facade the gaps and spacing of a colonnade, not from enough distance to see that what we had built, with its low-pitched pediments poised on slender columns, with its frieze and with its white finish, was indeed a temple of sorts—that was what Helen was after—a temple for an oracle on a cliff by the sea. A temple or the hollowed ruins of a temple that would be discovered and rediscovered by the centuries of boats that sailed by. Ruins that would be photographed from every angle. It was a timeless monument.

And I swam toward it, although I was very cold and had drifted very far out to sea. I swam toward the house, arm over arm over arm, but I was slowing down. But someone must have noticed me swim out too far, someone must have heard me shouting, and I saw the firefighters standing on the shore, I saw them waving to me, waving me in, and I realized that some of them, three men, were now paddling toward me, these professional saviors who were not about to let me drown.

A house in the distance. Who would live there? A family, a woman with her two sons. Lovers, two people who could not let go of their ancient passion. A lone exile from the city. Maybe no one would live there at all, and the house would by word-of-mouth become a free hostel where strangers wandering through town would stay the night, burning sections of the staircase to keep warm when it was cold. Someone would sleep in that house and sleep well.

A house that would age in the weather of the years. The paint would crack and chip and a column would rot and collapse. A rafter would break loose. Shingles would slide off the roof and a strip of siding would fall aslant. Windows would warp and refuse to open, a door would not close all the way. The house would yawn and creak and have its good days and its bad days, but it would live long enough to blend into the landscape, to become a landmark with its own myth. There is the one house that survived the fire. Travelers would use it as a marker: The white house at the top of the canyon would mean that they had almost arrived wherever they were going; it would mean that they still had a way to drive.

I knew that the canyon would be repopulated in time, that other people would return and build new houses, and eventually the brush would grow back along with the poppies and the bougainvillea and then the cypresses and the oaks, and I knew that it was possible, that it was likely that another fire would threaten the canyon, that it was possible and likely that this fire would burn out the canyon again and that our house might vanish in these flames. But the people who lived in the canyon would survive that fire, too, and they would return once again, a few of them at first, the impatient pioneers whom others would inevitably follow. One way or another, there would always be a white house in the distance riding the peak, a house that would be bright before the morning was bright, a house that would glow long after dusk.

I swam back toward the shore with a tired but even stroke and the push of the tide behind me and the knowledge that I would be rescued along the way. I swam with the same wind in my heart that now carries me north up a coast with a lost, found friend driving my car, both of his hands gripping the wheel—

North toward the promise of land and what we can build there.